Crashing on all fours through a tunnel, the gigantic rat left behind a choking stench. G'kaa slaughtered sentries as he found them and stamped their bodies to the floor. He almost split the tunnel walls with his monstrous, knotted shoulders as he drove forward in the dark. Behind him stretched a packed column of warriors two hundred strong, whiskers feeling the way through lightless, airless spaces. Tunnels echoed with the sound of hundreds of claws. . . .

In the darkness ahead, a sentry suddenly jerked awake. "Who's there?"

G'kaa struck with vicious fury. His blades punched into the body ahead. The enemy rat fell, the stink of death instantly filling the passageway. G'kaa's huge strength rammed against a press of panicked, shouting warriors. He struck left, felt something stagger, and then ripped past the milling guards and up into the only other exit from the room. His own fighters flooded into the chamber at his tail.

A bitter fight began, a fight only true Itheem could survive. . . .

ABBEY AND GREENWOOD'S

Tales of the

Mornmist™

Shared World

The Rats of Acomar

Paul Kidd

Vision Novels

THE RATS OF ACOMAR

First Edition, First Printing: October, 2000
Printed in LaVergne, TN, the United States of America.
Library of Congress Card Number: 00-100367

9 8 7 6 5 4 3 2 1

ISBN: 1-887038-05-1

Vision Novels
Imprint of Vision Entertainment
Post Office Box 580009
Flushing NY 11358-0009

For Alexandra, our "wee pink insect"
may she learn how to see the beauty
inside every living thing,
be it fruit bat, spider,
mouse, or vole.

Chapter 1

In a land lashed by winter winds, in a place where mountains overshadowed violent ocean shores, a peninsula ran out into the sea. It was a place of stark black rock and withered weeds, scoured by whips of sea foam and sterilized by sand, forever walled away from the green lands of the shore. Across the neck of the peninsula ran a rocky ridge, a plateau topped with a massive palisade and lined with mile forts and towers – the Great Shield Wall. To the inland side ran green fields half-covered in frost – the lands of the canine Uruth, patrolled by armored guardians. To the seaward side, out on the barren neck of land, there lay nothing but death.

Acomar was a land of dust and black obsidian, of poisoned springs and crevasses filled with rotting bones. Most of all, it was a place where life fought a bitter, endless struggle. The soil was a packed black mass of dead flesh and fur. Desolate and poisoned, Acomar stank of the life that seethed and battled in tunnels deep beneath the ground. The great wall made by the canines sealed Acomar away from the rich green lands beyond, leaving her inhabitants to starve and breed and die inside a prison of bones.

Legend said that Acomar had once been a lair of Giants, a place where near-gods had raised massive towers and dug lairs to the center of the world. The land was now a maze of titanic broken blocks. Veins of metal salts twisted through the earth below. At night, the soil itself glowed with tiny points of light like little stars – a drifting mystery that stained the rocks with sickly reds and shades of blue.

Within the peninsula was a heartland of utter lifelessness, where no weeds grew and sand dunes hissed beneath the breezes. Overhead, titanic metal pylons soared – great, curving bones of green metal that no steel tool could ever mark. Legend said they were the half-exposed skeletons of giants, buried long ago beneath the world.

And as the winds blew, the pylons softly sang.

The sound began as a low note humming from a single tower, a note ebbing and flowing with the power of a world gone by. Slowly the music traveled, spreading to one more pylon, and then another. Music rippled across the lifeless sands. It drifted from the dunes out into the oft-stormy sea. It sifted landward, too, sinister in the ears of the watchers on the mighty wall.

On the Great Shield Wall, canine soldiers stirred; guards changed and new sentinels looked out across the blighted lands. Eternally patrolled, the Uruth's wall sealed Acomar away from the living world. The seas tossed, the pylons moaned, and a cold dawn sun at last began to fill the world with light.

§

On a certain rock above the violent waves, the dawn always came crisp and clear. The lights within the earth soaked slowly back into the ground, leaving the predawn sky shimmering like distant rain.

Here the wind blew bitter-sharp with the scent of salt and spray. Here the cold and rock sealed away a world of hungry claws and teeming eyes. Utter isolation, but total freedom – a thing more valuable than food and mates and coin.

An *Itheem* lay atop a white-streaked rock; Ra'hish the rat – a child of deadly Acomar. His body stretched long and lean, ribs hidden by straps of raw, taut muscle. Long whiskers shifted in the winds. Fine gray fur matched the colors of the ruins. Cunning lines of black and white dye made the creature disappear into the angles of the rocky ground.

Long, lean, and brooding – a creature made beautiful by his feral, primal shape – Ra'hish rested lightly on all fours, gripping the boulders with long fingers and toes. His naked pink tail was the only sign of life, an extremity that stirred with a mind all its own. A blade-bearing steel tube had been lashed to each forearm. Even at rest, the rat lay tensed, instantly prepared to battle for his life.

To be Itheem was to be a thing of hunger. Born of the ruins, a child of Giants long dead and gone, the rats were as much a part of the desolation as the metal struts and tumbleweeds. And yet, *hunger* always stirred. Starvation made greed a virtue and life a battle. The cunning, the powerful, and the deadly survived – and so each generation came from terror into strength. . . .

And yet this morning, the solitary rat had eyes only for the dawn. While the metal towers sang their ancient song, Ra'hish merely lay and watched the patterns in the surging foam. The music vibrated through the creature's soul, shivering through his body and down into the stone. It felt powerful, majestic – a private silence filled with noise. He blanked his mind of mundane hungers and gazed upon an alien world. With unseeing eyes, he stared into the sky and let his thoughts drift away like thistledown.

Far across the barren rocks and dunes of Acomar lay the Shield Wall, eternally patrolled by the peoples of the green lands beyond. To them, Itheem were only goblins. On fine days, one could sit here at the shore and look across the savage riptides to a distant, fertile countryside, fields growing row by row and strange, dense-packed trees. Above it all floated Ghost Mountain, a titanic snowcap that appeared to hang high in the sky. The young Itheem lifted his eyes to gaze on the faraway peak, and then slowly frowned and wrinkled his fine pink nose. There was a stench upon the air.

Ra'hish wiggled his nose and made his whiskers quest. He reluctantly felt his gaze drift away from the horizon and down onto the rocks a dozen body-spans below . . . and discovered an utter fortune at his feet.

A carcass had washed up onshore – a blunt gray creature easily ten times an Itheem's size. Its flippers lay limp, and something had torn a vast chunk of flesh from the creature's side. It could feed an entire nest for many days.

The shore was dangerous. The dark waters hid deadly scavengers, and many explorers had simply disappeared. Still, the corpse should be traded away before other hunters could make a claim. Reluctant to reveal his private hideaway, Ra'hish flattened his ears and puffed an irritated breath into the wind.

From behind came a sudden *presence*.

Without bothering to turn, the rat pressed the catches on his steel batons. Wicked knife points snapped from their housings to tip the warrior's forearms with steel. Dawn light glittered from blades stained acid green.

With a piercing scream, a figure lunged across the rocks. Ra'hish parried, whirled, and slashed, feeling his left knife blade rip into flesh. He punched hard twice and felt bone splintering. The body fell. The young rat spun and killed a second enemy with a single blow, spitting his blade into the creature's skull. Blood sheeted Ra'hish's fur as he whirled to meet the next attack with crossed batons and chisel fangs.

More rats were coming for the beached carrion – three scouts with the markings of the East Tunnel Clan. They broke from cover and charged along the narrow path, forced to come one at a time on the narrow causeway above the booming surf.

Ra'hish streaked with blinding speed toward his enemies. The first scout leapt across the rocks. Ra'hish hacked him from the air, and he fell screaming into the raging tide. The second enemy blasted forward and punched its twin blades at Ra'hish's heart. Ra'hish parried in a blur of steel, matching speed for speed. Sparks spat madly out across the rocks.

He caught both of his opponent's blades against his own and lunged in to bite out the creature's throat. His enemy staggered back in foaming agony, falling as a wave crashed high to drag it into the sea.

The last scout came more slowly. The creature rang its blade points against each other and pounded the rocks with the steel ball threaded on its tail.

The two Itheem met, rage against rage in a spitting ball of hate. Foam soared high and wind ripped through fur. Batons blurred as the two creatures fought. Knife blades slashed and stabbed for flesh. Ra'hish fought the larger, more powerful enemy to a standstill upon the crest of jagged, windblown rocks. They fought with weapons flickering, hands moving almost too fast to be seen. Fur parted across Ra'hish's shoulder, and blood leaked across his skin. He broke one of his enemy's teeth and clipped a gouge into its ear. Ra'hish let himself be driven slowly back until he reached a low point on the rocks. Then he made an agile backward spring onto higher ground and let his enemy roar into the attack.

A wave surged, perfectly timed. It thundered across the rocks and crashed into Ra'hish's enemy. As it fought for balance, Ra'hish ducked and ripped a blade across its knees. The rat spilled into the surf. A second wave caught the creature and slammed it hard against the rocks before dragging it out to sea.

Ra'hish overleapt the waves and advanced, bristling, along the rocky ridge. There were no more East Tunnel warriors onshore. In their place sat a single rat that merely watched and drew the gravel through its claws.

The intruder reared, casting a vast black shadow out across the chill dawn. A gigantic creature fully twice Ra'hish's length, the rat's black hide was foul and knotted with battle scars. Through its one good eye, it watched Ra'hish approach, smiling with jagged, feral fangs.

The creature spoke in a voice that spat and coughed. "A fighter! It is a long time since I saw a *real* fighter." The rocks behind Ra'hish ran blood into the sea. "The East Tunnel Clan said you would be here."

Ra'hish, almost skeletal before the huge rat, seethed across the rocks, leaving bloody footprints in his wake. "I fight." Ra'hish's voice brimmed with an orphan's bitterness. "The Easterners can tell you I do it well."

The intruder lifted his massive, heavy arms – each one equipped with a war blade almost as long as Ra'hish's entire body. "Would you fight *me*, Child?"

"I'll fight you." Ra'hish crouched, instantly ready to streak into the attack. "If you want the food, go around! The rock is mine!"

"The rock?" Rising in confusion, the black behemoth let its red eye turn to gaze upon Ra'hish's chosen territory. "What in plague's name do you want with a rock?"

"I like the view."

Something moved behind Ra'hish. He spun to find his first enemy crawling across the rocks. Ra'hish leapt high, speared both blades into the creature's neck, and then whipped about with lightning speed to face the great black giant once again.

The giant slid its blades back into its war batons and gave a hissing laugh.

"*Ra'hish.* 'Blood and milk.' Why give a fighter such a name?"

Filthy with blood, the froth of battle still dripping from his jaws, Ra'hish crouched warily on guard. "I was a nestling. My eyes had been open for two days – new teeth, no fur. The nest was overcrowded, so my mother ate her young. When she came for me, I killed her with my jaws!"

"I heard of it. A good first meal." The black rat paused, the sea winds whipping through his ragged fur. "No mother means no clan. You are alone, Ra'hish."

"My blades are enough."

Grotesquely ugly, massive and vile, the intruder shifted to fix Ra'hish with its single eye. "We knew you were here. Few scouts dare come here; the lone rat of the rocks is no one's easy prey."

"What do you want?"

"I want *you*." The black rat stretched. Huge muscles shifted under his scarred and knotted pelt. He was fully twice as long as Ra'hish and stronger than a troll. "I want a rat that can live in the wilds alone. I want someone who would kill his own mother from the cradle in order to survive!"

Ra'hish blinked, feeling his hackles rise in wonder. His thin rat face tilted as he stared toward the other male. "Who are you?"

"I am G'kaa the Warlord. And now you have a clan."

The rocks amid the metal pylons were suddenly alive. The shadows moved. A hundred warriors shifted their concealment and drew closer to the shore. And beyond them were a hundred more, and then a hundred more, stretching back into the ruins in a blaze of watching eyes.

G'kaa; a name that brimmed with fear. The gigantic rat lead a war band of outcasts – an elite army that had become the spearhead of a dozen clans in a hundred wars.

Feigning unconcern, Ra'hish sat back upon his haunches and began to comb his whiskers clean. "I work alone."

"Then scout for me. Think of it as an *alliance* – nothing more."

Ra'hish paused and thought. The clans were swelling to the bursting point. Every scrap of arable land was under harvest. Hunting parties fought each other in endless battles day by day. Soon it would be impossible to stand alone.

The young rat finished grooming his whiskers, licked his pink hands clean, and made his blades slip suddenly back into their tubes. "I'll join."

G'kaa gave a savage laugh and signaled to his troops, who came spilling out onto the shore. They were pure Itheem – sleek, dangerous, and cruel, with nothing but their weapons, armor, and trophies made of tooth and bone. Turning his back, Ra'hish stripped the dead East Tunnel warriors of their blades and left the corpses to the teeth of G'kaa's men. He descended the rocks toward G'kaa and watched the other rats spill along the titanic carcass, stinking in the waves.

The warlord breathed in the stench and then fixed Ra'hish in a glare. "What would you have done with the whale carcass, Ra'hish?"

"Traded it for grain. Grain keeps – meat rots."

"I'll give you grain. The war band needs meat! How often does a rat get to feed on whale?" He gestured to the rocks above, where snarling Itheem tore the bodies of the dead scouts into meat.

Ra'hish ignored them. He fought through the surging waves to climb atop the beached whale. The flesh smelled strong and salty. Ra'hish sawed himself a piece of fin and dragged it clumsily back on shore. He found a perch and ate, his back to the rocks and all approaches covered – the life habits of an Itheem without a clan.

Below him, hundreds of Itheem came to throw ropes about the dead whale and drag it onshore. They would strip the flesh and blubber and scoop the marrow from the bones. In Acomar, nothing could be allowed to go to waste – not even the bodies of the dead.

G'kaa moved behind his females and warriors, snarling at the shirkers.

Ra'hish narrowed his eyes in thought. The war band must number two thousand, with nestlings hidden somewhere in the ruins above. For a male to command so many was utterly unheard of. The Itheem were matriarchal. A mother bred a dozen nestlings a year, all of whom would grow to be adults under her command – mother to grandmother, great grandmother to clan mistress. A female needed sons to fight for her and daughters to breed more warriors. More nestlings meant more mouths to feed. Rats bred, numbers swelled, the wastelands were scoured of every edible thing. . . . But without numbers, the war band would be consumed by their rivals, the warriors slain, the nestlings eaten. In the end, numbers were everything.

Numbers. Ra'hish had a clan at last. Now he would see if survival here was easier than living hidden and alone. With a long glance toward the rich green lands beyond the ruins, Ra'hish slowly narrowed his eyes. The piece of fin weighed heavy in his hands. Tearing with his incisors, the rat chewed his unlovely meal while cold breezes rippled past his fur.

§ § §

A lack of humor was the biggest problem in Tupan's life. Not in herself, of course, but no one else in the world seemed to know how to take a joke. The armed mob baying behind her was a perfect case in point – good people in their own way, but with no appreciation of the sheer *value* laughter brought to life! A joke was gold. Fun was treasure! Tupan could only sigh for the failings of an unkind world. Running fleet-footed across the icy mountains, smoke streaming from her tail, she pondered the sad state of the world and lengthened her stride.

Tupan sped away on all fours, through a landscape made brilliant with snow and ice. Icy wind coursed down her long, pointed nose and across watering, guileless eyes, rippling the golden fur on her skinny ribs. The coyote girl wore a fantastic motley of ribbons, patchwork, and bells, which fluttered all about her as she ran. Each tassel waved farewell to the lynch mob behind. Fleet of foot and lean of flank, the girl seemed half stick insect and half starved wolf, though she always claimed her sparse lines were a result of fashion choice rather than famished necessity.

She ran with the speed of long practice, practice forced on her by a sadly unappreciative world. On the whole, she decided, Uruth were a dull sort of breed. Other Uruth – Tupan considered herself outside normal considerations of species, intellect, or sex – valued toil too much. Surely a bright moment in their lives was worth the price of a little food, a little drink, and the high seer's prize-winning eels?

Life for a young coyote could often be a vale of woes.

The dogs lagged behind, not having had the advantages of a life spent in high-speed chase. The mountain air was fine and clear – perhaps a little sharp, but still, Tupan felt no reason to complain. She sped across the frosty grass, patchwork gloves protecting her pretty hands. The skies were blue, the bright sun shone, and it was promising to become a wondrous day.

A pine tree overhead suddenly exploded as a spell plowed into the boughs.

Blinking, Tupan launched into overdrive, almost running out of her fur. Behind her, a high priestess gave a triumphant scream and dragged another spell out of the air.

Tupan gave a sudden squeal of fear and dived across the ground. The flame dart skipped aside and buried itself in a hayrick in the fields, setting the pile of winter fodder afire.

The coyote girl had troubles of her own. She had entered a madly sloping forest of hawthorn thickets and tall pines – a place where

sunbeams never fell. A deep-dished mountain stream had frozen early for
the season, and it was into this slippery trough that Tupan tripped and
fell. She hit the ice and skidded off downstream, sitting on her backside
as she dazedly gathered speed.

"Oh, *pooh.*"

Tupan sat on her bottom, hands held out in front. Ducking beneath a
branch, she began to enjoy the ride. Landscape whizzed wildly past as
the slope grew ever sharper. The friction upon her bottom was hardly
pleasant, but it was at least less tiring than running. Tupan looked
owlishly about and decided to fit her chance discovery into a greater
plan.

Shouts and hunting howls came from far behind, where four pack
mates of the high seer had launched themselves belly down into the
frozen stream. It was all rather excessive for a few vegetables, a few
missing trinkets, and having the seer pitch into a barrel of live eels.

Tupan frantically paddled with her hands to get more speed, but the
belly riders shot forward at a fantastic pace, baying as they came. And
then the whole journey took a down turn.

Tupan blinked as she felt the stream bed slope even more steeply
down the mountainside. Wailing, she raced through a high-banked curve
and saw the stream bed end in open space. A pine bough slashed toward
her face. Tupan grabbed the limb and jerked aloft, her tail whipping out
above a dizzy fall into a lake below. She glanced down in time to see
four pairs of eyes looking up as they took the plunge. The last dog gave a
heart rending glance of disappointment as gravity took hold and flung
him into a freezing bath three dozen body-spans below.

Quick as a weasel, Tupan slithered down the tree and raced toward
the valley floor. She plunged in great leaps from tree root to tree root
above the hard-packed snow. Reaching a rocky ledge, she made a dizzy
spring out to the tip of a pine rooted in the valley below. Needles
exploded out as she took hold, and the treetop swayed dangerously. The
coyote shinnied down the pine until she neared the bottom. She couldn't
help making a joyous noise as she slid down the trunk in a shower of
bark. Once there, she ran on among steeply stacked boulders. A new
snowfall began drifting through the skies.

Across her path ran a dirt road, all black with slush and lined with
pony carts, creaking and swaying on their way. A quick run down the
slope brought Tupan to the road. She whipped between the legs of
frowning horses and raced along a line of carts. There were signs and
legends written on the sides of the vehicles. Had Tupan been able to
read, she would surely have taken great pleasure in seeing what each one
had to say. As it was, she shot beneath a cart laden with clay pots packed
in straw. There she found a suitable, if uncomfortable hiding place,
hanging upside down between the wheels.

Plodding stolidly along the road, the spotted pony towing the cart suddenly hung its head to peer awkwardly back between its legs. "What are you doing under there?" it asked in a slow voice – rather ponderous of thought, in fact.

Tupan cleared her throat and gave a gay swirl of her tail. "I am investigating the axles of your cart! Most fascinating."

"I don't think you should be down there." The pony had a bass voice, rather in keeping with its shaggy pelt and beetled brows. "It's not allowed."

From his seat atop the cart, the driver scuttled back and forth to peer beneath the cart. The young hound finally hung upside down, only to find himself snout to snout with a pair of guileless hazel eyes. "Hey, you! What are you doing?"

"Your wheel nuts were loose!" Tupan clung on with feet and fingers, making a show of hammering at one of the cart's solid wooden wheels. "Good thing I came along!"

"You can't stay down there!"

"Oh, thank you!" Slick as a snake, Tupan shot up onto the seat beside the driver and avidly thumped him between the shoulder blades. "Much better! Most neighborly of you. Oh, wow – you really have quite a view!" Tupan removed a folded black blanket from beneath the young driver's rump and whipped it quickly about herself as a shawl, utterly covering her eccentric finery. "Hey, I brought some beer. You got anything to eat?"

The driver flapped his lower jaw like a fish dragged from the river. He was a tall gray short-fur, a little on the stringy side, but smooth and sleek as glass. The greyhound stared at Tupan in bewildered outrage, only then noticing he had a small flask of beer in his hand.

A deep throated baying came from the woods above. Six or seven heavy canines – shag-furred creatures dressed for the mountain winter – burst out of the forest. They held pitchforks, clubs, and wooden rakes, and seemed more than a tad annoyed. The males ran along the slow-moving line of carts, leaping to peer into the cargo trays. Farther back, the females were down on all fours, sniffing hopelessly at the mud and slush in hopes of picking up a scent.

Still bemusedly holding his beer, the wagon driver was accosted by a warrior clinging to the cart. "Hey! Hey – seen a girl? Hey, you! Have you seen a girl go by?"

"Eh? A girl?" Tupan replied in a voice infinitely frail. She had tied one of her own ribbons about her eyes as a blindfold and quested blindly back and forth to find the speaker's face. "A girl, do you say?" She sniffed the air like a connoisseur. "No girls here. Last one I smelled was two hundred spans back along the road. She headed north."

"North? Thank you, Old One!" The black-furred hunter swung an arm and gave a howl to summon his troops. "*North! Spread out and head north!*" The newcomers rushed forward, leaving the carts to wend their way along the road in peace.

Slipping the ribbon from her eyes, Tupan vigorously scratched a flea or two and gave a happy sigh.

The wagon driver and his pony stared after the departing hunters, ears sagging in disbelief. "Who were those people?"

"Aaaah! Possibly the minions of an evil overlord! An overlord who has had his eye upon a certain beautiful young coyote girl and now intends to keep her prisoner!"

"What!" The driver gaped at Tupan in shock. "Really?"

"No, no – I said *possibly*." Tupan had found the driver's lunch under the seat and tossed an apple to the horse. "This meat cake is pretty good! Hey, are you going to drink all of that beer?"

On the road behind, four sorry figures trudged out of the woods. They were blue with cold, sneezing and dripping wet from head to toe. Leaving frozen duckweed in their wake, they shambled along past the wagons, heading on their comrades' trail. The last of the warriors gave a titanic sneeze as he came level with Tupan's cart.

The pony *tut-tut-tutted* and shook his head in evident sympathy. "Don't catch cold."

"Thanks." The frozen dog waved to the pony, lifted his head in puzzlement, and then wrenched about and looked straight into Tupan's eyes.

The girl froze to her seat and made an annoyed little noise. "Oooooooh. *fur balls!*" She stuffed the rest of the driver's lunch into her mouth and vigorously snapped her tasseled belt against the draft pony's rear.

The creature gave a squeal of shock and broke into a gallop, arcing off the road and racing crazily along the snowy ground. The cart bounced wildly in the pony's wake, pots all jouncing high for a moment only to land with a spectacular unison crash. In an instant, the cart had sped past the four wet and weary hunters, who raised a croak of alarm that their comrades could never hope to hear. The cart and pony careered southward, heading against the traffic flow, and then bumped across the road and landed with a bone-shuddering clatter.

Downhill offered the best escape route, and the cart bounded off hidden logs to ram its way madly down the mountain slope. The pony seemed to know where it was going. Tupan freed herself of the blanket and took a grateful draft of air, looking about as cart, driver, and pony jittered crazily across the ground.

"You know – one day I'm going to get myself one of these!"

As she spoke, the driver gave Tupan a look of absolute amazement. An instant later, one wheel rolled free and slowly wandered off across the snow. The cart slammed hard against the ground, breaking pots and jarring Tupan's rear. The pony galloped on, dragging the shattered cart behind him until at last the second wheel broke free. The cart slid down a great, steep hill, collected the astonished pony, and then tobogganed down the side of a ravine. With the greyhound wailing and the pony blinking great, sad eyes, the cart eventually shot down through a forest and slammed straight into a thorny stand of hawthorn trees.

An awful silence fell. Amid a scattered ruin of pots, straw packing, quaking ponies, and bits of cart, Tupan had emerged utterly unscathed. She dusted herself off, walked past the panting pony and stuck an apple in his mouth. Then she extricated the handsome young cart driver from beneath a bank of snow. "What's your name?"

"What?" The greyhound sat in a freezing drift of snow, almost knocked out of his wits. "It's – um, Surolf."

"Surolf? Tupan!" The beribboned coyote girl stuck out one wet, elegantly gloved hand. "How are you doing?"

"Not well."

"It'll be fine. Hey, I can catch a hare, and we can cook it over hawthorn twigs for tea! Did you see any berries on your way down?"

The driver and pony sat side by side in the wreckage and exchanged a look of bewildered horror. Surolf watched the coyote girl as she happily collected twigs in the snow. Stunned, he lifted his hands, trying to somehow shape a concept out of the empty winter air. "Tupan?"

"Yes?"

"I hate you."

The girl snapped her fingers, utterly oblivious to it all. "Hoopy! Hey, and you haven't even tried my cooking!"

Girding her bells and ribbons all about her, the girl went happily off to make a decent lunch. Lost and drained, her companions numbly sank into the snow and prayed that the bad dream would simply end.

Chapter 2

On a cold, ashen ruin, in a land made brittle by the sound of claws and shattered glass, Oosha sat and stared at visions that only she could see. She hunched atop a mound of broken stone stained with flecks of rust, like old, decaying blood. Her white fur shone clean as morning frost. She stared, hypnotized, through her strange, pink eyes.

Below her, Itheem swarmed in their thousands, her fellow rats chittering and smothering the very ground. There were weapon smiths and warriors, nests guarded by spitting females, blind babies, matriarchs and squabbling young. At the center of the swarming clan, two males fought each other over a scrap of food. Blades rang and fur flew as the enemies – brothers from the same mother's brood – killed each other over a withered ear of corn.

Oosha stared, seeing in this one fight the ghosts of a thousand other mindless battles. Small, delicate, and purest white, Oosha could only watch with saddened eyes and wonder at the emptiness inside her soul.

Another female crowded onto the rocks beside her; a sister, Teela, the liveliest of her mother's brood. The girl watched the two combatants fight and gave an admiring, anxious cry. "Look at him go!" Teela gripped the rocks and leaned forward in avid interest. "If the little one wins, I think I'll try to mate with him!"

"You what?" Oosha's voice drifted as though she had trouble returning from a dream. "What will you do?"

"You know – mate." Embarrassed, Teela kept her innocent black eyes on the fight. "It's all right. I know him. He's really nice – he came over last night to give me a piece of honey. If he wins, maybe I should. Strong mates make strong babies. Strong babies make strong bodyguards."

Astonished and uncomfortable, Oosha turned to look her sister in the eye. "We're too young!"

"No we're not! The sooner we start, the more clan we make! Faala already has a brood!"

"Faala is weird."

"Yeah – right." Teela looked into her sister's pink-within-pink eyes. "Eighteen months from now, she'll have ten grown kids to hunt for her and guard her!"

Oosha felt a nasty, crawling sensation in her fur. She turned to look carefully at her sister, and saw a fresh scratch across her nose. "Has something happened? Did someone try to hurt you?"

"No." Teela evasively turned away, but fluffed her pelt and made a lie of her own words. "Nothing's happened. I'm just thinking about the future, that's all. . . . You *have* to have babies. Lots of them; they'll never let you stop until you do." The gray rat carefully kept her gaze on the distant fight. "If you're going to, I will, too. It won't be so hard that way."

Oosha looked away and miserably ruffled her fur. Teela bit her lip and subsided into an uncomfortable silence. No rat *had* to breed, no one except Oosha. The two sisters nestled side by side and watched the fight from afar, their long pink tails hanging down into the breeze. "Teela?"

"Yes?"

"Don't do it yet."

On the dueling mound below, Teela's sweetheart screamed and died. He was instantly consumed by the crowd, the body disappearing beneath a rush of jaws. Sickened, Teela turned away and hid her face against Oosha's weird white fur, trying to shut the scene out of her mind.

Claws and hisses, babies screaming, bodies crawling over one another in the dark. Teela hunched against Oosha and put her hands against her ears, but then suddenly broke away and bolted down a tunnel mouth. Dismayed, Oosha ran after her sister and caught her by the tail, holding her still until she felt the quieting of her heart. Oosha nuzzled her pink nose against her sister's hide and led her into a black and silent world.

A narrow tunnel twisted down into hidden places, long feared and unused. Moving with sure instincts, the sisters climbed down a gigantic black crevasse, scattering blind crickets and walking along beside a bitter, sulfurous stream. They passed places where the rock had flowed like liquid night, solidifying into frightening shapes that twisted through the soil. The tunnels wound and crisscrossed in a twisted maze, each one scarcely wide enough for a single rat to travel on all fours. Great long clever whiskers brushed against the walls and read the currents in the air, moving the two rats unerringly through the kingdom of the blind.

The path sloped upward, ever upward beside a wall of freezing stone. Teela led the way to their favorite haunt – a place they had discovered together what seemed a lifetime ago. When they had first sat here, a year before; their eyes had scarcely been open for a fortnight, and all the world had seemed brilliant and new. They had wandered through forbidden caves and found a special place all their own. The tunnel rose through a strange buried tower of stone until it reached a square window that looked out onto open air. Perched high above a mighty valley, the little cave seemed a perch made for eagles; a place utterly isolated and alone.

In the valley below, countless bones rattled to the fingers of the wind. A mound rose in the center of the valley; the dark hummock of the oracle. Said to be a gift made by Giants to guide the Itheem, it was an place of dark, malicious power. Caves riddled the mound, black openings fringed with roots and sickly ferns. To these caves, Itheem came.

A cave could be filled with offerings – rusted relics or sterile seeds, iron ore or sickly young – and after many days, the cave would open its jaws and allow the rats to cautiously explore. Sometimes the oracle was kind. Rust-laden soil became steel ingots. Sterile seed grains suddenly shone with life. Other times, the oracle brought horror and pain. An injured child was liquefied. Metals turned foul and soft with rot. . . . As unpredictable as it was, the power of the oracle had caused countless savage wars. The vale of skulls was littered with millions of bones. When winds blew across the vale, they sighed between the empty skulls as though the dead still somehow found strength to moan.

The East Tunnel Clan was now guardian of the oracle – an honor for which five thousand of the clan had died. Yet they held the valley, and the oracle was now more often kind than cruel. The bloodline of the Hastaasi ran strong within the clan.

Most Itheem were gray, brown, or black. Of all the Itheem, the rarest were the Hastaasi – those marked by white. It was a coloring from the Before Time, from the ages of Giants and of gods. The white-furred ones had been servants to the Giants, it was said, and from time to time the oracles repaid the debt.

If a Hastaasi gave an offering to the oracle, the results were more often good than bad. It was a secret that brought prosperity. Other clans would trade food for the privilege of having the East Tunnel Clan present their offerings. Trade made the survival struggle easier, and so the East Tunnel Clan had begun to prosper and grow.

Then Oosha had been born. She was not patched or flecked with white. Her fur was a throwback to ancient times – a pure, unblemished white upon fair pink skin, with white whiskers, white claws, and pink eyes that could never stand strong light. When she came of age, the oracle would surely cherish her, and the clan's granaries would bulge. But day after day, Oosha sat in meditation in the caves. Never once had she felt the oracle reach out to whisper in her mind.

From their perch high above the valley, the whole scene seemed strangely unreal. The two sisters gazed past the plain of bones, toward the brooding shape of the oracle. Here and there, the bone piles shifted, making brittle tinkling noises in the breeze.

Oosha stared blankly down at vista, as stark-white as her own fur. "Kash the Maker said that if you sleep on top of an old machine, you can hear it whisper to you in your sleep. It will tell you what it used to do."

Teela kept her eyes upon the bones. "And what happens then?"

"You can make it work again. But only if you have the talent. Only if you really believe."

Teela – thin and pretty – turned an anxious eye toward her sister. "You're Hastaasi. You don't have to believe; you *know*."

"Do I?" Oosha wrung her hands, feeling small against Teela's simple, honest faith. "Yes . . . yes, I suppose I do."

"It will speak to you in time. You are Hastaasi." Teela reached out to touch her sister's strange white fur. "One day you'll make the oracle be good to us all the time."

At two years of age, the sisters were very nearly full grown. Another year might see them grow in size, but already they were almost a match for any other Itheem in the nest. In the meanwhile, they *learned*. Each young Itheem retained knowledge at a frightening rate, far faster than any other species. They needed the knowledge. Within two years of birth, they would be raising nestlings, battling enemies, and warring with other clans. Within four, they would probably be dead. Itheem never grew old; the vicious fight for survival claimed them sooner than later.

Rat games were simple games; rat art was simple art. Skills were crude, dictated by the brutal drive to eat, breed, and survive. As the ruins became more crowded, population pressures grew. The race controlled its numbers by gorging on its own blood.

Looking out across the plain of bones, the two sisters felt the future like a claw upon their hearts, and shivered, even though the tunnel air was still and warm. A long, uncomfortable silence fell as the sisters stared down at the hollow, dusty bones.

Teela picked at the stone window ledge with her claws. "I'll wait. Maybe I won't mate quite yet."

The sea breeze rippled through the plain of sighing towers. From the distance came a deep booming sigh of sound – a vibration that made fur rise in simple awe. Gazing off toward the north, Oosha and Teela felt the music like a caress upon their skin. This was why they came here, to feel the touch of mystery. The sighing bones, the distant sounds . . . the oracle asleep beneath their feet. For a few brief moments, the world seemed something more than nestlings, fangs, and war.

As clouds came in from the north, the music swelled. It ebbed and flowed like magic into the sisters' souls.

Entranced, Teela lifted her hands, as though feeling the music in the wind. "It's there again! Isn't it wonderful? It's like the whole world can sing!"

"It's strange." Oosha – small, pale, and fey – seemed to watch the passing music with her eyes. "So beautiful, even here, among the bones."

Teela swayed, utterly entranced by the sounds. "It's from the plain of sighing towers. Nest-mama K'shh says it's a place where nothing lives. She says there are gates that suck lost rats into the land of Gur, where the ghosts of dead things go." The thin young rat tried to touch the music with her hands. "But it can't really be bad, can it? When it sings, I see beautiful things in my mind."

"When you go there, I wonder if the music talks to you in your sleep." Oosha drew in a long, cool breath, slowly blinking herself awake. "That would be better than talking to oracles and Giants."

"Yes." Teela tilted her head to weigh the thought, and then noticed that Oosha had suddenly slipped through the window and was walking headfirst down the wall. The cliff face hung a hundred dizzy spans above the valley floor, yet Oosha scarcely seemed to care. Her feet gripped the bricks with unconscious skill and let her walk easily toward the ground.

Teela half stuck herself from the tunnel mouth and blinked in alarm. "Oosha?" There was no answer. Testing her grip fearfully one foot at a time, Teela started down the wall. "Oosha, there might be enemy patrols out there! Maybe we shouldn't go."

Deep and powerful, the music of the towers came. Teela jerked her head in awe. With bright eyes and a surging heart, she instantly shot down the wall and joined her sister as she perched upon a mound of bones. They both quested with clever whiskers and listened to the skies, feeling the music washing through their fur.

Oosha suddenly felt utterly alive. Her pink eyes were fixed and bright, and her white fur stood stiff and tingling. "We could try to sleep there, just tonight! We could see if we hear the words!"

"All night?"

"Yes – all night!" Oosha turned and took her sister by the hand. "We can sit and hear it sing!"

One tiny strand of caution tugged at Teela's thoughts. "If the matriarchs find you're gone, they'll pop their skulls!"

"No one will notice! No one saw us leave the nest!"

To be almost grown was to be one part child. The sisters felt adventure call and suddenly went scampering on their way. They ran across the fields of bones, slowly leaving the sinister valley far behind. The black mound of the oracle lay forgotten in their wake. White fur and gray fur slithering through the bones, they slipped off into the piles of skulls, and went to hear the singing of the world.

§   §   §

"Come on! Let me make it up to you!"

"Go away!"

"Oh, please!" Tupan's banter took on a deliberate, annoying whine. *"Please please please please please!"*

Twilight in the mountains seemed almost black as night. The snow fell thick and hard enough to fill the air like fog, swirling in stinging flakes between the trees. Frozen, shivering, and annoyed, Surolf plodded side by side with his partner the pony and kept his ears hanging flat against his skull. "Sod off!"

"Are you mad? With me?" Tupan recoiled as though the thought were sent from a far-off world. "With *me? What for?"*

Utterly agog, Surolf stopped in his tracks, up to his knees in freezing snow. *"What for?* My pots are broken, my trip is ruined, and now I'm lost in the damned snow! You have *personally* destroyed my entire life!"

"Oh, well – like *I'm* responsible for your pots deciding to just fall apart!" Tupan crossed her arms, her whole body miming a magnificent sulk. "So, what were you doing? Trudging along the road to nowhere. I brought a little fun into your life!"

Dragging the shaft poles of the broken cart as a shoddy travois, Hern the pony frowned and rumbled at the ground. "I don't like fun."

Tupan ground her knuckles into the creature's skull. "Hey, beetle brain – *everyone* likes fun!"

"Oh." The pony looked slowly about at the snowy wastes. "Is this fun?"

"What – walking through pristine woods, having adventures, talking to friends." Tupan threw open her hands to encompass the great outdoors. "Of *course* it's fun!"

"I thought so." The pony heaved another sigh. "I don't like it."

Tupan sucked a tooth and looked at the creature from the corner of her eye. "Just pull the damned travois."

"Okay."

Surolf lifted his burden – a stretcher filled with the few unbroken bits of earthenware. "Thanks to you, we're hungry, cold, and about to die, lost in a damned empty wilderness!"

Her fur and ribbons covered in falling snow, the coyote girl lifted her arms. "Hey, are we lost? Did anyone *tell* you we are lost?"

Hern the pony raised his head and gave a sigh. "I did."

"Did anyone with *opposable thumbs* tell you we are lost?" Tupan threw a hand across Surolf's snow-slathered shoulders. "Of course not!"

Surolf kept his head down and trudged uncomfortably through the snow. "Look, lady. It's nightfall. We missed the road. We are *lost!*"

"Ha!" Tupan snapped her fingers in the air. "Well, it shows how much you know. Because I know exactly where we are!"

"Oh, yeah? *Where?*"

"We are standing at the beginning of something beautiful."

They had come to a halt beside a sharp ridge of rock from the mountain above. The coyote girl's bells tinkled all about her as she bent and lifted a hatchway covered by a layer of fresh snow. Beyond the hatch was a clean dry cave – a long rock tunnel made smooth by a layer of fine, springy silk. Warm, dry, and empty – and big enough to hold Hern the pony and a dozen of his breed. Surolf scratched his long gray muzzle and shot a sidewise glance toward the girl.

"How did you know this would be here?"

"Seemed the right place for it to be." The slender, sloe-eyed coyote gave a bright flick of her tail. "Get ol' hoof-head in out of the snow, will you! I'll build a fire."

Surolf kept himself well away from the opening of the tunnel. "Lady, this is a spider cave – and I don't think we can really deal with giant arachnid carnivores right now!"

"Ha!" The girl danced happily inside the cave, Hern plodding at her heels. "Well, *laughing boy*, it just so happens that arachnids have dirt-poor respiratory systems. They don't breath properly in the cold. So, if there was a spider here, he'd have lit a fire! No fire, no spider!" Deep inside the cave, Tupan made a bed for herself out of a great wadded pile of spider web. "Relax!"

Annoyed, Surolf petulantly stood his ground out in the cold. "They do *not* have bad lungs!"

Hern trotted around and around in circles, enjoying the feel of springy silk underfoot. "Oh, they do, you know."

"Hern, you are *not* helping!"

The tunnel ran about a dozen spans back into the rocky ground, swelling out into a considerable cave, notably lacking any giant spiders.

Reluctantly edging farther in, Surolf sniffed at the air with his long, lean nose and felt the hackles rising on his spine. "I don't like it."

"Hey, beats the snow!" Tupan cleared a space of webbing and found a few twigs for a fire. "Hey, can you get me some pine cones from outside?"

The irritable greyhound shot a dark glance at the girl. "I thought *you* were going to start the fire?"

"I'll start it! But it needs something to feed on, hey?" Tupan's bells and ribbons swirled dreamlike as she walked. "Big cones are the best. The little tiny ones explode!" The girl's voice chased Surolf out into the cold. "And try to get a few branches, maybe a log or two!"

With a savage hiss of dislike, Surolf stalked back out into the freezing snow. Flakes fell soft and heavy, landing with a hush that muffled every other noise. The huge feathers of snow settled onto needles, branches, leaves – they smothered Surolf's footprints and filled the air with an impenetrable haze of white. Surolf pulled his shabby woolen jacket tight about his frame and simultaneously managed to lose a boot in a drift of snow. He retrieved the garment, pulled it back on – and felt the ice inside melt around his foot. Freezing wet and with his temper frayed, he eventually found his way back indoors and dumped a double armful of firewood down onto the floor.

A cheerful yellow fire had already sprung to life, filling the silk-lined cave with warmth and light. Much to Surolf's annoyance, he found his pony partner warming his backside and eyeing the ribbons now braided through his tail. His slow, thoughtful voice boomed richly through the cave. "I just don't know."

"Hey, it suits you! And ladies really go for these things!" Tupan had already begun braiding Hern's long, flowing mane. "You need more confidence! And a confident creature always knows how to groom!"

Surolf noisily dropped half a dozen pine cones on the fire. "Hern, what are you doing?"

"Grooming." The pony gave a long slow swish of his braided tail. "It feels rather odd."

"Right. Whatever." Surolf poked his way through the bundles rescued from the cart wreckage and found carrots, more carrots, and a solitary onion. There wasn't a steak or a piece of jerky in sight. "Hern, I thought I asked you to find food in the wreckage?"

"I did find food. Lots of food." Hern dipped his head into the bundles on his travois and came up with yet another bunch of carrots. "See? There's plenty for everyone."

"Great. Two hundred raw carrots, and one onion."

Suddenly interested, Tupan eagerly jerked her head. "Hey, I'll eat the onion!"

"Somehow I knew you were going to say that." Surolf tossed the thing toward her, where she caught it and began to eat it like an apple, skin and all. Surolf winced at the awful smell. "Stay over there!"

The coyote girl made herself obscenely comfortable, flopping back onto a spider-silk cushion and stretching out her tawny legs. Her long, toeless boots were pointed at the fire, her claws wriggling with pleasure as heat stole into her pads.

With an audible crunch, she bit into the raw onion and chewed while she talked, having to shout to be heard over the noise of Hern crunching scores of carrots. "So, hey, laughing boy! Surolf – so what's your story?"

The gray-furred young canine looked at a carrot as though it were poisoned, and then held it out to toast above the fire. "I am not telling you one solitary thing about my life."

"Fine. Shall I tell you about mine?"

"No!"

Hern worked big yellow teeth, consuming his carrots, tops and all. "I can tell you about mine."

Tupan gaily took a bite of onion. "Hoopy!"

"Hern!" Surolf shot the pony a dire, dark glance. "She probably just wants to hit you up for money!"

"I don't have any money." Hern took a fresh bunch of carrots in surprisingly nimble lips. As he ate, the carrot tops traveled to one corner of his mouth. "No pockets. Can't carry any."

Tupan decided she could go for a carrot or two; she polished a root against her tawny fur and gaily crunched it between her fangs.

"Thought you pony guys mostly hung out with cats?"

"Cats make me sneeze."

"Hoopy! They make me hungry. So, hey, you pull wagons, though!" Tupan flipped over onto all fours, hoisting her skirt to present her bottom to the flames. "Is it fun?"

"I don't know. I've never done it before. This was our first time."

"Hern!" Surolf put down his scorched carrot on a stick, trying to avoid looking up Tupan's skirt. "She doesn't need to know!"

"So, this was your first time off the farm! Hey, hoopy!" Tupan rested her bright-eyed face upon her knuckles. "And you met me straight away! That was lucky!"

"Yeah. *Real* lucky." The male dog chewed on a scorched and stringy carrot. "Be still, my beating heart."

"But it's great! I mean, we can go wherever you're going – together!" Tupan sniffed, decided her tail might be singeing, and spread her skirt to the sides. Damp clothing gave off a visible cloud of steam. "Now no one gets a boring trip!"

Lean and gray, Surolf hunched like a ghoul over his wretched meal. "I *wanted* a boring trip. I wanted to sell my pots and get the futz back home!"

"Why's it so important to sell so many pots?"

Surolf kicked at the floor in anger. "Because I need to be rich!"

Tupan's skirt had turned transparent against the flames. "Will you sit down! You're being annoying!"

"So, I'm sitting!" Tupan perched herself prettily upon a wadded roll of silk. "See? Sitting. Now what's with this 'rich' stuff? We've got fresh snow, wide skies, good company! What do you need that you don't have now?"

Grumbling, Surolf decided to feed the fire. "I need to meet a bride-price. That's what I need money for."

"Oooooh!" Tupan slitted her lashes and gave a gleeful sidewise glance toward Surolf. "Romance in the air?"

"He howls for her." Hern had turned his side to the fire and had gone back to admiring his plaited tail. "On the mound in the village center, he puts his head back and howls."

"Mmmm? How interesting!"

Stung, the gray-furred youth pitched a pine cone at Hern's flank. "Thanks for keeping your mouth shut!"

"No problem." Hern blinked, slowly organizing thoughts. "Her name's Aela. Her brothers chased Surolf clean out of town."

"You fought her brothers?" Tupan's face showed mock disapproval, and she fanned herself with carrot tops. "Eeeew, that's just *so* uncouth!"

"I did *not* fight her brothers!" Surolf speared pine needles into the flames. "I ran away! If her family knew it was me courting her, I'd be a laughing stock!"

"Oh, why?"

The young dog jabbed angrily at the fire. "Because I'm poor! I'm from a no-account pack from a tumbledown house, and she's the daughter of the village alpha pair!" Surolf hugged his arms against his knees. "I worked for a year to afford all those pots. I was going to sell them in Kamla town and make enough profit to prove myself to her parents."

Tupan tilted her head, mouth open and eyes shining bright. It took a moment for Surolf to realize she was almost moved to tears. "Surolf – that . . . that's so beautiful!" Suddenly the girl sat up, inspiration dawning inside her like a golden light. She radiated an inspiration so pure, so primal that it filled the air like a song. "Okay, we're going to win you your bride!"

Panic plunged into Surolf's heart like an ice-cold stone. "Oh, no."

"Yes! Hern and I will do it with you! We'll help you get that bride-price – just you see!"

"No, now look. Just *don't* help!"

"It'll be magical!" Tupan rose, staring into the flames as though gazing at a vision only she could see. "A stalled romance – lovers imprisoned by the chains of fate! And together we three can forge the keys to unlock your happiness."

"Oh, no." Appalled, Surolf tried to back away. "Look, I'll think of something on my own! Maybe make more pots or something."

"I'll help." Hern had retreated from the fire and sat down on a lump on the ground. "I'm good at treading clay."

"We don't want to spend weeks making pots! Someone will have stolen the girl by then!" Tupan paced on all fours, her shadow looming huge on the wall. "No, we need quick, decisive business! Let's find what assets we have at hand and get you your bride-price! We'll have you tucked up with your wife in no time!"

Throwing a pine cone at the fire, Surolf merely looked miserable. "Assets? What assets!"

The girl happily rattled a little canvas bag. "Hey, we have potsherds!"

"Very useful." Surolf rested his face on one hand and stared at the flames. "We'll really make it big with those."

"There's a way! There's always a way!" Sitting on her haunches, Tupan gave a vast, expressive wave of her hands. "Hey, you're with *me* now!"

"Yes, I forgot. I'm with you." Surolf hung his head. "I feel so much better now."

The coyote girl crouched down and lifted Surolf's chin, suddenly seeming quiet and intense. "Look, true love is hoopy, and the world likes hoopy things to happen!" Tupan tugged at Surolf's ear. "You can't argue with the world! It's taller than you are and has an awful lot more teeth. Just hang out with me; Tupan fixes things!" The coyote scratched Surolf happily between the ears. "Relax. Hey, Hern, what's so good over there in the corner?"

"It's warm here." Hern had made himself comfortable atop a strange swelling in the cave floor. "I like it."

The girl frowned, abandoned Surolf, and made her way to the far end of the cave. She leaned over and put a hand on the floor, feeling the rock glow warmly beneath her hand. She sucked one tooth as she sniffed a slight hint of sulfur in the air, and then saw a tiny volcanic stream leaking through the rear of the cave. The hot water made that area toasty warm.

Tupan instantly became a whirlwind of activity.

"Ooookay! Um. Hey, have you boys done much traveling in the mountains?"

Hern blinked. "No."

"Well, the secret is to always travel at night. Navigate by the stars! That's the way it's done."

"Well, it's almost night now." Hern thoughtfully swallowed a last carrot top. "We ought to be going."

Quickly repacking the rations and storing the potsherds stored, Tupan made ready to go.

Surolf could only watch in shock. "I am *not* going out into a mountain snowstorm at night!" Surolf planted both fists on his hips and glared at his two brainless companions. "It's freezing out there!"

"Hey, at night we can find lights and watch fires easily. Basic travel procedure!" Tupan had already packed Hern's travois, moving with unseemly haste. She hastily stamped out the campfire, producing a bed of coals and a prodigious amount of irritating pine smoke. "Come on. Better go quick, or we'll lose valuable darkness!"

Spluttering in protest, Surolf had no choice except to follow as his two companions bustled swiftly out the door. The lean greyhound gathered a final carrot, shot one last, wistful look toward the coals, and followed the others out into a sharp and chilly dusk. The threesome blundered swiftly through the trees and lost themselves in a universe of snow.

§

Back at the cave, the evening shadows fell. Muted by snow and the gentle hush of pine needles, the winter breeze was full of endless peace.

Pad-pad-padding through the snow, there came a bumbling visitor. White furred and splay-footed, all eight eyes shining puppy bright, a gigantic spider scuttled down across the ridge. The hunting had been good – a large deer wrapped in silk trailed the creature. The spider dragged its winter food toward its front door, deftly pulling a strand of web to lift the hatch high.

Eight bright black eyes glittered in innocent puzzlement as the creature smelled the smoke inside its lair. Little paps pumped like white gloves shadow-boxing at the air. The spider smelled food – warm bodies and the reek of fresh-crushed onion. Moving cautiously, the creature found his way indoors and tested out the spaces deep inside. He found onion skins, carrot tops, and the coals of a well-laid fire glowing merrily in the middle of his floor.

The visitors had gone, leaving his house in a state of disarray. Still, the gift of a fire was much appreciated. Moving swiftly against the chill, the silky spider gathered in his evening meal and battened down his door, expecting the freezing cold that every creature on the mountain knew would strike before dawn.

Chapter 3

"There!" Poised whip-slim against the evening light, Teela quivered her whiskers as though she could somehow even *smell* the sounds. "It's stronger over there!"

Oosha and Teela skittered to the top of a pile of strange, rusted shards, there to sit with sea breezes lifting their fur. The sun sank across the violent ocean, spreading blood-red stains through the thickening clouds. To the north, the titanic metal pylons towering above the forbidden plain cast shadows as stark and black as night.

Light had begun to leak up through the soil – a tiny twinkle that moved in rivulets of scarlet, blue, and gold. It grew point by point, grain by grain as the sky darkened into evening. The light cast weird hues across Oosha's stark white fur, making her merge into the land.

Moving slowly, carefully, the rats placed their fine pink feet upon the sands. Their toes sank into the cold granules and took grip, feeling the strange sensation of clean grains sifting through their feet. With a glance at one another, the sisters walked out into the dunes, losing themselves in the plain of sighing towers. The music of the pylons hummed and throbbed deep into the young rats' hearts. Fascinated, they slid down a sand dune and took shelter from the cold.

"It's wonderful!" Dazed with excitement, Teela groomed her whiskers with her hands. "Don't you think it's wonderful?"

"It's empty. So peaceful. . . ." Her pink eyes adrift with the lights of another world, another time, Oosha felt the vibrations travel up into her flesh. "But nothing grows here. No weeds, no ants, no grass. I wonder why."

"Maybe the soil's too salty." Teela scratched behind her ear with one hind foot. "That happens by the seashore, doesn't it?"

"Someone said it did." Oosha had her usual abstracted, interested air, reading wonderful depths into everything around her. "But not here. I'd smell it."

"Yes, I think you would." Teela lifted her eyes toward the nearest pillar, a thing like a gargantuan rib rising from a buried monster far below. "Maybe we might find out?"

"Maybe."

Teela ran ahead, her bright eyes questing. Oosha came behind, thoughtful and aware, reading the strange currents of the world. The two young sisters walked in silence through the moonlit dunes, pink tails swaying gently as they went.

From the shadows behind them, something slid briefly into view; something pale and squat that watched the girls through glittering compound eyes. The shape waited – made a rhythmic clicking of its claws – and then slid in silence to follow the sisters' trail.

§ § §

G'kaa's war band numbered over two thousand Itheem of fighting age. Though he knew no mathematics, Ra'hish counted very well. Two thousand fighters – half of which were first quality – two thousand half-grown nestlings, and perhaps a hundred females too busy nursing to take positions in a battle line. It was a good combination, not too tail-heavy to pick up and move as needs demanded. G'kaa had recruited mostly males, savage young Itheem desperate for food or outcast from the clans. After two years, he had only just begun to breed his own warriors from the nest to the blade.

Two thousand elite warriors and a few sharp, controlling brains. Warriors needed weapons; they needed occupation; they needed food. The war band was too big to hide and lacked the females to sustain a long war with a proper clan.

And so it traded. G'kaa sold his services in war, spearheading assaults for the East Tunnel Clan against the Upsiders, or raids against hives of insect Thoud. Combat won rewards of food, and females would switch allegiance to join a victor. As his reputation grew, G'kaa became a power broker – a savage weight to tip the scales of battle. With the passing years, G'kaa had built an empire on a foundation of blood.

In the evening, the war band built fires and made meals. It had carved a new nest in unwanted territory, in a place where ridges ran crazy crisscrosses through hard mounds of crystal salts.

Alone as always, Ra'hish had wandered far from the nest and its sounds of violence and merriment. On a far-off hill, he dug patiently at the base of a basalt rod thrust into the ground, piling poisoned, rusted soil behind him.

The task interested him. There was a vein of discolored earth here, the usual sign of some strange treasure buried in the soil. The mystery of it tingled under his hands. What might it have been, and who might have made it so long ago? To creatures living in the ruins of Acomar, the Giants of ancient legend were very real. Their poisoned legacy remained as rust and salts and crystals twisting down into the dark heart of the world. No Itheem had ever made such terrifying, deadly things. No dog or cat or mad raccoon had ever raised metal pylons to the clouds. And so Ra'hish dug with tireless energy and wondered what it might be like to look into a giant's eyes.

He had gone three full body lengths down into the stinking soil before he heard the voices – a dozen voices, chittering, high, and brimming full of hero worship.

The sound came from twelve nestlings who stood in a semicircle behind him. They were half grown and bubbling with energy, a pack of avid little beings with the perfect memory all Itheem had at such an early age. Their ability to recall details would be only one of their irritating traits. Another would be that manic enthusiasm found only in the truly young. Their mother – probably a tousled, saucy piece of work with an eye for shiny baubles – must have abandoned them to beget another brood.

It was not Ra'hish's problem. The little rats could go off and survive like any other children. Fluffing out his fur, Ra'hish dug busily at his hole and hoped the growing problem would just fade away. In time, he looked back. At the rim of the hole, twelve young faces hung down to watch their hero at work. Shaking his head in annoyance, Ra'hish kept up his digging, flicking rust flakes out behind himself in the hope of hitting one of his audience in the nose.

He followed the rust vein down deeper in the earth, and suddenly felt something hard and ragged against his claws.

It was a characteristic of the Itheem that they usually knew what their fellow Itheem were thinking. Deep in his dirty hole, Ra'hish suddenly stopped his excavations and flattened his ears. "No!"

"Just one?" An eager young voice came from above. "Just learn us one?"

"That's *teach* you one – and *no*. I'm busy!"

To demonstrate his point, Ra'hish gave a brisk flurry of his claws, shooting dirt high up out of his tunnel. Having lived a life well outside of rat packs and crowded nests, Ra'hish felt he had excuse enough for being poor with conversation.

There came a sound of busy claws above. Ra'hish's audience had decided to help by dragging the spoil away from the edges of his tunnel. Feeling annoyed, the lean gray rat tugged at something heavy in the soil. He freed a heavy plaque of shiny metal from the rust and felt the acid deposits on the artifact burning his skin. Scrubbing his tattooed hands in the dirt, Ra'hish dragged his newfound treasure backward up the shaft, scrabbling out into the open air and shaking the debris from his fur.

Twelve tiny nestlings, bright and skinny and only half grown, ran around Ra'hish in a fascinated ring. Their fur had not yet been painted into protective stripes and lines. They wore no talismans, no feathers, no clan marks, but only the painted tails of G'kaa's followers. The youngsters fearlessly mobbed about Ra'hish, trying to help him dust off his new trinket and clean off his fur, more hindrance than help. Surrendering to the inevitable, Ra'hish let them struggle the heavy plaque over to a rock and industriously clean the dirt from the crevices in the surface. Some of the youngsters unoccupied by cleaning tugged at the fur of G'kaa's most introverted, solitary fighter and pestered him with a hundred thousand questions all at once.

Combing rust flakes from his whiskers, Ra'hish heaved a little sigh. "One each! One question each – and one at a time!"

The nestlings instantly gathered around, fighting for places as close to Ra'hish as possible. One, a thin female with startling tawny fur waved a hand and managed to speak first.

"What is it? What did you find?"

"How did you find it! How did you know it was in there?" Other brothers and sisters crowded close. "Does it work? Is it magic?"

Waving down the questions that surged toward him, Ra'hish settled the fighting batons lashed onto his arms.

"It's old, and it isn't metal, and it's hard. I won't know what it is until I've had a look at it! And how I found it is by looking." Ra'hish, who had a particular talent for locating strange junk, irritably shook the rust flakes from his fur. "Why don't you all go out and give it a try?"

Unfortunately the baby rats were not immediately seized by the desire to practice looking. Instead, they crowded closer about Ra'hish as he pulled a tuft of grass, dipped it in a rainwater puddle, and used it to scrub the deeply encrusted rust and crystals from the surface of his find.

It was a slab of pale blue material that seemed to almost sparkle with a light all its own. The hexagonal plaque was perhaps a finger's thickness and a forearm in length. One surface was smothered in tiny scored marks, cut with infinite precision, forming patterns that almost hypnotized the eye. On the front surface there were yet more markings – crisp shapes carved with cunning artistry.

As Ra'hish dusted the last of the dirt out of the lines, he knew he had made an extraordinary discovery.

A whip-thin boy rat turned his head sideways to stare at the markings on the plaque. "What are those?"

"Talk-marks. No one knows what they mean." Ra'hish touched them with a reverent, wondering hand. "But they say the marks keep ideas in them forever."

"Like the oracle?"

"No, not like the oracle. Talk-marks come to your eye and not your mind. Someone makes them, like painting clan marks with a stick."

The little rats all turned to stare in unison at the plaque. "Who made it?

"It's from the Before Time. Giants made it."

"Heeshan says there *are* no giants." One haughty little nestling spoke out from the rear, brimming with the certainties of youth. "He says they're nothing but a story."

Sitting beside a tunnel he had dug deep into the littered soil, Ra'hish raised one brow. "What's your name?"

"Jez. We told you; it's Eeka, Rika, Shika, Oota, Goota, Koopa, Marta, Barta, Loopi, Hoopi, Shoopi and Jez." The baby boy rat made a lofty little sniff. "And *I'm* Jez."

"Well, Jez, personally I'd avoid asking Heeshan for advice. He clearly has the brain power of a cuttlefish." Ra'hish gave a superior sneer. "If you want to know something, just ask me."

It was perhaps the defining mistake of Ra'hish's life. Nestlings instantly crowded close, clambering over each other in their eagerness to tug Ra'hish's fur.

"*Where did the Giants go?*"

"*Are they still here?*"

"*Why did they put talk marks in the dirt?*"

"*Do mole crickets have ears?*"

"*Where do stars go in the daytime?*"

The adult rat made a helpless noise and pressed his hands against his skull. "I don't know . . . maybe . . . no idea . . . yes . . . and they're always there, you just can't see them when the sun shines bright!" Ra'hish scuttled forward, trying to pull free from his swarm of admirers. "Enough! That's more than one question each! Why don't you all go learn something useful?"

"You can show us how to fight!" Male nestlings surged to the front of the pack. "We can be your war band when we get big! Can you show us what blades work best?"

The tawny-furred female looked up at Ra'hish with big, grave eyes. She blinked at him, and Ra'hish suddenly wondered if she was shortsighted. "Ra'hish – will you tell us about the Giants, please?"

"I'm not going to tell any more stories!"

"It isn't a story – it's an answer to a question." The girl blinked again. "You said you'd answer questions."

Ra'hish sat back and tried to knock some sense into his own mind. "What do I know about Giants?"

"More than I do." The girl strolled beside Ra'hish with infinite calm.

"I'm only ten months old, you see."

"And I'm forty months old. You want someone really old to tell you all of that. Someone older than the hills."

"Are there any Itheem that old?"

"There are no old Itheem."

Ra'hish slitted his eyes to fight the cold. Itheem lived short lives; Ra'hish had never heard of an Itheem living past eight. Age never killed them – it was violence. War and combat were as relentless as waves smashing the shore.

The little rats sat about in a trusting circle, trying to press closer to Ra'hish. They were thin, abandoned by their mother, too young to draw combat rations, too small to fight for food. Ra'hish remembered a smaller self, tiny and embittered in his fight to stay alive. He shook the images away and sank uncomfortably down into his skin, trying to busy himself by combing fingers through his muzzle fur.

"Have you decided what you're all going to do?"

"Oh, yes!" Eeka sat pertly upright, joined by her tiny brothers and sisters, all in a row. "Mother threw us out – so we want to be solitary rats, just like you!"

"All of you together?"

"We can be solitary together!" Eeka blinked. "I'm sure it's allowed."

A strange sensation prickled at Ra'hish from the inside. Finally he hissed and rolled his newfound treasure out into the starlight. "You children don't fight enough. Tomorrow we'll sell this to the East Tunnel trade post and buy you each a set of blades."

Her tiny jaw hanging open, Eeka stared. "But it's *your* treasure!"

Ra'hish gruffly hid the metal plaque beneath a pile of shale. "We'll buy them tomorrow, and I'll show you how fighting's done."

The nestlings made an excited surge of noise, and then crowded in Ra'hish's wake as he led the way back toward the warmth of G'kaa's fires.

They walked to the edges of the light. Here, among the sharp rocks bordering the plain of sighing towers, G'kaa had made his war band a home. Two thousand Itheem mated, ate, and fought beneath shelters of half-cured skins. Fires of thistle and driftwood spread a crackling heat, casting light by which warriors bandaged wounds and sharpened blades. The hiss and slur of whetstones made a background to the roar of voices chasing around the fires. By one fire sat G'kaa – a hideous black behemoth covered with a network of scars. At his side, a blood-covered shaman gnawed a piece of uncooked meat, laughing loud and exposing crooked yellow teeth.

Ra'hish took a seat on a ridge nearby and watched it all, a stranger peering across an alien landscape. Sadness struck him as he looked for beauty amid a swarm of fangs and claws. Eeka and Jez sat down beside him, their tails curled identically about their feet.

With her head tilted, the girl rat watched warriors fighting in the dust. "Where do we go when we die?"

Ra'hish shrugged as though he scarcely cared. "I don't know."

"Ma said we go into our children – but *her* ma died last month, and I don't feel any of her inside me."

Ra'hish watched as two fighting warriors were separated by a huge backhand cuff from G'kaa. "You can't affect it – so don't worry about it." Ra'hish stood, stretched, and stalked over to sniff at a thistle bloom. "Just work to deserve the best if anything comes hereafter."

Something big suddenly took the girl; one moment she sat talking to Ra'hish, and the next she was smashed aside and dragged into the brush. Her brother sat, shocked, looking at his own broken arm as a high pitched squealing came from the bushes.

Three warriors from the nearby fires had pinned the girl, laughing as they cuffed her. One rat struck the girl – and then jerked as a blade punched out through his chest from behind. He fell screaming. Ra'hish ripped free his blade, cut the rat's throat, and hurled the corpse away.

With barred fangs Ra'hish attacked. In a frenzy of hate, he flung himself at the other rats, making warriors scatter. His enemies tumbled back in panic. One stood his ground and died, staggering as blades punched a dozen times into his hide. Ra'hish let the body fall and surged toward the last warrior, blades dripping and yellow fangs howling. *"No!"*

G'kaa, huge with anger, slammed Ra'hish aside. The leader snarled and bared his fangs, facing down the angry warrior as he came back onto his feet and gave a snarl. "Ra'hish! No!"

Shocked, the nestling Eeka crawled slowly from the weeds and clung to Ra'hish. The warrior stood, craving blood, his fur filthy and his blades dripping. He stared at G'kaa, and then slowly hissed and slid his twin blades back into their tubes.

"I was talking to her." Ra'hish's mad-dark eyes were colder than the stars as he scanned the warriors. "These are *my* war band. You touch them, and you touch me!"

Leaving bloody footprints, Ra'hish turned and made his way back up the path to where the other nestlings sat and stared. He passed the girl back to her siblings and licked the blood that had spattered his fur.

"You should have heard him coming. Next time, don't freeze – dive and strike!" Ra'hish turned to find himself facing a dozen pairs of bright, frightened eyes. "Always attack! Speed brings fear. Make the enemy panic! When he can't think, he has already lost the fight."

Jez still sat where he had before, cradling his injury.

The warrior settled beside him and looked him slowly up and down. "Does it hurt?"

"Y-yes!" The young rat blinked his eyes, swaying with shock and pain. "Yes, it does."

"Good. Pain is a lesson, too."

Ra'hish jerked the limb straight, feeling the bone click into place. Staring hard into his eyes, the nestling never even squealed. He blinked and let a tear slide in silence down his cheeks.

Itheem healed quickly. In a week the boy would be running and fighting with the limb again. Ra'hish showed the other youngsters how a splint was tied.

Then he went to scratch at a patch of soil. He came up with a great earthenware jar. "Honey. I traded for it. There's grain to make bread. Bake it, and we'll all sit here and eat honey." It was good honey – dark and thick, still mixed with bark and dead, drowned bees. Ra'hish had been saving the treasure for a private feast. "Leave the corpse to those that want him. There's better food at hand."

At his instruction, the children started a fire and heated flat stones on which to bake fresh cakes of bread. Soon, the smell was clean and delicious in the air. Ra'hish went to find a trickle of water outlined by the glowing soil of nighttime Acomar and washed himself fastidiously nose to tail. He felt tainted by the dead rat's blood and annoyed at showing weakness over a mere child.

Something heavy moved in the dark, blocking the shining pinpricks in the soil. Emerging from the rivulet, Ra'hish shook out his fur and combed his whiskers clean. He elaborately pretended disinterest, grooming with rodent pride until G'kaa coalesced out of shadows.

The huge, sinister rat spoke with a voice of sugared ice. "You have cost me two warriors."

"If they'd been worth their feed, they would have defeated me."

G'kaa's fangs gleamed in the dark. "Then I would still be poorer one warrior. I have work to do. I will not have my forces thrown away in brawls."

"What work?" Ra'hish spared G'kaa a calculating, wary stare. "More fighting?"

"Yes, fighting – for a cause." Huge and terrible, the black rat had settled on all fours. Light gleamed from the tubes lashed to his forearms – the war blades that never left a warrior's side. With his scars reflecting the sickly lights from the soil, G'kaa gazed out across the chill wastelands of Acomar. "By spring, the new nestlings will be grown. Acomar's population will have doubled." The warlord was a savage, brooding shape against the stars. "What will happen then?"

Ra'hish shrugged the problem distastefully away, as though the affairs of other rats hardly concerned him. "Instant famine. Instant war. Most of them will die – the rest will have enough food."

"Yes – they'll kill each other, as they always do." The warlord tilted his head to fix Ra'hish in his gaze. "But what if the numbers stayed high, Ra'hish? What if the Itheem were to find enough food?"

"Food from where?"

"From *there*." G'kaa's blinded eye was sickly white with the distant gleam of mountain clouds. "The dog lands – the lands beyond the wall."

Rising onto his hind legs, Ra'hish turned to scan the empty night.

"You mean a raid for food? It never works." Every season a few rats had the same idea. A hundred warriors would cross the wall to strip the canine's fields, but the raid was always bloodily repulsed. "The wall's high – your war band could never defeat the dogs."

"Then it will take more than the war band. We have killing to do before we can go to war. . . ." The warlord spoke with a sinister, calculating thirst for blood.

With a distasteful glance toward G'kaa, Ra'hish shook a foul sensation from his fur and turned away. "I will be gone for four days. I will take my nestlings out into the wilderness."

"Ra'hish the teacher?" G'kaa hissed, his throat bubbling with twisted laughter. "Teach them well, Ra'hish! We need fighters."

With little care for G'kaa's plans, Ra'hish turned and scuttled his way back toward the fires. The nestlings had made him fresh bread running with honey, and for once the fires warmed Ra'hish clean through his bones.

§ § §

In the plain of sighing towers, a chill wind blew sleet from the sea. Pylons caught the sharp throb of the wind, and harmonies traveled up and down the night. Each new hum set another tower thrumming, the titanic sounds crescendoing and diminishing until they led the mind off into strange worlds of dreams.

A wave of sound broadsided Teela and Oosha, a tide crashing hard against the shore. The sisters staggered, arching their whiskers and blinking as vibrations thundered through them. The force took them in its hands and lofted them, making their souls surge and soar on the breeze.

When the sounds faded, Oosha found herself walking through the sand in a strange, unsteady daze. She lifted her head to taste distant life going by. Storm winds blew, and strange wreaths of ghostly force crackled at the heads of the metal towers. Here and there, lightning arced between the pylons and threw out great sheets of pale blue.

Teela panted, arching to watch it all, wonder shining in her dazzled eyes. "Beautiful."

A sharp scent filled the air – the stench of lightning strikes or ancient machines. In massive grandeur, the scent seemed pure and clean. Teela reached out to let sand run through wondering fingertips. Oosha swayed with visions of a long-ago universe.

"There once were Giants – and they must have walked like gods!"

"Oosha?"

"Gods." Oosha turned to follow a sight that only she could see. "Ancient and full of learning. So old. so old."

"Oosha – there's machinery beneath us." Gripped by senses Oosha seemed not to possess, Teela arced her head, questing whiskers through the air. "Don't you hear them sing?"

"What would it be like to be so old, do you think?" Oosha breathed with shallow little gasps, feeling the smell of lightning in her lungs. "A dozen years – then ten dozen more! Learning every minute of every day! Wisdom growing year by year until *everything* is possible." Oosha stared in rapture at the towers.

Teela blinked and turned upon her sister's face. "No one gets that old, Oosha."

"No. Especially not Itheem." Oosha reached out to touch the cold night air. "But if there really were Giants, we could make them do it. We could make them let us grow wise and old."

Life was short and always ended with claws and jaws and knives. Have a hundred offspring, grow in power, and fight to survive – these were the only hopes of an Itheem's life. And yet, here among the towers, far from nests and death and young, it seemed almost possible to dream.

Out across the sands, something hissed and smoked with cold. It rolled languidly forward, a gigantic sphere of purest black. Numbed by the strangeness and the isolation of the night, the two sisters watched the apparition pass, trembling, without once exchanging a word. When it was gone, they hurried on into the sands and lost themselves inside the maze of thrumming towers.

"Where will we sleep?" Teela stopped at the edge of a shallow depression about a pillar. The pylon had been broken off high overhead, and vast chunks of shattered metal lay sprawled about the sands.

Her white fur gleaming in the storm light, Oosha looked about and shivered with cold. "Somewhere out of the wind. Somewhere deep – but beside a pylon, where we can hear it sing."

The wind was joined by rain. In distant mountains, blizzards would be blowing. The chill struck through the sisters' fur and froze them to the bone. They had fled the nest without blankets, food, or even steel. The raindrops fell harder, hissing to the dirt like knives. The two girls ran for cover and found themselves slithering down a steep slope of old, dry shells. They slid to hit hard against the pylon base, then found a crack between two gigantic blocks of obsidian.

Teela hastily dug into the sand, and then disappeared snout first into a deeper darkness beyond. "Oosha! Come inside! There's some sort of light down here!"

Hesitating at the threshold, Oosha touched the giant pylon. She instantly turned to stare out at the world, her whiskers trembling with fright.

Something sat perched upon the edges of the shell pit, its armored skin glittering with reflections of the storm. Pale and stinking, it slithered slightly forward, the skyline showing the silhouette of its arching, deadly tail. A second shape slid forward to join the first – and then a third and a fourth.

Oosha felt herself turn weak with fear. "Teela?"

They were scorpions – gigantic scorpions, easily three times the size of the two young rats. Their deadly tails curved high, sting bulbs glinting with nearby lightning. The scorpions surged forward, claws gaping wide.

Oosha instantly backed into Teela's cave. Inside was a huge, echoing space – a deep crack between vast blocks of stone and the metal tower. Oosha felt herself cram against her sister, who screamed in fright.

A giant scorpion hurtled itself against the door.

Teela ran and toppled over a block of stone, walling the scorpions back behind a sudden avalanche. Oosha shook dust from her eyes, and then lunged flat. A vast claw rammed in through a gap in the walls. The claw scythed a whisker's breadth above Oosha's head, clashing shut with a force that could have cut her clean in two. The claw drew back and struck again, this time gouging sand out of the floor. Oosha bit the reaching arm on the wrist and felt her teeth sink into stinking flesh. She spat scorpion blood. The claw whipped past her, flailing in pain as it jerked itself outside.

Outside the tunnel, scorpions flung themselves into the attack. Teela frantically tried to dig deeper in the sand, but her claws hit a floor of seamless black volcanic glass. She screamed again as a new hole opened in the roof above her head, a scorpion's claw tearing at ground.

Teela panted in terror. Oosha desperately shoveled loose sand back at the ever-growing holes. She backed herself against the cold, thrumming metal of the pylon's buried base. The metal shuddered to rhythms from above. Oosha slowly forgot the scorpions and turned. Her pink eyes staring, she reached out to touch the metal column with her strangely delicate little hands.

Teela stared at her. "Oosha, you're Hastaasi! Make the towers do something!"

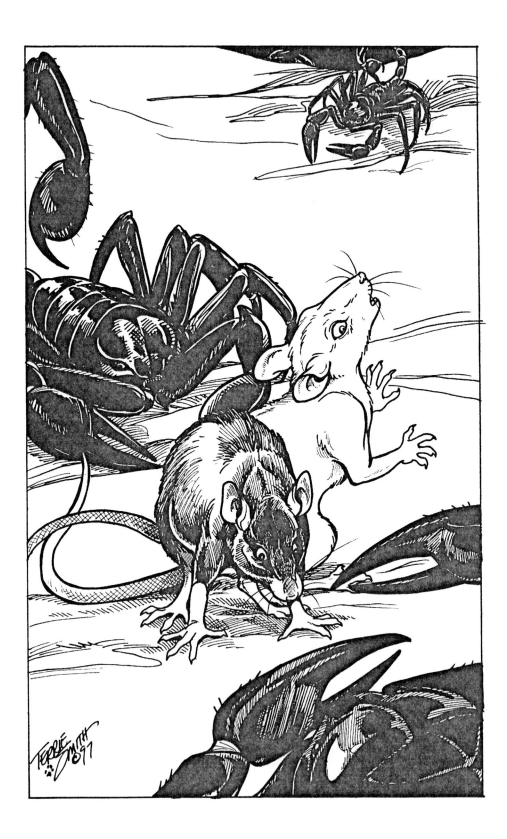

"I. . . I don't know how." Oosha touched the metal. No ancient voices spoke inside her mind. "I don't know how!"

"I believe in you! You can do it!" Teela closed her eyes, hunching as if to add extra force to her prayer. "Hurry! Hurry, or we're dead!"

The music moved through Oosha, and the girl felt her legs buckle with its power. Behind her, the ceiling crumbled. Teela gave a wild cry of despair – and suddenly the night turned brilliant white.

§

Through a smell of burning and scorched, hot dust, Oosha felt herself being pulled across the sand. She vainly tried to fight the scorpion's claws only to feel strong hands grasp her by the tail.

"Come on – quickly! We have to climb the pylon!" Teela pulled at Oosha's arms, hauling her out from under a pile of sand. "Oosha! Come on!"

The white rat dazedly sensed a slope of scorched shells and sand beneath her. To one side, a scorpion lay on its back, its legs curled upward in death. Oosha found her feet and stumbled onward, vaguely aware she had burned both of her hands. "What happened?"

Teela pushed her sister's rump, propelling her upward. "You called the lightning on them! Now come on! Up. Get up! We have to climb the tower."

"T-too high!" The white rat numbly stared into the sky. "Can't . . ."

"It's broken on the side. It's rough there – climb!"

Oosha cried out in dizzy pain as metal tore at her burned hands. She felt herself thrust up a vertical surface and gripped rough metal ridges with her long toes and her claws. She climbed. Her limbs gained a mechanical rhythm. The climb took her impossibly high into the sky, into a world where storm winds hammered her fur. She found a ledge and edged along it, clinging to bare metal. Teela scrabbled into place beside her and planted her face flat against the shuddering tower.

Scorpions moved down in the ruins. Four lay dead, blasted by lightning. Another four had righted themselves and now surged toward the pylon's base, lifting claws and screeching for their prey. Oosha stared down at them in a daze. She pressed her face tightly against the pylon as wind whipped her fur.

Far below, the huge, strange black sphere ran hissing against the bottom of the tower, sucking in a dead scorpion and swallowing it without a trace. The evil apparition made sparks fly from the sand. A distant lightning strike smashed against a pylon, and the sphere instantly rolled away. Oosha released her breath and watched it go. When it was out of sight, scorpions crept again from hiding and scuttled toward the metal tower.

The scorpions could not climb; their feet were too primitive. The monsters clambered upward again and again, rising a few body lengths before tumbling to the ground. Teela watched the creatures in numb fright, and then raised a worshipful face to meet her sister's gaze.

"You called the lightning. You called for it, and it came."

The wind howled, and the sisters clung on tight as rain and sleet lashed across a frozen world.

§ § §

"Now, spread out a little! Just feel with your whiskers. Metal makes currents in the ground. Feel for them – don't see with your eyes, don't hear with your ears. Keep those to watch for enemies."

Ra'hish directed his chain of followers out into the empty dunes, walking behind them and overseeing their work. He'd roused the nestlings before dawn – the perfect time for hunting. Already they had caught and dined upon a giant centipede. Ra'hish led them far from the war band with its prying eyes and savage fights, showing the little creatures how to survive on their own.

"Nests are dangerous. Other rats are dangerous. In the wilderness you can find food, but you have to be wary. Never lose concentration; always look for danger." Ra'hish threw a rock at the rump of the tawny-furred girl, and the sting of it made her yelp. "You! What's your name?"

"Eeka!" The girl rubbed a hand across her stinging bottom. "It's Eeka, Rika, Shika, Oota, Goota, Koopa, Marta, Barta, Loopi, Hoopi, Shoopi and Jez." The girl nodded her chin toward a sibling. "He's Jez!"

"Well, watch behind you!"

"But *you're* behind me!"

"And if I died, whatever got me might get you, too!" Ra'hish threw a rock at another nestling, and was pleased to see the young rat dodge. "Trust no one! Watch your own arse, or you'll be dead!"

It was a quiet morning. Evening storms had blown the foul weather away, and a winter dawn bloomed fragile, bright, and clear. The morning light slanted through the gargantuan pylons on the empty plains, making the whole world stream with yellow light.

Ra'hish knew the dawn would be good at the seaside. The storm would have washed a bounty of dead animals from the ocean. To reach the shore before the rats of other clans, Ra'hish and his followers would have to take a deadly shortcut between the poisonous green towers.

Ra'hish measured the danger, shrugged, and waved his party on. "Watch carefully. There's a danger here – the Gur gate, a hole into another world." Ra'hish scanned the surface of the dunes. "If you see it –

run!"

"What does it look like?" Rika, the tiniest nestling of them all, curiously waved her little tail. "What sort of world does it lead to? Is it nicer than this one?"

"It looks like a huge black ball – and no one who goes in comes out." Ra'hish quickly waved the nestlings on. "It's not dangerous as long as you see it coming. Now, close up and watch your flanks."

Cradling his broken arm, Jez hung back and stared in amazement at the massive metal towers. "What are they?"

"The towers? The bones of the world, made from a metal that never rusts and never wears away." Ra'hish drew in a deep, fresh breath of the dawn. "Peaceful. No one comes here."

"Why?"

"They fear the Gur gate. They think the Giants use it to stare out into the world."

The Itheem were not a reverent race. They had no gods, no beings to whom they groveled; but myths of the Giants always caused a thrill of dread. The twelve young nestlings crept fearfully into the forbidden lands, looking up in fright as they walked into the shadow of the towers.

The silence in the ruins was profound. Shells and sand made for muffled footfalls, and the strange metal towers cut away the sound of ocean waves. Eagerly questing for treasure, Eeka twitched her whiskers, running them just above the ground.

"Is there treasure? Shall we dig here?"

"No good." Ra'hish wrinkled his nose. "It's sea sand over a layer of solid rock. And the rock's seamless – like molten metal left to set and seal."

"You dug here?"

"Only a little. There's nothing to find, but it's a good place to be. Quiet; empty. You can sit here and look upward, and sometimes the pylons sing."

The little rats all instantly sat down and parked their tails on the freezing sand, hoping the metal towers would hum. A little weevil pattered past, leaving a trail of funny footprints in the dust. Its footfalls sounded strangely sharp and loud.

The only other noise was faint and tenuous. A sharp clicking sound came from the east. The rats frowned, sank into the shadows, and flitted up a shallow hill to peer across the crest. Just ahead, a broken pylon stood in a depression of metal shards and sand. On a whisker-thin ledge half way up the shaft, two rats clung, slipping and swaying with fatigue. Below them, four hideous creatures clustered at the tower's base – putrid white scorpions three body lengths in size. The creatures climbed and climbed at the pylon, rising a few spans, falling, and tirelessly climbing again. Their claws clicked and rang against the metal tower, the noise sharp as knife blades in the dawn.

"Scorpion folk." The deadly creatures sometimes risked coming into Acomar. They were tough opponents and unpleasant to eat. Ra'hish scanned for a covered route out of harm's way, but then turned around to find that he was suddenly alone.

He blinked and felt his heart lunge into his throat.

Twelve tiny figures pelted eagerly across the sands, racing straight toward the scorpions' tails. The nestlings gave a twittering little battle cry, and then leapt like maddened wasps onto their foes.

The scorpions reared and lurched, each covered with numerous biting little shapes. Ra'hish gave a noise of fear and frantically launched into a charge.

One nestling girl was hurtled clear, and a monstrous scorpion pinned her against the wall, arcing back its tail. Ra'hish ran first on four legs, and then rose to two without breaking stride. The vicious steel blades snapped from their tubes. He sped past the scorpion, and the creature staggered as the stinger was hacked from its tail. Spraying blood, the monster lurched away. Cheering nestlings beat at its claws.

Two other scorpions stayed to fight, throwing off the nestlings and scuttling to the attack. Ra'hish leapt atop one. Instantly the creature began to bob and sway, unable to reach him with tail or claws. The monster's partner made a lightning lunge with its tail. Ra'hish leapt off the beast's back, felt the stinger whip past, and saw it stab through the chitin of the scorpion's shell. Poisoned, the creature arched in agony.

Rallied, the nestlings chased the last two scorpions away.

Ra'hish staggered, stunned. He reached a hand down to feel where the deadly stinger had actually parted his fur. Mouth open in shock, he met little Eeka eye to eye.

"What in plague's name did you think you were doing?"

"You said to always attack!" The tawny girl had managed to pierce a scorpion's foot armor with her fangs. "So we attacked!"

"I didn't mean you have to do it every time! You pick your . . ." Words failed him. Ra'hish snapped his blades back into their housings and wiped his snout with his hands. "Just hit what I hit, and run when I say run! *No one* is to attack *anything* unless I tell you to!"

A nestling – possibly Oota or Goota, scratched in puzzlement behind his ear. "What if we're ambushed?"

"Oh, all right! I mean obviously you attack what you *have* to – but nothing you don't *specifically* have to – okay?" Ra'hish ran confused fingers through his fur. "Just hit the things that are going to hit you! Is that clear?"

"Should we ask them, or wait until they hit?" Eeka frowned, trying to get her instructions clear. "And if we ask them, how do we know they're telling the truth if they say no?"

Confused, Ra'hish felt his temper start to slip. "Well, you don't go around asking things if they're going to attack! I mean, nothing's going to *tell* you!" The warrior looked at the attentive little faces all around him and made a desperate noise. "Look, all I'm saying is don't deliberately *make* trouble – okay?"

"Yes." Eeka frowned. "But always make sure that we attack first?"

"Ooooh – just stay here and watch for scorpions. Tell me if you see anything move!"

Annoyed, Ra'hish left his addle-witted students far behind as he clambered up the rough, broken edges of the metal tower. He rose halfway to the ledge above and called out to the rats clinging there. "Come down. The scorpions have gone."

The two rats had their eyes closed. Exhausted and terrified, they blinked and gazed about in bewilderment. Ra'hish watched them, unable to help them climb down.

"Come down. There'll be more scorpions later."

With that, Ra'hish picked his way back down to the sands. He dropped onto all fours, piercing one foot with a broken piece of seashell. He ended up sitting on his backside as two nestlings solicitously helped pull the splinter out.

Annoyed, Ra'hish could only look at the half-grown youngsters and grumble. "Charging a pack of scorpions, indeed." They didn't even have a war weapon between them. Ra'hish would have to find them war blades and teach them how to tunnel fight. He should have stayed down his rusty hole last night and let the little drips get eaten to the bone.

Meanwhile, the little drips had discovered a new diversion. With a breath of awe, the nestlings watched the two stranded rats descend.

Eeka stared in wonder as the fugitives reached the ground. "She's Hastaasi!"

Ra'hish looked up in amazement. His gaze met a pair of haunted pink eyes. The girl was slim and perfect, as small and delicate as a fragile winter flower. The shock of her pink eyes made her white fur seem almost normal. Her pelt was clean as gleaming silk, a pure, unblemished white. As she moved, the light rippled through her fur. Ra'hish stared at the sight, almost hypnotized.

Staring back at him, the white rat spoke – her voice slow and dreamlike with fatigue. "They saved us."

"Come on! Oosha, come on!" The other female – this one a pure iron gray – dragged at the white rat's hand. "Come on. They're not clan! Let's go!"

"But they saved us."

"Come on! *Run!*" The gray rat dragged her companion into the sands and forced her into a run.

The white female regretfully stared back at Ra'hish and his band, her alien eyes gleaming with a strange and yearning light. The two fugitives disappeared into the sand, and soon nothing could be heard except the whisper of the breeze.

The nestlings stirred. They looked about to see Ra'hish still staring out across the empty sands. Smitten. Filled with glee, the children made a unison high-pitched hoot.

Annoyed, Ra'hish shook himself and mustered a pompous dignity. "Close up! I believe we were headed to the beach."

The nestlings smirked and whispered. Ra'hish puffed out his chest and whipped the laggards onward with his tail, deliberately turning his back on the white-furred girl, dead scorpions, and broken shells. He nipped at Eeka's flanks to keep her from giggling, and marched his charges off toward a dark and restless shore.

Chapter 4

A night of freezing cold had turned into a frostbitten dawn. Emerging from foothills and wallowing in a bitter powder snow, the travelers made straight toward a thick, rich plume of smoke that hung above the trees. The mountain slopes ended, and the woods began to disappear. Beside thawed brooks were fields crowded with winter crops and captive herds of sheep. Beyond the farms, the smoke of many fires promised a large and busy town.

It was the coldest winter in living memory – frosts had swept down from the mountains to freeze the valley plains. The three travelers crossed freezing brooks and wandered out into the brisk sunshine of a frosty winter day. Tupan, holding aloft a crude umbrella of leafy pine boughs, had scarcely a snowflake on her. Surolf had refused the umbrella she had made for him. Thin, gray, and shivering with cold, Surolf hugged his arms about his wet coat and wallowed in utter misery. He stumbled along through ice and snow, dazed by the freezing temperature and cursing his luck with every painful step.

Wearing a snow-proof coat Tupan had made for him from green pine boughs, Hern the pony lifted his great broad nose and took to sniffing the wind.

"Cabbages. I rather like cabbages."

"We'll get you cabbages!" Emerging from the trees, Tupan took a peek at the clearing sky and then slung her shaggy umbrella across one shoulder. "What sort do you like? Red or green?"

"Red."

"Hoopy!" Tupan brushed the frost off a cabbage and plucked it. "Here you go!"

Frozen and shivering, Surolf managed to give a bark of indignation. "That's stealing!"

"It's a wild cabbage! It's just growing in the ground!"

"Growing with a whole lot of other cabbages?"

"A whole lot of *wild* cabbages!" Tupan split the cabbage by bashing it against a fence post, then fed the leaves to Hern piece by piece as she walked. She walked past a large and carefully lettered sign. "Hey, there'd be some indication if the cabbages were private."

Sick and frozen, Surolf shuddered.

Tupan gaily kicked her feet through the brittle grass beside him, her bells tinkling in the clear winter sky. "A town! We could get some soup with barley in it. Do you like soup with barley? I had some once. It was great!" Tupan's diet often consisted of frogs, field mice and stolen pies, so anything fancifully cooked won her instant admiration. "We could even get someone to make us a pie!"

"How?" Surolf shivered, too proud to admit to himself he should have taken Tupan's offer of a pine-bough coat. "We-we have no coin."

"We have everything we need!" Tupan jingled a bag of small clattering shards of pottery. "Do you like mutton shin? I think I'd like a mutton shin."

A sheep bleated in the cold; Surolf firmly took Tupan by the arm and led her past a pasture of sheep, ignoring her hungry protests.

§

With the ground underfoot slowly becoming a dirt path, the trio crossed a rise and gazed down the valley.

A great, sinister jut of land stretched out into a cold and savage sea. A towering ridge of rock sealed the peninsula from the valley lands – a rock plateau topped by a grim, efficient palisade. A road ran behind the wooden wall, linking mile forts and lookout towers – a road that ran straight into the gates of a town.

The town looked like a deadly star. Tall wooden battlements were ringed about with barricades of sharpened branches. Catapults and ballistae were mounted in a dozen towers. In the center of the star was a gigantic artificial mound that rose far above the tallest tower roofs. The roads around it were mud, the walls were manned, and the gates were guarded by a row of fleshless skulls.

Tupan stood on a rise and propped one fist on her hip, casting a thoughtful ever over the decor. "Oh – wacko."

Annoyed, Surolf gazed on the town and slowly ground his teeth.

"I thought you said we were heading south! This is the border! This is west!"

"West-south!" Tupan twirled a finger as though people spent too much time over meaningless names. "It's a town! I told you I'd get you to one!"

"I was heading south! South to sell my pots! This is *Sentinel*, not

Kamla town!"

Tupan gave an easy shrug.

"Do you have pots?"

"No. You broke them!"

"So, it doesn't matter what town it is, then! See?"

Surolf limped on feet that had turned strangely numb. His open-toed boots were wet, and his feet felt frozen through and through. "At least we're only about ten miles from home. Maybe we can beg a ride back somehow."

Hern finished a mouthful of cabbage and swished his plaited tail. "I thought you needed to make money first."

"I don't even know if I can make it to town." Suddenly feeling sick, Surolf grabbed a handful of the pony's mane. "I think I feel a little ill."

"Do your feet hurt?" Hern leaned his head down and cocked it to one side to bring one great brown eye close to his friend's feet. "You ought to take care of them, you know. Soft feet can't be very sturdy."

With her own feet bound in great clogs made of yet more pine needles, Tupan padded over and easily hoisted Surolf onto Hern's back.

The hound tried to fight her as she inspected his feet, weakly swatting at her with his hands. "You keep away from me!"

"Hey, shut up and let me fix them!" Tupan tugged the hound's frozen leggings free. "You just need to warm them a little. It's no trouble."

The girl cupped Surolf's cracked, frozen footpads in her hands and blew across them, warming the flesh clean through to the bone. Surolf jumped in sudden pain as circulation came rushing through his toes.

He jerked his feet free and held them up, looking down at them in utter disbelief. "How did you do that?"

"I told you – I fix things!" The coyote gave an easy click of her fingertips. "It's what I do."

"You must have brought the circulation back. That's all."

"Like I said! I fix things!"

His frostbite was gone. Surolf cautiously wriggled his feet. Perhaps the damage hadn't been as bad as he had thought. Tupan slapped him on the calves and drew in a happy sigh, tugging at Hern's mane and leading him down toward the road.

It was an impressive Uruth town – a typical dog town, its spiked palisades, watchtowers, and abatis giving it a dark, unfriendly look. The town's titanic howling mound stood so high it even dwarfed the wooden walls. Canine figures armored in steel moved with deliberation back and forth along the road. Tupan raised a friendly hand to hail each group as it went past. After being ignored three times in a row, the girl became annoyed and went into a sulk, haughtily ignoring other dogs that marched by.

Feeling hostile, cold and ill, Surolf shot a dark glare at the girl. "Where were you planning on getting soup, anyway?"

"I'll buy some!" Tupan spoke with a simpering, prickly dignity. "Hey, look – I admit it may have been a bad night for walking. No fault of mine – but I feel I ought to make it up to you. A hot meal is the least I can do."

"We don't have any money!"

"We don't *need* any!" Tupan gave the airy wave that so grated Surolf's nerves – an appeal to unseen powers that seemed to somehow guard everything she chose to do. "I told you – I'll take care of it!"

The thin greyhound watched the girl in suspicion. "This is *Sentinel* town, lady! Do not do anything remotely dishonest."

"Dishonest? *Me?*" Tupan was outraged, dropping her toothy jaws in betrayed innocence. "I've never ever done any such rotten thing! – And, anyway, why not?"

"Because it's a border town. See the Shield Wall?"

Tupan looked at the vast, spike-topped wall that ran for miles and miles beside the road. Craning her head, she walked. There were Uruth soldiers behind the battlements, all looking out across the plains and sniffing at the breeze. Without a clue as to what it all meant, Tupan merely gave an airy shrug. "So? What's the wall for?"

"Goblins – Itheem!" Surolf jerked his chin to indicate the blasted wastelands on the far side of the wall. "That's Acomar the poisoned – ruins from the dark time. And inside those ruins are millions of rats, just waiting for the chance to kill everything that lives and breathes. . . ."

"Really?"

"Yes, *really*. They put the wall up to stop them raiding out into the fields."

Tupan scratched at her ear, her wrist-bells tinkling. "Why do they attack the fields?"

"They don't need a reason! They're *goblins!*" Surolf shivered. "Just pray you never see one face to face!"

Tupan, who honestly seemed to take delight in everything, immediately looked about, hoping to see a rat. "Rats are small guys, aren't they?"

"Not these. They're only a head or two shorter than you. And they're numerous!" Surolf sneezed with the cold. "You don't want to see one."

"I slept in a cave with Amiir once!"

"Well bats are not rats. Try sleeping with a goblin, and you'll end up with an apple in your mouth and served in a bed of lettuce."

Rapt in thought, Hern lifted his long ears. "I like lettuce."

Surolf gave a snort. "Yes – well if you ever also decide to eat your own young, you might have a career in Acomar."

The road led up to a gate, which was flanked by barricades of sharpened branches and tall towers of pine logs protected by leather hides. The guards were heavyset canine warriors, each armed with spears and armored in suits made from slats of lacquered iron and horn. They cast a disinterested eye across the travelers before rising on hind legs and stalking forward to order a halt.

Tupan confidently waved Surolf to the rear. "All right! Here we go! Just leave it to me – I know exactly what these guys want."

"Tupan – what they want is *order*. An alpha pair, an alpha pack – duties and regulations."

Tupan seemed honestly puzzled by the thoughts of other Uruth. "I can never figure that. Sounds pretty boring."

"It sounds just great." Surolf sulkily thought of home. "Security, honesty, and industry."

The girl looked Surolf pityingly in the eye. "Oh, I have *got* to get to work on you. You have a cute butt, but the soul of a total numbskull."

Hern's hooves were loud on the sodden ground as he passed Surolf by.

"I don't think his butt is all that cute."

"Shush! Let's go talk to the guards. . . ." Tupan and the pony approached the soldiers and made a friendly bob of their ears.

The chief guard sighed and looked the travelers up and down. "No weapons?"

Armed mostly with fleas, Tupan looked down her long nose and pondered the question. "You don't want us to have weapons?"

"No, we *do* want you to have weapons." The commander of the guards, a tall, trim smooth coat with a handsome black countershade on his snout, leaned on the shaft of his spear. "If you have weapons, you can do guard duty on the wall. No tax, see? If you can't do guard duty, we tax you – helps pay for weapons for other people."

Tax. Tupan daintily furrowed her tawny brows. "Girls don't fight! I don't see why *I* should have to pay."

"Most girls do fight. And those that don't fight do make weapons, make armor, or serve lookout duty up there." The handsome guard pointed to the high, chilly looking wooden towers far out along the barrier wall. "You can do that instead of paying tax, if you like."

Tupan's current ambitions extended to a warm bed, soup with meat and barley, and a few new bells for her tail. The prospect of spending a night or two atop a windswept platform was rather unappealing.

"Ah, well, we usually don't do much in the line of armor making." The girl held up her little bag of potsherds and let it clink like a heavy pouch of coin. "We'll pay if we must – but we prefer to offer our services – just to ensure that the frontiers are *truly* secure."

The guards pricked their ears. "Services?"

"Oh! Well, we're Howlers."

Howlers! The word worked like a magic spell. Tupan's bizarre dress made it all seem all the more real.

The guards straightened, their eyes alight with sudden anticipation. "Howlers!"

At Tupan's tail, Hern shook his head and made his ears flop noisily from side to side. "What's a howler?"

A sharp-eared guard gave a frown. "What?"

"He said the weather's getting fouler!" Tupan gave the pony a sharp swat across the rear. "Yup! Sure snowed last night, huh?"

The chief guard had already begun clearing his men from the road to let Tupan's entourage pass. He nodded his snout toward Surolf, who stood out of earshot, scowling at one and all. "What about him? Is he a Howler too?"

"He's *the* Howler! He's the channeler. But you have to be a little careful with him. He's . . ." Tupan let her words trail off, and then sadly tapped her head. The guards at once gave her an understanding look. "He tends to be a little *sensitive*, you know? Not, well. . . quite as *quick* as he could be . . ."

The guards all put on strange, friendly smiles as Surolf approached, and they made a great show of giving him enough room to pass. The three travelers made their way through the tall palisade and its earth-backed walls and out into streets lined with hummock-shaped houses, warm with glowing fires. Raising one eyebrow, Surolf tilted his head curiously toward the girl.

"What did you tell them?"

"Nothing!" Tupan straightened Surolf's clothes. "Hey – you know, when you look all stern like that, you're quite handsome! Have you ever thought about doing public performances?"

Surolf gave her a dark, suspicious look. "Why?"

"No reason! But hey – lets go find a fire! Barley and mutton soup – and a rack of ribs for dinner! Smells like an inn over that-a-way!" Tupan took each of her companions by the shoulders and walked between them on into the streets. "Relax! I said I'd pay for it."

Convinced he was going to be embarrassed, harassed, or killed, Surolf glumly let himself be led off to his fate. "Something horrible is going to happen, isn't it?"

"No way!" The girl's bells jingled merrily in the air. "What could go wrong? Dinner, fire, and a job. My dears – we have it made!"

The trio walked their way through muddy, undrained streets, past houses sunk deep into the ground. There were building sites where carpenters measured wood and raised new walls, and practice grounds where youngsters drilled in the arts of sword and spear. Tupan ignored all signs of tedious activity and homed in upon the elusive smell of beer. She finally found the doorway to one of Sentinel's inns and triumphantly led the way inside.

The inn was a large, low-ceilinged hummock-house dug deep into the ground against the cold. The roof beams were pine carved with images of ancestral dogs chasing fleeing, naked rats. The room was dotted with earthen tables both big and small, where Uruth clustered, enjoying a respite from the daily grind. A cat sat primly in one corner, delicately reading through a paper scroll. The Lammada took one scathing look at Tupan's ribbons and bells – sniffed at the thought of a coyote being allowed indoors – and then disdainfully went back to sipping at a dainty cup of broth.

A pair of bats hung in the rafters, drinking beer upside down. Tupan craned her neck to see just how they did it, and then spied a canine waitress drawing near.

"Can we have mutton ribs, soup, beer – and something pony-ish for my friend without opposable thumbs!" Tupan found a table – a hard-packed hummock of earth about which animals could recline on blankets and eat their food. "Hey – do you have any pickled onions? A jar of them, if you've got them!" Tupan dropped her pouch of potsherds on the table, where it thumped to rest with a heavy chinking sound. "Ooooh, this is just so much better than outside. Hey, sour snout – come park your arse beside the fire!"

Tupan circled on all fours, treading a blanket into a nest for herself. It took several rotations before she was happy enough to sit down, by which time Surolf had managed to perch himself beside the table. Hern clopped in through the swinging door, clumsily turned about and drew the draft curtain shut with his mouth, lumbered over to the table, and sat down.

"Hey-la! Any luck on those ribs?" Tupan called to the waitress.

The Uruth serving girl raised a haughty brow. "Well done or rare?"

"Burnt to a cinder! And with sauce! Lots of sauce!"

"It will take a while." The waitress shifted her tray full of beer cups. "It will also be twelve dinkets. Fifteen if you want lamb instead of mutton."

"Lamb! And make it two big servings!" Tupan freed herself of her makeshift clogs, accidentally pushing her heavy purse so it clinked with promises. "Ooooh, I am starved!"

The serving girl made a note upon a slate hanging from her belt. With one brow raised, she jerked her chin toward Hern. "Ma'am? Ponies usually go in a stable outside."

"Are there any other ponies in there right now?"

"Um – no."

"So he'd be lonely!" Tupan signaled for the beers to be delivered to her table. "It's okay – I housebroke him myself."

The beer came thick as honey and dark as scalded oak. Tupan drank from her bowl, lapping with her tongue, heaving a sigh like a creature who had just run a hundred miles.

Surolf peeled off his sodden coat and hung it by the fire, holding out his hands and fingers toward the circular central fireplace. "They are going to put you running in a wheel, lady! You are going to be powering a grain mill for the better part of a month, and I am going to buy wheat just to watch you work!"

"Hey – she'll be paid! Did I ever say she wouldn't be paid?"

"Just remember." Surolf wriggled his fingers toward the flames. "Round and round, squeakity-squeak. That's what they do to debtors around here."

Tupan gaily licked at the bottom of her bowl. "Say, this girlfriend of yours; she's attracted by your sunny disposition – right?"

"Oh, go sit on an anthill!"

Depressed and annoyed, the handsome greyhound tried to nurse his irritation. Three days ago, life had been a thing of clear goals, noble struggles, and hard work. Now he was broke and stuck with a thieving coyote, and his partner was already half under the creature's spell.

Leaning over to Hern, Surolf nursed his beer bowl in his arms and whispered in the pony's ears. "Now, remember – we have nothing to do with any of this. When she gets caught, we just let them know it's all her fault!"

"Oh, okay." Hern had drunk a bowl of beer, and now discovered salty biscuits on the table. He delicately picked up one with his lips. "And then we can help her run in the wheel."

"No! *We* do not go in the wheel! This is her theft – it's her fault."

"But we've already drunk the beer."

"Only because she offered it to us!" Surolf was an engineer, a creature dedicated to hard work. Tupan's parasitic lifestyle made the greyhound seethe – mostly because she seemed to somehow trick the universe into keeping her happy and alive. He pulled a tiny wooden wallet from his belt pouch and opened it up, staring at the picture that had been painted within. He leaned down to breathe the scent of the few precious hairs he had begged from his true love's tail, and then closed his eyes and tried to think calming thoughts about her amber eyes.

He slipped into a brief, unintentional, and much-needed sleep, awakening slowly to a scent of sausages and tea. Shouting, cheers, and excitement now filled the hall. Surolf opened his eyes. A table at the middle of the room was crowded with dogs and curious raccoons. Even the bats had moved to the rafter above it, flapping their wings in simpleminded excitement as they watched something at the center of the mob.

"We have a winner!" Tupan's voice; the girl leapt triumphantly up and down amid the roars of approval, doing a gleeful little dance of joy. "Yes! Take that, Black-Chops!"

A huge black dog cursed vigorously and began frantically winding a length of string around a metal cone. He worked with great enthusiasm, cunningly crisscrossing the string before demanding that the crowd draw back to give him room.

Sitting cross-legged on the ground were a scholarly little family of Miir-mice dwarfed by the tall dogs all around them. Their ears scarcely reached the waistband of Tupan's skirt. The creatures were examining metal cones and lengths of string, turning the whole affair into a science project. They wrapped cones in string, and then solemnly fought to make a place beside the table

"All right – all strings wound? All bets placed?" Tupan blew on her own metal cone and shook it, making her wrist bells jingle. *"Go!"*

The contestants whipped their strings and sent their cones buzzing out along the tabletop. The cones balanced on their points, spinning around and around until their painted surfaces blurred. The crowd shouted and cheered their choices. The tops began to clash and battle, bumping each other aside and veering about the table like a swarm of angry wasps.

"Number One – *out!*"

A top had veered too close to the table edge and had fallen to the ground. The mouse who had wound its string cursed, and then immediately began to rewind the top, planning an even more cunning attack for the next game.

Tops clashed, showering impressive streams of sparks. The heavy little objects bounced and jarred, hurtling each other off the table in spectacular attacks. The players and the spectators crowded forward, having the time of their lives as the metal cones fought themselves to a stop.

"We have a winner!"

Tupan grabbed the hand of one small mouse and held the victor aloft. There was a great cascade of coins as money was swept off a nearby table and given to the mouse – followed by a storm of noise as spectators eagerly fought for the right to play the game. Tupan shared the four heavy brass tops out among the crowds, ushering new players forward so that one and all could take a turn.

"Okay, ante up! You spin a top, you pay a dinket. All bets down and winner takes all! Any top for anybody – there's no way to cheat! Pure luck, pure skill!"

Curling sinuously through the crowds, the scroll-reading feline had come to watch the fun. She relieved the huge black dog of his top and inspected it, weighing the iron cone inside her hands.

The black dog gave a snort of mistrust. "Are you strong enough to even lift it, *cat?*"

"You do not flick your wrist properly." The cat, sourly superior, took the launch string away from the dog. "Uruth muscle will always bow to Lammada intelligence."

Winding her own top, Tupan walked past, scuffing her feet upon the woolen blankets covering the floor.

"Oh – so you're *that* smart?"

Black snout and black ears tilted as the cat gave a haughty sniff. "Far superior to a mere canine – as I shall now demonstrate."

Tupan shuffled back and forth across the blankets, chuffing her feet across the pile. She called out to start the contests, threw back her arm, and cast her top furiously across the tabletop.

The other player's simultaneously threw. As they did, Tupan stopped shuffling her feet and touched her finger to a puddle of spilled beer. At the far end of the puddle, the cat gave a yowl of fright, and her fur stood on end. The cat's top miscast, veering hopelessly across the ring to be bashed aside by a top from an excitable bat.

Hern loomed over the table with its cheering crowds and sparking tops. He rumbled slowly into Tupan's ear. "Maybe I can help. I can't pull a string, but I'm very good at counting. . . ."

"Hey, okay! So, you can watch the money table. Winner takes all!"

Tupan stuck a little rake into Hern's mouth, and he set to work with an amiable diligence. He was still hard at it twenty-one games later when the waitress returned with both of her parents in tow and tugged at Tupan's tail.

"Hey, you! Your meals are here – and that's thirty dinkets for the lamb and six more for the beer!" The two parents, large and hardened by years of watch on winter walls, glared dire promises at the coyote girl. "You can pay me now, before you eat."

"Now? Why not?" Tupan managed to bob her head above the crowd and find the pony. "Hey, Hern? How much of mine do you have there?"

"Forty-seven."

"Hoopy! Pay the waitress, can you – and give her another two dinkets if she can give us a smile!"

The waitress shot a look toward her parents, and then glumly accepted a pile of triangular copper coins from the pony. Once her grim parents had gone, the waitress shot Hern a watery, apologetic little smile, and he duly passed over two coins all her own.

Tupan sat heavily down at the dinner table, gleefully bouncing her tail as a great plate of sizzling meat and bones slid beneath her nose. She breathed in the savory steam, instantly forgetting hundreds of meals of toadstools and water bugs – and set to work frenziedly stuffing her face.

Behind her, the top fights went on. More people entered the tavern, all wandering over to the arena to discover what the fuss was all about. Noisily sucking the marrow from a rib bone, Tupan watched the action with a smile. "We need some metal! Pig iron will do, but brass is nice! We can have a mold made and cast some tops to sell tomorrow – we should sell forty or fifty in a week!"

Trying to ignore the loud sounds of Hern eating a bowl of apples, beets, and carrots, Surolf irritably nibbled at his meal. "Where did you get those tops? What *are* those things?"

"Plumb bobs! I found them at a construction site along the town walls. But they make great tops! You should feel the way they spin!"

Agog, the greyhound looked at Tupan with shocked eyes.

"You just invented that whole game – just then?"

"It's what I do. I show people how to have fun!" Tupan gave a shrug, immodestly lowering her lashes. "It's a holy calling. The universe loves me."

Surolf ripped ribs apart and fed, not trusting himself to say a word.

Leaving his greens to start upon a bucket of barley mash, Hern flicked his long ears at the girl. "Why do you win the game so often, then?"

"I'm left-handed. Most people are right. They wind the string a different way to the way I do." The girl gave a smirk. "Makes you hit with more of a bash! You circle the arena until the other tops have hit a few times and lost momentum. Any idiot could figure it out. They'll all be doing it by tomorrow!"

"Even the cat?"

"Maybe. If she doesn't win first time, she probably won't play again; it's a feline thing." Tupan cracked a bone between her sharp back teeth. "But, hey, we've started a craze here! Isn't it nice to hear people having fun?"

Hern nodded, impressed, and then immersed his head in the feed bucket. Suddenly bereft of conversation, Tupan finished her meat, soup, and kibble, and wriggled about to present her bottom to the fire.

It had been a good day after all – and tomorrow there would be money for sourpuss Surolf to go buy his bride! Heaving a sigh of love for the workings of the world, she flipped her tail across her nose and quite simply fell asleep.

§ § §

"Ra'hish – Are there plants that walk?"

"*No.*"

"Are there plants that move?"

"*Yes!*" Ra'hish grumbled, persecuted by questions and crowded by eager, worshipful nestlings. "There's some that catch flies."

"Can they catch people, too?"

"Only if you sit on one." Shouldering a badly made seaweed bag full of crabs, Ra'hish was keenly aware he could be smelled by every hungry enemy in a thousand spans. "Look – Eeka – keep an eye on the others. Make sure they're scouting properly."

The nestlings should ideally be moving in pairs, each pair backed up by siblings in cover, the whole team flitting through the ruins with infinite cunning. Instead, Ra'hish half suspected the curious little creatures were digging up plants to see if they moved, or were busily chasing one another with their newly purchased blades. Trudging along under their bounty of food, Ra'hish could only quicken his pace and keep to the abandoned lands.

There were frequent moments when he wondered why he had ever taken on the trouble of guarding an energetic band of overly curious pip-squeaks. But the little creatures trusted him – almost worshipped him. Ra'hish made an effort to break long habits of solitary silence and tried to dredge out answers to the nestlings' incessant questions.

"Ra'hish? How do talk-marks work?" Oota and Goota, two identical males, walked in perfect step beside Ra'hish. They wore matching frowns, and each carried a large dead crab across his back. "We should like to know, since we feel it would be useful."

"I can't tell you how they work." The long, lean guardian rat could only give a shrug. "Maybe someone really old could tell us how."

"Are dogs old? Would they tell us how?"

"Yes, they are old, and no, they would never tell us how. Dogs are enemies."

One of the twins gave a puzzled frown. "Are all the other animals our enemies?"

"All of them. Everyone hates Itheem. That is why we are trapped in Acomar." Ra'hish shifted his heavy burden and trudged up a hill of broken glass. "If you want to know why they hate us, you'll have to ask the oracle. I can't tell you."

"G'kaa says its because we were chosen by the giants to rule the earth. He says that's why the other creatures fear us."

"G'kaa – " Ra'hish gave a slight twitch of his tail " – G'kaa has too many thoughts. Listen to *me,* and you'll live longer."

They came to the edge of G'kaa's new camp and peered down into a smoking pit that stabbed like a scar into the earth. G'kaa's war band had invaded the plain of towers, lice crawling ravenously onto naked skin. Precious steel had been fashioned into picks and mattocks, and the rat warriors swarmed about the ground, digging holes into the hard, brittle rock. For once, there were no food raids, no war parties out to snatch harvest or fight at the command of other clans. G'kaa had gathered all his power in one place and bid it crack holes into black obsidian. The gigantic, scarred black rat hunched in consultation with his plague-shaman and the leaders of his warriors. Above them, a vast metal tower moaned softly like a giant crying in its sleep.

Ra'hish felt his senses tingle, the old caution stealing out to taste danger in the wind. Letting his bag of crabs slip down, he kept his eyes fixed on G'kaa and called out to the nestlings. "And what did we learn?"

The nestlings sat up on their rumps and gave a unified little chant. *"Hit them fast and from behind, and then you'll always victory find!"*

"Good. Now, give me the biggest crab and hide thirteen others for us, and we'll get busy."

The nestlings bustled about to do as they were told. Ra'hish walked alone down into the pit, moving past struggling teams of Itheem hauling sleds of rock and spoil. Savage fights broke out among the digging teams – fights stopped short of murder only by war chiefs forcibly dragging battling warriors apart. A huge crab cradled in his arms, Ra'hish made his way up a mound of stone to where G'kaa and his plague-shaman – a stinking creature smothered in dried blood – surveyed the work and snarled orders across the dusty hole.

G'kaa caught sight of Ra'hish and instantly turned on him with bared fangs. "Where the plague have you been? We need every pair of claws!"

"Finding food. We put out pots for crabs." Food was inviolable; no one could fault a rat for hunting.

But G'kaa wanted a fight. Seething with frustration, he moved into attack range, fangs bared and eyes red with rage. "If I wanted food, I'd order you to hunt it!"

"I don't ask for permission to feed." Ra'hish suddenly knew he would have to fight G'kaa. *"Never."*

Ra'hish shifted his weight forward, ready to attack an instant before the first strike came. He let the crab fall and crouched on all fours, dwarfed by G'kaa's huge body. G'kaa hissed, baring his fangs, and shot his war blades out from their tubes. Ra'hish shifted, sleek with promised speed.

Even if he killed Ra'hish, G'kaa would be mincemeat at the hands of his officers. Seething with anger at being forced to dig, they would be happy to pull down a weakened overlord.

Ra'hish settled his weight and gripped the handles of his blades, ready to dive aside the moment G'kaa made his attack.

Bristling with fury, G'kaa hesitated; Ra'hish could move with blinding speed. The warlord bunched his muscles to crush Ra'hish like an insect, and sensed the other rat already anticipating the move.

Down in the digging pits, there came a scream of fear. All eyes had been locked on G'kaa and Ra'hish above, and now the Gur gate had burst out from between two metal towers. The vast sphere of darkness thundered down a slope of sand, crashing into the excavations below. Rats screamed as the gate touched them and sucked them from the world, their bodies disappearing the instant the evil sphere touched them.

"Clear out of the way! Run! Run downhill!" G'kaa had turned his back upon Ra'hish, and his huge voice galvanized rats into action. Warriors hurtled aside tools and scrabbled out of their holes, fleeing in terror as the black sphere rolled crackling across the sand and inexorably through the camp.

Lightning arced from the black surface. Where the sphere passed, the ground smoked with cold. Ra'hish stared at the enigma, seeing strange shapes inside the blackness – images of a foul landscape made from tortured bone. The sphere lurched out of the camp and veered toward one of the humming metal towers – then slid off into the windswept wastelands of the plain. Rats emerged from hiding, whiskers quivering with fear.

G'kaa roared out across the chaos, sending warriors racing back to their posts. *"Get back to work! It's only a few casualties! Dig! Dig and be careful!"* The warlord lashed the steel ball upon his tail, cracking one of the black rocks of the plains. *"We need treasure. So, dig!"*

His quarrel with Ra'hish ignored, G'kaa stalked the ridge of rock like a demon brooding in the night. His tail dragged, sparks slithering all about him as he walked.

"No one has ever prospected the plain of sighing towers!" G'kaa paused, reaching out to snatch a chip of black obsidian. "No one! Not in the generations we have been trapped here has anyone penetrated the obsidian shield to look beneath the towers. We need treasure. We need a weapon. We need a key to unlock the cage."

"We need Hastaasi, Lord." The seer's fur rattled with pendants of black, dried blood. "If we find a weapon, we will need the oracle. Only the oracle can bring a dead machine to life."

"Then we must hunt for white-furred rats. We must take them from the East Tunnel Clans and breed Hastaasi of our own." G'kaa compressed his hand and his own blood leaked slowly as he crushed the obsidian in his palm. "Ra'hish! You are still here."

"I am." Ra'hish watched, fur bristling to fight. "Here I stand."

"Then go elsewhere! Have your useless nestlings hunt for treasure!"

"As you command." Ra'hish slid slowly backward, his face chill and deadly.

G'kaa raised his savage head upon its bull neck, coldly catching Ra'hish in one corner of his eye. "Call me *lord.*"

"Lord." With barred fangs, Ra'hish retreated back down the slopes. As he moved back into the cover of the rocks, he knew G'kaa watched him, could feel other warriors gathering near. Ra'hish hissed at a rat that came too close, his blades snapping out in warning, and then retreated out of the excavation pit to find his own followers.

The nestlings had made a fire and were toasting crabs. They sat beside the sizzling shells, trying to defend their meal from lurking warriors. The passersby retreated as Ra'hish came near – some glaring at him with pure venom, and others hissing promises they were not bold enough to fulfill.

Ra'hish took a quick look across the nestlings' campsite – there were clear avenues for vision, and rocks to guard them in case of attack. They had chosen well. Ra'hish sensed Jez's hand in the matter, and praised the injured boy with one sharp monosyllable.

The crabs were cooked to perfection and sizzling hot. Ra'hish, a long practiced scavenger, showed his pupils how to lever the food from the fire and let it cool enough to eat. Soon cracking shells filled the air with the comforting sounds of greed and hunger.

Nursing a gigantic crab claw, Eeka and two sisters simply sat and watched Ra'hish. "Are you going to fight G'kaa? Will you be warlord then?"

"G'kaa wants to fight the whole world." Ra'hish sniffed the wind, sensing the stench of burning in the wind. Of the black, all-destroying sphere, there was no sign. "And no, I will not become a warlord."

"Why?"

The adult rat turned his slim face, with its pattern of camouflage lines, toward the little girls. "Do you remember how I showed you the sunrise over the sea? How the colors lit the breakers at the very tops, but the sea stayed dark?"

"Yes, Ra'hish."

"Good." Ra'hish split a crab leg with sharp fangs. "I kill because if I were dead, I would never see such perfect things again – nor could I share them with you."

Eeka seemed to understand. She stared down at the excavations, hordes of workers hunting for ancient weapons hidden in the earth. She gave a frightened blink of her eyes. "Will you give us camouflage today, Ra'hish?"

"We'll dye your fur, and then scavenge rations and get out of here. I want us away from this camp by nightfall." Ra'hish pushed his food away from himself. "Out into the plains, where we can be away from all of this."

The nestlings paused and stared out toward the plain of sighing towers. Her fur ruffled by the breeze, little Eeka watched the world with dark, deep eyes. "Will we see the white lady again, Ra'hish? Will she show us how to cast a magic spell?"

Ra'hish deliberately turned his back upon the plains. "Eat your crab claw, Eeka. Crack it here, and the meat is just inside."

A cold wind blew. Empty crab shells rattled off across the hills. The nestlings ate.

All the while, somewhere in the maze of towers, a black globe scarred the ground with frost. . . .

Chapter 5

Morning began with a frosty breeze and the solid, busy sound of marching feet. Orders were called and guards were mounted.

Peeking from his blanket nest beside the embers of the tavern fire, Surolf stretched, shook his body with a great flap of dangling ears, and then gave a mighty gape-fanged yawn. Shivering virtuously with the bite of the new dawn's wind, the greyhound drew on his pants and wandered outside into the morning cold.

Much to his annoyance, he was the last one awake. Hern stood outside the tavern door, one lip curling in ludicrous ecstasy as Tupan worked his coat with a hog's-hair brush. Weak-kneed, the pony made ridiculous sounds and drummed one hoof against the ground. Surolf walked past, skimmed the ice from a water trough, and almost killed himself by splashing freezing water across his hide.

Warmly dressed in a blanket coat and a new fur hat, Tupan shot a quizzical glance at Surolf as he took his morning bath. "Hey, Grizzle-Face! Isn't that cold?"

"In *civilized* circles, we keep ourselves clean." Surolf shook himself dry, spraying water out across the street. "I take it we won't see *you* using the water trough today?"

"Naaaah, I used the warm water and soap they have at the back of the inn." Tupan clicked her tongue, and Hern raised one back foot to let her brush the long hair upon his hocks. "Got to take what pleasures out of life that you can!"

A squad of soldiers walked past, their lamellar armor clanking in the frosty air. They saw Tupan and her furry hat, and then Surolf, wet to the waist and dripping in the snow. The soldiers made kindly faces, politely nodded Surolf's way, and walked on, sadly shaking their heads and whispering to each other.

Surolf narrowed his eyes. "Why do they keep doing that?"

"Doing what?" Tupan had found some soot and candle wax. He

began polishing Hern's hooves into a lustrous shine. "Being nice to you?"

"Being nice to me?" The greyhound cast a suspicious eye over Tupan's new clothes. "Where did you get the gear?"

"Gifts from admirers!"

"Really?"

"Close enough. Hey, they'd admire me if they only knew me." Tupan gave a last swipe of her cloth across Hern's hooves. "There we go, Old Snout! Bright as a new pin!"

Hern went to look admiringly at his own reflection in the water trough and gave a great, delighted smile.

As he stood there, striking noble poses, a file of cold and windswept citizens made their way into the inn, waving brightly to Tupan. "Howlers! Good morning!"

"So it is! So it is!" Tupan produced a sausage from somewhere in her clothing and snapped the thing in half. "I'll have those fighting tops for you tomorrow."

"How's your partner's head?"

"Fine, fine!" Tupan gave Surolf a rough rub between the ears. "See? He does all right. We look after him."

The citizens piled into the inn, looking for a hot drink and a warm fire, leaving Surolf to drag in deep, indignant breaths and glare at Tupan in building rage. "*How's my head?*"

Hern rolled innocent eyes toward the clouds, his voice rumbling as he cleared his throat. "I'm won't tell him if you don't."

Faced by a seething greyhound, Tupan steepled her fingers and produced a large, false, brittle smile. "Um, look – I may have *just* managed to intimate that you have a few *special* needs." The girl kept her fake grin and looked about the streets, marking avenues for flight. "Just for tax purposes. It's all for your own good!"

Hern rolled one droll brown eye toward Surolf. "She told them you were loony."

"Shush!" Tupan's hands made genteel motions of placation. "I didn't say that at all."

The greyhound slowly flattened his ears. "*Howlers?* You told them we were speakers to the dead, didn't you!"

"Um – well, that is. I mean, everyone prays to the ancestors! I may have just intimated that we – that is *you* – do so in a more publicly visible fashion."

Stifling an urge to choke Tupan with his bare hands, the greyhound bared his teeth. "You lying, cheating, swindling, rag-tailed, worthless *thief!*"

"Rag-tailed?" Tupan hastily inspected her tail. "Who's rag-tailed?"

"This is blasphemy. This is dishonest, and I am not going to do it!"

"Do it? Well why not do it!" The girl spread her arms in amazement. "It's only talking to dead people, for the Huntress's sake!"

"Tupan – I am *not* talking to dead people!"

"Whaaaat? But it's easy! You just . . ." Tupan suddenly broke off, rolling her eyes to gaze worshipfully up toward a blank patch of air. "Grandmother? Is that you?"

"Stop that! It's irreverent!"

"It's a coyote thing. You doggie types take life too seriously!" Tupan twirled one slender finger in the air. "Like this girlfriend of yours. Snooty, serious, and dull. I'll bet she's haughty, tall, and svelte, with rich red fur and legs that just go and go and go. Yes?"

Snorting derisively, the greyhound looked Tupan up and down. "You've been looking at my picture of her. You didn't even have the decency to ask!"

"Naaaaah, what would I need a picture for?" The coyote girl gave a huge, sharp-fanged yawn, shading her mouth with her hand. "I mean, she's standing right behind you on the street."

Surolf dived for cover behind the water trough and stared down a muddy street thronging with soldiers and travelers. There, in the center of the street, a litter suspended between two black ponies rocked slightly as a female dog extended a startling length of leg to the ground. Slim and brimming with absolute hauteur, the girl adjusted her white fur robes on her gleaming chestnut hide. Beside her stood two hefty armored dogs with identical coloration – clearly a brother and an uncle from the same alpha family. The trio conferred with local soldiers before walking down the street toward the local alpha clan group's house. The house was missing one of its draft curtains at the door; the surviving curtain matched Tupan's new blanket coat and furry hat.

Surolf flapped his jaw in outrage, only to have Tupan shove the rest of her sausage inside. "Hoo hoo! So, am I right?"

Hern crouched behind the water trough, wishing he could hide behind his own hooves. "Hide. Hide now."

"What for?" Tupan's voice was the gayest sound on the street, and half the town seemed already to know her. "Surolf can just stride over and tell her that he's here! He can tell her why, too!" The girl noisily swallowed sausage. "It would sure as plague impress *me!*"

Instantly dissolving into a ball of neuroses, Surolf tucked his tail between his legs and watched his idol from afar. "She'd be mad at me! She'd think I was following her!"

"Ha! Well, I'll do it, then! She has to know you love her!" Tupan tipped her fur hat aggressively across her eyes. "This is romance, boy! I told you – Tupan fixes things!" The coyote girl had taken five long strides before Surolf unfroze and lunged after her.

He wrestled her to a stop and wailed with fright. "Don't! She'll see you!"

"Hope so!" Tupan stuck up an arm and waved madly to Surolf's girl. *"Hey, there! Look who's over here!"*

The greyhound frantically tried to clamp Tupan's muzzle shut, and the girl struggled to fight free. They fell in the frosty street, kicking and fighting like vindictive pups. Surolf ground Tupan's face into the mud, only to scream like a girl as she bit him on the shin. Tupan half lunged from the ground to signal to the nobles, and then squawked as Surolf tripped her and rolled end over end with her into a patch of sooty snow. He managed to wrestle Tupan's mouth shut, gave a wild look of triumph – and found himself eye to eye with the love of his life, who stared at him from across the street.

"Aela." Surolf spoke her name and felt his heart sink as he read the panic in her face.

The girl stared at him, appalled, her mouth opening briefly, and then snapping shut. She turned, pretending not to meet Surolf's eye. Drawing her fur robes about her, Aela stepped back into the shadow of her relatives. The two polished, armored males shot a look of cold dislike toward Surolf and ushered their charge in through the door of the town's largest, tallest house.

A stark old canine strode from the house and leaned on a staff hung with bones. Beside him came a tall, powerful young dog in polished armor and embroidered clothes. The old man took a look at Surolf lying there in the mud and gave a loud snuffle of the air. "Frogs – water bugs – pine needles! Koja – I smell a vagabond!"

"Yes, Spirit-Father. They are visitors."

"Visitors?" The ancient man leaned forward, squinting at Surolf. "Oh, yes! But why's he flapping his mouth like that? Catching flies? There's no flies in winter, boy! Keep your trap shut!"

The polished youth cast an eye over Surolf, and then murmured politely in the old priest's ears. "Spirit-Father, it's the slow boy – from the Howlers."

"Ah – yes, yes, I see." The old priest looked at Surolf and wrinkled his nose. "Well, keep him from fighting on streets! It's an embarrassment to his calling. Even if he's touched in the head, he should understand that!"

Tupan emerged from the snow and mud, poking out her tongue at Surolf as the priest and his handsome, red-furred guide made their way back in through the door.

Surolf merely stared after them, his face sickened and his body slowly draining of all will to live. "What's she doing here?"

"I don't care." Tupan adjusted her clothing, sinking into a magnificent huff. "You punched me!"

"You stuck snow in my pants!"

"I was only trying to help, and you hit me!" Tupan stood with elaborate dignity. "She's here to marry someone. They have a priest and everything. So it just serves you right!"

The greyhound's face whipped up, appalled. He felt each word like an icicle forming in his soul. "It's true." Surolf sank into the snow, staring desolately at the lavish house. "Her family – they're making her marry. She's going to be forced to become a bride!"

"Ha! Told you!"

"But she said it was forever!" Surolf stood and began to pace, unable to take his eyes from the household's door. "She *said!*"

"Oooh!" All wrongs forgotten, Tupan picked her teeth and sidled nearer, sensing scandal. "Hey, you didn't . . . you know . . . did you?"

"Well, yes! No! Well, almost." Surolf looked as though he wanted to run around in circles wailing like a child. "They're taking her away from me!"

"*Almost,* eh?" Tupan made a face as she rolled a few unsavory thoughts through her head, and then clapped Surolf between the shoulders and propelled him back toward Hern. "Tupan fixes things. So, we'll just have to win your bride for you before she can get hitched!"

"B-but how?"

"By making you lots of riches. By making you the success of the century! By boldly venturing where everybody else is afraid to tread!" Tupan found a perch for herself on the water trough and ran a hand along Hern's nice warm neck as the pony came to join his friends.

The coyote looked toward the soaring wooden palisades. "Look – we just go where the metal is! We find some scrap iron and cast it into fighting tops using the mold these people use for plumb bobs. Sell them for, say, ten dinkets each. We'll have two hundred dinkets – maybe even five hundred in the next couple days. So, there's a start."

Hern wrinkled his spotted nose. "I think we need two thousand."

"So, we'll make two thousand!" Tupan gave one of her airy little shrugs. "If it's hoopy, it'll happen!"

"But iron!" Surolf simply shook his head. "Where do we find iron?"

Tupan jumped off her perch and beckoned to the other two like a mistress calling puppies. She marched up the long earthen ramp that led onto Sentinel's walls. By the time the other two had caught up, the skinny coyote was already leaning on the point-topped battlements, her black nose pointed to the wind. A cold breeze rippled through Tupan's tawny golden fur and stirred music from her countless little bells. "What's two hundred spans high, weighs more than a pussycat's ego, and shines when you polish it?" The girl pointed a finger out across the hideous landscape.

Hern joined Surolf in peering across the ramparts into the poisoned wastes of Acomar. It was a foul country – dead and gray and leached of life. The soil formed sinister geometric patterns, following the shapes of things hidden in the earth. There were streaks of rust like leaking blood, the glint of acid crystals rimming pools of rainwater. Wind hissed across the corpse of a world, bringing the stink of poison to the sky. In the far distance – far beyond mazes of tumbled blocks and swamplands venomous and green – the shapes of huge towers could be seen. Dawn light made the towers spark with a bright, metallic shine.

Tupan leaned her chin on her hand. "Hoo, hoo! See, I found metal, and it isn't even breakfast time! Am I hoopy or what?"

"Acomar . . ." Surolf was horrified. "No one goes into Acomar!"

"Oh, *phtttttbt!* We can go in a little way. It's like going into haunted caves on a dare! How many rats do you see?" Tupan cheerfully studied the lands of the damned, already utterly in love with her plan. "Look, we volunteer to man a guard post waaaaay out in nowheresville! We jump the wall when it gets dark, grab some handy lumps of ore, and get back safe and sound before dawn. You'll be on the path to marital bliss by tomorrow dinnertime!"

Biting his lip, Surolf let the dangers fade before the splendor of the rewards. "I'll need a spear."

Tupan made a magnificent, scornful noise. "Look, if you carry a weapon, you get dumb ideas like fighting! No weapons, and you do the proper thing and run. It's good for everybody! *You* feel clever because you escape – *they* feel clever because they've chased you off. Gets the heart in condition, brings a shine to your coat . . . I'm onto a better way here, trust me!"

"I want a spear!" Surolf shot a dark look toward the girl. "You have no idea what's out there, do you?"

Hern frowned. "I can't use a spear."

"I can." Surolf let his spine straighten as he drew in a deep, brave breath. "A spear, and bags to carry metal, and shovels and a pick."

"Hoopy! We'll get it! Easy as pie." Tupan nudged Hern. "Hey, do we have money left?"

"No."

"Well maybe we can rent a spear. Or maybe find one!" Tupan began to drag her companions back into the town. "There's lots of armed people here. They must lose spears every now and then."

"Tupan – please don't steal a spear."

"It's not theft, it's relocation. The spear will still be perfectly happy, I swear!" The coyote led the way toward the town, sparing a glance of annoyed pity for Surolf. "You dogs have *got* to learn how to live!"

§ § §

All alone and with her fur tingling, Oosha sat in a deep, dark cave and wished she *believed*. The ground beneath her feet held a strange, faint hum. The cave around her was lined with root tendrils from the weeds growing in the earth above. Sitting in the oracle cave, Oosha closed her eyes and tried to will her mind to hear the thoughts of the oracle – and as always heard nothing but the movements of her own mind.

Oosha was Hastaasi – forever marked as a voice of the ancients. Her pure white fur made her the most recognizable creature in the clan, a creature of whom great things were expected. Oosha's mother had wormed her way into the council of the matriarchs, and Oosha had been spared the hardest tasks out in the flinty fields. But if she did not deliver, the clan would eat her alive. Of that, she had no doubt.

The valley of bones lay outside like a vast field of staring eyes. Countless skulls forever watched her. Oosha imagined them whispering as she passed. Each day she came to the oracle hill and found one of the changing caves that yawned like hungry, bearded mouths. She would push through the twisted, sick-smelling foliage and crawl within, sitting amid the root tendrils and straining to catch the slightest whisper.

The oracle had not yet killed her; that fact offered some hope. The oracle could destroy as readily as it could create. Every day, the clan's few Hastaasi took supplicants and cargo to the caves. Sometimes the oracle gave a wealth of metal. Sometimes it brought forth plague. Once it had unleashed a storm of rust that had consumed every piece of metal in the clan until the zone had been purified with fire.

Oosha perched upon the threshold of a malicious, uncaring god; few envied her the terrifying days of her life.

When other Hastaasi approached the oracle, they said they could hear unspoken whispers in their minds. When they raised spirits, they claimed to sense voices that no one else could hear. To Oosha, there came nothing but the sound of her own thoughts, made clear by long hours in emptiness and solitude. She would perch just inside the predatory mouth of a cave and stare out at the bones and their hungry, empty eyes. The little white rat would stare and wonder at the futility of life, and let her thoughts chase their own tails.

Of all the rats in Acomar, Oosha was the only one faced with endless daily solitude. She would sit in the cave mouths, an outsider – an observer. Oosha watched the Itheem with an alien's eyes, studying the cruel irony of their lives.

Rats begot rats begot rats. Each female bred a dozen young a year in a ploy for food and safety. Their numbers rose like fleas on a diseased hide, eating everything until famine caused one and all to fight in a wild frenzy of despair. The numbers dropped; there was plenty; breeding swelled the numbers all over again. They were fleas – vicious parasites. In her heart of hearts, Oosha forlornly craved to be so much more.

Behind her, the cave lay silent. Before her, a small figure waited fearfully at the edges of the bones. The day grew old, and no oracle would speak Oosha's name today. Perhaps none ever would. Oosha reluctantly drew herself away from the peace and quiet of the deadly hill and walked out across a floor of clinking vertebrae, her feet making little slide falls as bones rattled in the breeze.

Her sister waited for her, hunched and cold. Tired from gathering tubers that twisted through the rocky soil, Teela sat in a miserable heap. Her hands shook. There was a fresh wound on her flank – a terrible tear made by Itheem teeth.

Frozen in shock, Oosha stared at her sister. "What happened?"

"Kee'kas attacked me." Teela was shaking – dear, sweet Teela, the kindest thing to ever stalk the earth. "She – she took the grasshopper bread I was bringing for you." Teela hunched, shivering with aftershock and shame.

Oosha flowed up to her and anxiously touched Teela's hide. "Just Kee'kas?"

"Just her." Teela hid her face by brushing at her whiskers with her hands.

Oosha saw the ragged edges of the wound and felt a wave of sickness ripple through her heart. "It's filthy. Let me clean it."

"It doesn't hurt."

"I know." Oosha could feel her sister's body was taut with pain. "But it should be cleaned." Oosha licked at the edges of the wound, trying to gently worry away the outer crust of blood. The deep tear began to bleed again; Oosha let it flow, working to clean away the dust and dirt and fang-filth left by Teela's enemy.

Spiderwebs made a dressing, and dry grass stalks bandaged them across the wound. Teela sat stock still and neither flinched or cried all the while the work was done. Finally, Oosha sat on her haunches and cleaned the blood from her own snout, brushing away the unpleasant taste with obsessive washing of her paws. Teela tentatively nuzzled Oosha in the flank, making the white rat lean her head into her sister's soft, warm fur.

"It will heal, Teela. In a week, you'll scarcely even know it happened."

"*I'll* know." Teela hid her face. "She – she thinks she can do anything she wants, just because she had a mating!" The girl drew short, sharp breaths and stared blindly out across the valley of dry bones. "I'll make sons! I'll make a hundred of them, and they'll tear that scum apart!"

Infinitely saddened, Oosha put an arm about her sister's back. "Let's go. I'll find you something sweet to eat, and you can sleep right up close to the fire."

A tunnel mouth stood nearby, guarded by two clan warriors with ever-watchful eyes. The two females slipped past and down into the twisting mazes far beneath the ground, their whiskers reading all the tiny currents in the dark. They passed other rats – felt teeth bared in annoyance, only to have them fall back once they recognized Oosha's peculiar bonelike smell – and finally emerged inside the great clan caverns in the heart of Acomar.

The forges were busy, smiths heaping fresh-mined metals on the fire. The metals were a gift from the oracle, who gave metal-seed, a liquid that made ore veins grow in earth. At the fires, ore-striped rocks were heated and the metals drained away. Rats hammered iron into sheets and pounded it with carbon, folding it end over end to make the core of battle blades. Others made springs, traps, catches, and other bits of Itheem trickery that sent deadly darts and blades leaping up from concealment – products of devious, cruel and brilliantly inventive minds.

Oosha's mother sat beside the forges, archly waving her tail and flirting with the hard-working artisans. She spied her two daughters as they passed by the red glow of the ironworks and turned her eye on Oosha's freakish fur. "You! *Stay.*"

Oosha and Teela froze, and their mother scuttled toward them, teats heavy from her latest nest of young. She had thirty-seven surviving offspring and had given birth to the purest Hastaasi the Itheem had ever seen. Overnight, Oosha's mother had become someone to be reckoned with. She thirsted for power, craved it like a hideous drug. Already she had begun to gather allies to her cause.

The matriarch looked her daughter up and down, running her eyes across the shocking fur and pale, pink eyes. She sniffed at the scent of defeat on the air. "Nothing yet?"

"It's . . . it's still waiting." Oosha could not bare to meet her mother's gaze. "It will come."

The older female made a noise of pure disgust. "How much longer do you think they'll wait! Make it happen, Daughter! I'm warning you."

Mother lashed her long pink tail, seething with ill will. Oosha was a creature of many promises and no deliveries. If she proved to be a dud, a great many plans were foiled.

"There's a consignment of ore arriving soon. Bits of machines and metal belonging to G'kaa. They'll take it to the oracle to be refined." Mother wrinkled her nose as she spoke, as though Oosha's strange smell offended her. "You are to remain out of sight when G'kaa's men are here. No one must know the clan owns a pure Hastaasi."

Oosha sank down and made to go. "Yes, Mother."

"Have you selected a mate?"

The slim white rat froze. Her mother's words ripped her like a knife. "No. No, Mother."

"Don't. I'll do it. There's males who'll pay good metal to have a chance at a Hastaasi female." Mother suddenly cast an eye over a powerful weapon smith who passed by. The man wore ornaments and seemed sleek and full of wealth. "Never relinquish your resources. Remember it, and you'll live well."

"Yes, Mother."

The two sisters retreated from the fires and into the gloom of the overcrowded caverns. They stared briefly at the packed masses chewing and fighting and working around them, and then made their way into their own secret tunnels and escaped into the dark.

The dark, humming caverns shut away the world of rats. Moving among blind crickets and over forgotten, hissing streams, the two sisters instinctively fled their own kind. Finally, they made the long, slow climb to their private balcony, where they could sit and stare across the desolate vale of bones.

Standing poised at the brink, Oosha made to walk straight down the precipice.

Teela hesitated in the dark. "Oosha – we can't leave."

"I want to leave." Oosha's face was stiff and set. "It's destroying you, Teela. I won't let you become like *her!*"

"But there's nowhere else to go, is there?" Teela edged closer to the precipice as if dragging herself slowly from the dark. "Another clan would get us, or those scorpion things. We can't live in the wilds."

Standing poised at the edge of the open world, Oosha turned her whiskers to the wind. "I don't want to be a part of it anymore, Teela. I want to find the beauty in us and somehow make it live. I think about it, day after day inside those awful oracle caves. The oracle could kill me anytime – but never does. So, I sit and look for beauty, and wonder why we choke it with the ugliness of our lives."

"Can life be made beautiful?" Teela felt the pain of her wound – remembered bared fangs trying to kill her for a piece of bread. "Perhaps all life is ugly, because all struggle is ugly?"

"Not all struggle is ugly – not when we're striving to do something wonderful."

The winds changed – and a sudden, quiet song came drifting through the stones of Acomar. Oosha blinked her pink eyes and felt the ripple of music across her skin. "Do you hear it?"

The sisters lifted their delicate pink ears. Distant pylons sighed beneath the touches of the breeze. Oosha strained toward the sound, her face made blank by the wonder in her heart. "It's only metal stretching and shrinking in the cold; only wind across cold steel." The white rat put out a foot to walk down into the valley far below. "The pylons are not beautiful. There's something in us that reads beauty into the mundane." The white rat spoke quiet words into the breeze. "I want to find that part of us, Teela. I want to give it a chance to be alive. A chance for everyone. . . ."

With Teela at her back, Oosha flowed down the sheer sides of the cliff face and descended into the valley of dry bones. With the remains of countless ancestors rattling under their feet, the sisters once again passed out into the wilds and left the clans behind.

They walked through withered fields, and finally found the waiting dunes. The plain of sighing towers drew them as a lodestone drew chips of iron. The two sisters wandered onward through an afternoon that turned to eventide, watching the sun unwind great flags of smoking pink into the darkened sky. Long shadows faded into night, and magic came creeping from the depths of Acomar. Distant soil and rock faces began to drift with tiny lights, making the dead land swim with streams of gold and red and blue. The two rats climbed atop a dune and looked out toward a phosphorescent sea, and then sat with their tails hanging and new life shining in their eyes.

A flash of light came from the left, and the sisters slowly turned. There, sizzling and drifting across the broken ground, came a great sphere of darkness – a thing two dozen rat-spans wide. Sparks arced out from its surface, climbing at the rocks and touching metal fragments in the soil. The two young rats stared in awe as the apparition moved past, and they saw the eerie silhouettes of mountains buried deep in the sphere.

"Oosha – what is it?"

"The *Gur* gate." The little white rat sniffed at the air, sensing the sharp crackling of magic. "It's a hole into another place. A place where monsters live and daylight never comes. A place giants went when they were finished with the world."

Teela blinked, frightened to move in case she would somehow break the spell, "Did you call it, like you called the lightning?"

"I don't know." The white rat felt her whole world tingling across her fur. "I don't think so."

With a sudden flash, the sphere changed color. One instant it was an insensate juggernaut, and the next, a thing of purpose. The black shape swam with colors that flickered like a giant, seething eye. Air hissed against the sides of the sphere, smoking with a stone-cracking cold. A gaze seemed to turn upon the two little rats – eyes unseen but felt. An ancient intellect seared them with alien disdain as the Gur gate scored a trail of frost across the sands.

Oosha stared. The little rat swayed, and then slowly crept along her perching place. Teela dared not stop her as she edged out to place herself before the passing sphere.

In a daze, Oosha rose and spoke. Her voice rang strangely clear across the deathly still. "Did you make us? Are we your children, or are we just discarded parasites?"

The sphere halted and seemed to somehow turn itself about. Crackling with power, it loomed above the delicate white rat.

Oosha stood her ground, shaking with fright, but with a voice still soft and pure. "I have questions! I need to be wise!" The Gur gate swiveled, and Oosha stumbled as she kept herself before its face. "Show me how to grow old enough to be wise! I'm not afraid!"

Something stared out at her; Oosha suddenly felt its mind like a blow between her eyes. She sank back into the sand, her senses swirling. Stunned, she let her gaze drop blankly to the sand and her limbs turned vague and numb.

A *snap* of light, and the Gur gate became dull black once more. The controlling mind had closed its eyes and gone.

Time passed. The evening wind had long been replaced with a quiet nighttime breeze before Oosha stirred. She slowly blinked pink eyes and found herself sitting quiet and alone, her skin icy as though touched with the Gur gate's smoking cold.

The gate had gone, leaving nothing but frozen scars on the sand. Creeping into view, Teela hesitantly climbed from her hiding place and stared off toward the plain of sighing towers. "Was. . . was it a Giant?"

"I don't know." Oosha seemed to drift in and out of the world. "But I saw its eyes. It looked into me, and it knew that I could sense it in return. It has a mind like broken glass. . . ."

Teela looked at her, utter worship shining in her gaze. "You called a Giant. You wanted answers, and so you made it come." The girl reached out to touch her sister in awe. "What did it tell you, when you spoke to it? Did it hear?"

"I . . . I don't know." Oosha moved slowly, as though the life had half been drained from her limbs. "But it was *old*. I could feel it! Older than the hills. Surely it must have heard. . . ."

"But it came because of you!" Teela helped her sister stand. "It came because you called. Shall we follow it, or shall we go to where it came from?"

"It's searching for something. Maybe that's why the gate is here." Oosha unsteadily moved her feet, feeling her legs like distant blocks of wood. "Let's go back to where we first saw the gate, and see what it was looking for."

The frost-scarred trail led into the metal towers, off into the plains where music swelled and stirred. Unafraid of scorpions and dazed by the legend that had roamed the earth, the sisters quietly walked on into the night.

§   §   §

"All right. what if it *isn't* attacking us, never *has* attacked us, but looks like it *might* attack us?" Jez the nestling frowned as he walked, clumsily clasping his baton-equipped arms behind his back. "Is that okay?"

"No! Look – it's perfectly simple!" Ra'hish walked amid his nestlings, rubbing tiredly at his eyes. "You attack when it's to your advantage. Like, always hit an enemy, but think about it!"

Following in Ra'hish's footsteps, Eeka gave a thoughtful frown. "Think about it while he attacks you?"

"No! What's the point of thinking about it if he's already doing it? If he attacks you, then *kill* the bastard! Murder his family! Find his favorite tree and cut the damned thing down!" Ra'hish grew passionate with frustration. "That's the point! Hit so hard and fast that no one bothers you again!"

Little Eeka and her sisters padded along solicitously at their hero's side. "Your neck is all stiff, isn't it. Shall we rub it for you?"

"It's all right." Ra'hish grumbled, more out of habit than annoyance. "We can do it when we stop. I want to find someplace out of the wind – somewhere G'kaa's damned scout parties won't go."

Overhead, the towers boomed and echoed to each others' song. Now that night had come and the tainted earth had begun to glow, the plain of sighing towers took on its accustomed majesty. The little procession of rats – thirteen of them, big and small – climbed onto the rocky shore to sit with their tails hanging in a little line.

They had traveled long and far to watch the moon rise above the ocean waves. Perched at the shoreline, the foam surging bright and white and clean, the little rats all looked where Ra'hish pointed. They gave a breathless sigh as a great yellow disk arose far our across the black-purple waves.

Light shimmered yellow bands into the glorious sea. Ra'hish passed his little followers their dinner – big sand locusts he'd killed with a bite beneath the head – and the rats happily crunched the tasty morsels as they sheltered from the breeze. The moon rose overhead like a mighty eye, and the nestlings reclined and climbed about Ra'hish, who lay in soft sand and wriggled his long toes.

"Ra'hish – do you know what the moon is?"

"It's a far-off land. Another world up in the sky." The long, lean rat pointed skyward with a thistle stalk. "See? It has valleys and shadows – I think those are seas. Maybe even ruins like Acomar."

"Are there people on it?"

"Who knows? Maybe they stare at us and wonder the same thing. That would be hoopy, don't you think?"

Drawing a breath of chill sea air, Ra'hish relaxed into the sand and closed his eyes. "Have you seen thistle seeds, how they fly? I used to dream that I could find a giant thistle plant and hang onto the seed. Then it would blow me high into the sky, and I could travel far across the Shield Wall and off to other lands. I'd reach the moon and walk along the ridges and the plains – I'd fly above the sea and stare down to watch it passing my tail. At night, we'd find islands with tall, strange-smelling trees and sit in lush, warm sand, wriggling our toes."

There were no warm sands in Acomar; a winter breeze blew hard enough to strip skin off the bones. Sitting in their thin shelter in the rocks, twelve small faces stared at Ra'hish in wonder.

He merely rolled his head to see the moon. "I never found my thistle plant."

"We'll make it for you." Eeka and her siblings gazed at Ra'hish in utter trust. "We'll find the thistle plant – and then you can show us how to fly."

The youngsters gathered to watch the moon, their whiskers silhouetted against the starry sky. They lifted their faces and began a strange, soft song that set the fur rising all along Ra'hish's spine.

The sound was haunting – pipelike tones that rose and surged in wondrous little waves. Each voice matched the others – sometimes echoing, sometimes countering, but always forming clear parts of one blended melody.

They swayed as they sang. Eeka's sweet, high voice made sounds without words as she closed her eyes and faced the moon. Her singing wound above the other little rats' until it hung and shimmered in the crisp, clear air, awakening images of strange journeys on the breeze. Waves surged, moonlight shone, and the little rats made beauty with nothing but their souls. When they finished, the little nestlings kept their faces craned toward the pure light of the moon.

Ra'hish waited in wonder, fur prickling with the same strange feeling he sometimes had when the sunrise came across the waves. Finally, he stirred, letting the small sounds of his movements herald the coming of his voice. "That was . . . very beautiful." The words seemed almost ridiculous in the face of what had come before. "Have you always done that?"

"We thought of it as we walked among the sighing towers. When you took us there." Jez, still favoring his injured arm, blinked eyes half lost in a dream. "It was so magical. We wanted to make some magic, too."

Eeka's smallest sister, Rika, combed her whiskers in the wind. "It makes me feel funny inside."

"Well it was good." Ra'hish gazed at the little faces gravely staring at him in the gloom. "We'll find other places where you can sit and sing."

"Places like this?"

"Oh, there must be all sorts of places we have never seen." Ra'hish drew in a long, slow breath of winter wind, feeling himself awaken piece by piece. "We'll find them. We'll find all the strange, wild places where you can sit and sing."

They were alone now – no clans, no war band, and no G'kaa – alone to somehow survive the wars that inevitably would come. The rats watched the surf and let their private thoughts drift with the wind.

A strange ringing sound echoed in the breeze. Eeka sat upon her haunches, lifting her ears and giving a little frown. "Excuse me, but I hear something funny!"

They all rose together and lifted their painted ears. Above the churning of the nighttime sea, the air held a distant ringing sound.

Rika blinked. "Listen! The towers liked our song!"

"Maybe." Ra'hish heard the deep, discordant clang and gave a frown. "It sounds odd tonight. Not like the normal night music at all."

With one accord, the group of Itheem slithered out of their sheltered nest and perched above the shore, their fur blowing in the steady winter breeze. The creatures frowned in puzzlement, and then scattered out into the scout formation so patiently drilled into them by Ra'hish.

Painted tails a-twiddle, the rats marched toward the music, slipping silently through the eerie, ghost-lit ruins of Acomar.

Chapter 6

"Tupan? Tupan – *not* a good idea! Tupan? Tupan, no!" Surolf tried to keep his voice to a low hiss while snapping whiplash orders through the wind. "Tupan – I forbid it!"

Ignoring Surolf and having the time of her life, the coyote girl cheerfully took a hard grip on a mattock and swung with all the might in her scrawny body. The steel tool clanged against the vast metal column, shattering the nightscape with a wild, unholy blast of sound. The sheer noise made Surolf's eyes almost burst from their sockets. For her part, Tupan gave a great roar of glee and hauled back her mattock to make a second blow.

Pulling his face into a frown, Hern sucked thoughtfully at his upper lip. "Loud."

"*Yes!* Yes, thank you, Hern! Thank you so much for pointing out the bleeding obvious!" Surolf screamed as a second howling note clanged out across the plains. "Tupan – knock it off!"

"But it's great!" The girl stood on an obsidian outcrop, shouting against the sudden ringing in her ears. "Hoopy! Hey, did you hear the noise it made?"

"The whole valley heard you!" Surolf managed to grab hold of the mattock and firmly take custody. "Will you knock it off!"

"Look – the tower isn't even marked." Tupan's tail wagged from side to side behind her skinny bottom as she inspected her handiwork. "Hey, you know what? I don't think this thing is metal after all!"

"No! *Really?*" Surolf firmly steered the girl away from the titanic metal column. "What was your first clue?"

Tupan nastily stuck out her tongue.

Thin, cold, and leaning on a "borrowed" spear, Surolf hugged an old sheepskin coat about himself and tried to ignore her. The night was full of thousands of eyes. Sands shifted in the whispering wind. Surolf's bravado eroded in the freezing cold as his breath hung frosty in the wind.

Out in the ruins, something made the crooked metal towers moan. They stuck from the sand like the ribs of a gigantic beast – all curving identically, all pointing toward the sea. Two hundred body spans tall or more, they gleamed arsenic green and copper blue, throbbing subtly in tones that made fur stand on end. Sharp grains of sand rang faintly from the pylons as wind blew in from the sea, bringing with it a sharp, bitter, salty smell –

– and the stench of untold hordes of goblins.

The soil *stank* of them – the rocks, the weeds, and the earth itself smelled of the ancient enemy. Millions of rat-kind had scuttled over every inch of this unholy place, generation after generation of clicking teeth and claws. In their careful, creeping march from the Shield Wall, Surolf and his companions had encountered not a single goblin, yet there could be no question the rats were there. The soil was marked by narrow feet. The teeth and bones of rats lay churned in the soil. How many of the creatures had lived their foul lives here and died? How many swelled and festered beneath the ruins like a waiting plague? Surolf shivered, awash in dread, edging toward the great warm presence of the pony at his side.

Hung from end to end with blankets, Hern looked like a strange plaid hut. "I hear something."

"What?" Surolf's ears were less an asset than his nose. He lifted his muzzle and sniffed the stench of goblins and rotting seaweed. "Where?"

"Everywhere." Hern's deep voice held a note of fatalism. "I think we're all going to be eaten alive. . ."

"What? No way!" Back on her perch beside the vast metal column, Tupan posed and opened her arms. "Look at all this metal! We just chip a piece off, run back to town, and we're in business at last!" The girl turned to gaze out across the fantastic, glowing, twisted ruins of ancient Acomar.

"Uh-oh . . ."

"Uh-oh?" Surolf felt a sudden chill as he saw Tupan's face fall. "What 'uh-oh'?"

"Um. Are goblins, like, about chest-height, with really pointy faces and skinny tails?"

"Yes." Surolf took a grip upon his spear. "Do you see one?"

"Aaaah – not exactly."

Frightened, Surolf vaulted onto the rock outcrop and crouched with Tupan beside the pylon's base. The moon wavered out from behind scraps of cold gray cloud – and a sickly light shone out across the plains.

The dunes beneath metal pylons stood empty, cold, and clear; but out across the ruins, the whole ground seemed to flow. Tides surged and moved, screams sounded in the night, and countless claws scratched at the soil.

"Oh, pooh." Tupan blinked, a tad crestfallen as she gazed across a land that boiled with squeaking, chittering enemies.

Rat forage parties were scouring distant rocks or dragging nets across shoreside waves. Goblins stood guard on hillsides, snarling and fighting as hunting groups came to blows. From the high vantage point of the obsidian block, Acomar suddenly seemed frighteningly alive.

Surolf found Tupan pressing close, and he took a firm grip on his spear. "It's all right – they're miles away. They're not coming onto the sand. See? They – they mustn't like the pylons."

"Bad. Very bad." Hern's voice rumbled from below. "I don't like it."

"Why?"

The pony gave a heavy sigh of doom. "Because there's something here so horrible that even goblins are afraid of it."

The two canines froze to ponder the notion – Surolf biting his lip; Tupan tilting her head and dismissing the idea.

"Naaaah! They just don't like sand! Rats tunnel, see? You can't tunnel in sand."

"I think we should all run away." Hern noisily worked his big teeth. "I like running. It keeps me warm."

"Look, just . . . just stay on watch or something and let us find some metal, okay?" Tupan twirled a finger next to her ear and whispered a quick aside to Surolf. "Boy, is this guy oversensitive or what?"

Heaving a weary sigh of exasperation, Surolf ignored her, dropped back onto the sand and staggered off into the waiting dunes. "Come on. Get down, or they'll see you. Let's find this metal and get back as fast as we can! I want to be home before dawn."

"Why?" Tupan made a swan dive from the rock above, turned a somersault, and landed perfectly on her feet. "Is Mama keeping dinner hot?"

"No, because if we're missing, Aela will worry!"

Hern plodded through the sand and gave a thoughtful snort. "She looked comfortable enough to me. She was with that big tall chap with all the money and muscles."

"Hern!" Surolf seethed with injured sensibilities. "Just . . . just listen for goblins, okay?"

"Oh, okay."

They walked upright through the sand, feet sinking into the shifting stuff and making the travelers slide constantly to their knees. It would be impossible to find metal buried in the sand. Finally, the light of the moon shone upon a shattered column standing stark as a broken fang. Of one accord, the three travelers moved toward it, climbing over metal shards bigger than houses. Tupan stood high upon one chunk and opened her arms in relief and glee.

"See? Metal! Now lets go find little pieces to take home."

"Tupan – this stuff is really hard – I don't know of we can melt it in a fire."

"Well, we can figure out how to do it when we get back!" Tupan leapt down and ground her knuckles into Surolf's skull. "Hey – were you worried about me back there, protecting me from all those rats? You look cute when you go all protective!"

Surolf mustered an enormous store of dignity. "I was not *protective* – I was merely *concerned*. It's not the same thing."

"Right." Tupan danced gaily off, her bells tinkling in the wind. "Oh, well – you stand watch, and I'll find metal. C'mon Hern – lets go prospecting!"

With his nose to the ground, Hern began rolling over rocks and peering behind great square boulders of obsidian. Tupan left him alone and went sliding down into a great sand pit at the base of the broken pylon

Surolf stood on a rock and held his spear. The wind froze his tail, and he pulled his coat tightly about his shoulders. Trying not to listen to the happy tinkling of Tupan's bells, he scanned the empty wasteland and wondered why they remained so conspicuously clean and clear.

From behind the rocks, Tupan's voice rose into a little cry of delight. "Oh, wow! There's dead bugs here!"

Annoyed by her lack of caution, Surolf answered without bothering to turn around. "So?"

"They're really big!" Tupan surfaced from the sand pit, dragging a scorpion that was at least three times her own size. "Check it out!"

Surolf almost expired in fright. He leapt down from his guard post and ran frantically to save the coyote girl's life. "Tupan! Look out!"

"What?" The girl dropped her find and actually began to walk all over it. "Isn't it neat?"

"Tupan! How do you know it isn't still alive!"

"Oh, I can tell things. I can't feel its dreams." Tupan opened and shut the dead scorpion's claws, utterly fascinated by the articulation. "Well – that and it has a hole burned clean through its guts. Come and check it out!"

This was the final straw; Surolf jabbed his spear butt-first into the ground, planted his fists on his hips and confronted Tupan eye to eye. "Now, look, you! I have tried and tried to teach you how to stay safe and alive! So, from this point on, you just listen to me! You *don't* make noise, you *don't* touch alien monsters, and you *don't* dance about like an idiot in the middle of Itheem lands. We are going to do this in a proper, military . . . " Surolf skittered to a halt mid-rant as Tupan stared off across the rocks. "What? What is it now?"

"Something's coming!"

"How do you know?"

"Because it just sneezed." Tupan stretched out her hand as though sensing something chill and deadly in the air. "Get down!"

"Hide, now." Hern came plodding down the sand slope and into the shadows beside the pylon. "I rather like the look of this bit down here."

Jumbled blocks of obsidian lay half covered in dry sand. The three travelers dived down into the cracks between the rocks. An instant later, the shifting sand above began to shift to the sound of furtive feet.

They came softly and timidly, their pink toes scarcely disturbing the sand. The two little rats moved on all fours, their long naked tails slithering in the sand behind them as they slid down the slope and came to rest amid the blocks. The two creatures shook grit from their fur, and then tenderly groomed each other with perfect little hands. Long whiskers twiddling, they sat side by side and stared up at the broken pylon, their eyes wide and shining.

Moonlight glinted on one of the rats – the clean, pure white of fresh-fallen snow. One white and one gray, the rats were otherwise identical – slim, frail, and alien. They moved with a serpentine grace, flowing across obsidian blocks – halting, sniffing, and slithering onward again. They crossed the deep hoofprints left by Hern without so much as a glance, yet circled warily around the bodies of the long-dead scorpions left lying on the sands.

Fascinated by the view, Tupan shifted to get a better view. Her countless tiny bells tinkled.

The two rats froze and searched the air about them.

Surolf saw the goblins tilt their heads and look at the pylon, and his heart clenched with dread; Tupan! He should have cut the bells off her himself! Now the two goblins scuttled closer, homing in on the sound. They halted and spoke to one another in soft, high voices, and Surolf took a grip on his spear and prepared to fight for his life.

With a wild cry, he sprang out of hiding and lunged with his spear. The gray goblin squealed and tumbled wildly aside, falling among the cold stone blocks and slamming to the ground. The albino rat leapt high atop a piece of stone. Surolf stabbed at the creature, missed, and then leapt back to run the first rat through as it lay kicking helplessly on the ground.

The white rat sprang at him from above, thumping between his shoulder blades and sending Surolf sprawling in the sand. He scrabbled to his feet and found his spear – and discovered the white rat sheltering its injured partner, hissing with bared teeth at the spear.

Surolf gave a yell of satisfaction and made to run both creatures through – only to recoil as a lump of stone went bouncing from his skull.

"*Ow!*"

Tupan threw a second rock at Surolf for good measure. "You hurt her!"

The coyote had come slithering out of hiding, bells and ribbons fluttering about her in a wild, gay cloud. The girl ran past the dazed, smarting Surolf and slid to her knees in the sand in front of the two little rats.

The gray rat held a broken foot and whimpered heartrendingly in pain. The white rat – a creature with shocking pink eyes and a body quaking in fear – bared its long incisors and gave a frightful hiss, pulling away from the intruders and sheltering its companion's life with its own. Tupan tried to wave her hands and make friendly little noises in her throat.

"It's okay! He didn't mean it! He's just an idiot!" Tupan wrung her hands as the injured rat made a little cry of pain. "We're sorry! We're really sorry!" She made to approach the injured rat, only to recoil as the white-furred Itheem hissed and snapped its jaws.

Behind her, Surolf sat in the sand and looked at the coyote girl in hurt. "You almost killed me!"

"You hurt her!" Tupan edged back and hit Surolf right on his injured skull. "You moron! You should have left them alone!"

"So, they can tell their whole tribe we're here?" Surolf angrily took hold of his spear. "Do you know how long it takes goblins to strip a living creature to the bone?"

"They don't even know how to fight! You're beating up on little girls!"

Surolf bridled with injured pride. "So how do you know they're girls?"

"The lack of testicles is usually a giveaway." Tupan pulled her own clothing straight and shot the dog a scathing look. "Didn't they teach you how to recognize body parts back at home?"

Surolf took a firm hold of his spear. "Male or female – they're goblins! I say we get rid of them!"

"You so much as touch them, and I'll *bite* you!" Tupan sheltered the little rats behind herself. "You – you damned *dog!*"

The rats could only watch in a daze, panting softly in fright. Surolf pulled back to grumble – Hern padded out from hiding to gaze at the two rats with his strange, soft eyes. Tupan sat cross-legged in the sand and reached carefully out with one hand, her bells tinkling softly as she carefully touched the gray rat's fur. Sobbing softly, the gray creature let herself be touched. Tupan made little sounds of comfort, and managed to enfold the creature's injured foot between her hands. The white rat held the gray in comforting arms, watching with wide eyes as something sparkled between the palms of Tupan's hands.

Hern and Surolf frowned, ears rising as the blue glow spilled into the rocks. Tupan quietly massaged the gray rat's foot, and then held it up and watched the rat girl wriggling her toes. She stroked the girl's pelt, smoothing away a bandage and healing the cut underneath. All pain gone, the rat turned and spoke in clear astonishment to the other Itheem.

Surolf sank into the sand and stared. "How in the name of Sheer did you do that? You're no sorcerer!"

"I told you; Tupan fixes things." The coyote gave a prim sniff of her long nose. "There, now enemies are friends. All fixed and done."

The two rats stared at the healed injuries, their pointed faces filled with childlike wonder. They spoke to one another in their hissing, clicking tongue, talking half with words and half with motions of their whiskers, ears, and hands. The gray one looked to Tupan and made a speech of astonishing politeness, laying a hand on Tupan's tinkling bells.

"Oracle! I caught that." Her beautiful eyes luminous in her thin waggish face, Tupan patted the small rat on the hand. "You're barking up the wrong pine tree there, Ratty! I'm not an oracle. I just happen to have all the answers." Tupan gave a vain little peek toward Surolf. "Infallibility and charisma – they're such a burden. . . ."

The gray rat spoke, motioning from the white rat to Tupan – much to the protests of the white-furred girl.

Hern pricked up his ears and raised one shaggy brow. "Oh, dear. She said oracle again." The pony gave an eloquent swish of his plaited tail. "I don't like oracle mounds; I fell into one once, and it grabbed my legs with scratchy ferns."

"Really?"

"Yes." Hern made a serious face. "I ate them. They tasted bad. . . ."

A high, piercing scream came from the sands above. The two rats, two canines, and pony almost died with fright. They darted back into the obsidian blocks as a dozen Itheem warriors burst across the dunes and charged.

Tupan took one look at the wave of Itheem and felt her tail sag. "Ooooh. . . . *rats.*"

With piercing cries, the onrushing rats leapt spectacularly among the rocks. Striding through their midst came an Itheem giant – a rat twice the size of the others, and that moved with shocking speed. It streaked past the smaller rats, bounding from vertical rock faces and blurring through the air.

Surolf leveled his spear and tried to cover the rest of his friends. He yelped with fright as the huge rat simply cut the spear shaft clean in two.

One of the smaller rats had stopped to help a fallen comrade. Another slipped and skidded on its bottom, shooting down the sand dune with a plaintive wail. Tupan raised one brow and watched the creature as it passed, suddenly realizing it scarcely stood high enough to reach her thigh.

As the largest rat came in for the kill, Hern calmly turned about and began stamping his hooves. Each powerful blow sending shockwaves through the soil. Seeing the clear threat of the hooves, the large rat checked – a short spear lashed to each forearm glinted, and yellow fangs hissed in bloodthirsty madness as the creature took stock of its new foe.

§

"Don't hurt them! They're nice!" Skittering forward, Teela spread open her arms. "Don't do it! Don't hurt them!"

Nestlings gathered in confusion. They bubbled with excitement as they saw the sudden gleam of pure white fur. Oosha dazedly came out from behind the giant pony, saw the nestlings and the handsome warrior at their head, and felt an instant surge of relief. The warrior recognized her and spun to fight the canines for her freedom.

Oosha simply walked out and parted the battle lines. "It's all right. Don't hurt anything. Please – no fighting."

"Are they holding you captive?" The warrior's voice was a thing of beauty. He looked at Oosha with ferocious dark eyes. "They were fighting you?"

"We aren't captives. My sister hurt her foot, and they made her better. Their female is a shaman." Oosha sat quietly on her rump. "But you came to save us again. I never thanked you last time."

"You are welcome." Ra'hish kept his pitiless gaze on the dogs. "But they're Uruth. What are they doing here? Scouts? Headhunters?"

"They're not very good fighters." Oosha said the words almost in apology. "I don't think they came to kill anything tonight. But they did a very good job of fixing Teela's foot."

Ra'hish gave a feral glare toward the canine male, and then flicked the catches on his blades. With sinister efficiency, the knife points snapped back into concealment inside their staves. "Then they can live. So can their four-leg."

The canines gave a relieved sigh as the blades disappeared.

The nestlings crowded curiously closer, and Eeka reached out to touch Oosha's fur in fascination, running the fine white strands between her fingertips. "Is it real?"

Oosha's pink eyes were pale and strange in the filtered light. She made a wan little face and shrugged in reply. "It's real."

"Are you a *real* Hastaasi? Do the Giants talk to you?"

"I don't know. Maybe I'm not." Oosha spared a wistful look toward the canine shaman. "Things don't speak to me the way they should."

"She *is* Hastaasi. She can call lightning, summon Giants, and make the pylons sing!" Teela avidly took station beside her sister, winding her tail with Oosha's own. "She killed a dozen scorpions – a hundred of them! You can still see them lying here. One day she'll even make the oracle become kind!"

The nestlings "oohed" and "aahed" as they saw the dead scorpions on the rocks amid bitter rainwater pools. The moon bathed the shadows with an eerie light, almost making the dead monsters seem alive. The nestlings cautiously drew away.

"I like this one! This one's funny!" Rika, the runt of the nestling litter, perched on Hern's back. The pony turned to meet him eye to eye and spoke slow words in a deep and rumbling voice. Rika touched the pony's lips, as if to feel sure the apparition was real. Emboldened, he crept up to touch the monster nose to nose.

Trying not to jump in fright, Ra'hish instantly moved close to hand. "Rika! Be careful! It probably has fleas!" The nestlings were always meticulously and immaculately groomed. "Don't let it bite!"

Jez looked up from where he sat, gravely studying the slim male Uruth. "Fleas? In winter?"

"Dog fleas. They're tougher." Ra'hish, thwarted of bloodshed and quite at a loss, groomed his whiskers nervously. "Keep out of arm's reach. Canines can be strong."

Indeed, the aliens seemed huge – almost half again as tall as an adult Itheem. They were Uruth – the ancient enemy; for generations untold they had lived behind the great barrier, keeping the Itheem locked inside sickly Acomar. The nestlings felt a sudden chill and looked at the aliens in dread, wondering why such terrible creatures had entered their home.

Overhead, pylons moaned. Sand whispered among dunes. Against the deep sounds and sparkling stars, a weird, merry tinkling filled the air. Confused, the rats quested with their ears, entranced by the strange new noise.

One canine seemed blissfully happy with the truce. Long and skinny, spreading weird bright music with every jiggle of her tail, the creature had Eeka perched between her shoulder blades. Suddenly feeling a hundred spans tall, Eeka called gleefully down to the other rats and waved her slender hands.

"This one's the best! Her clothes make sounds!" Eeka gleefully gripped the canine's ears. "Come and ride!"

The strange Uruth was decked out in skirts and ribbons covered in tiny metal spheres, each one jingling a different note. Oosha, Teela, and the nestlings instantly crowded near to look and touch, poking the tiny spheres.

Delighted by the audience, the canine girl performed a strange, gay pirouette, put Eeka down, and turned a cartwheel on the sand. Skirts whirled and ribbons flew. The music surged in marvelous melody. Chased by cheering little rats, the coyote danced into the rocks and sat down, surrounded by nestlings. She began babbling away in her barking tongue, telling a story – or perhaps a monstrous lie. With Oosha propped there at her feet and nestlings on her knee, the Uruth held her listeners spellbound.

Abandoned by the other rats, Ra'hish joined the gray male dog in staring irritably at the scene. The rat heaved a sigh and pointed one hand toward Tupan. "Is that yours?"

The canine made a weary sound of annoyance in reply. Ra'hish and the Uruth simply sat down side by side, wondering why so much chaos ruled their lives.

§

"Tupan." Surolf was stiff, half expecting to be pulled down and eaten alive. "Tupan – don't mess with the goblins."

"I like the little teeny tawny girl. She's cute!"

"Goblins are not cute, Tupan. Goblins are giant maggots with teeth."

"You've got to look at things through other eyes!" Happily surrounded by chattering, curious rats, Tupan held aloft a nestling, studying the creature's nice pink feet. "When you look at a tree, be a tree! When you hold a rat – be a rat! When you look at the sea, be the sea, and the world suddenly seems pretty fun and hoopy!"

"Yeah, right." Surolf shook his head and let the subject die. Tupan would wail for help soon enough – and when she was being bitten to the bone, Surolf would be there to say I told you so. . . .

Quite buried under nestlings eager to ride, Hern padded from the pylon base and politely swished his tail. "This is a very interesting place. It has nice sounds." The pony did not seem to mind when a tiny rat walked up to perch on his head. "By the way, did anyone else notice there's light coming from between these rocks?"

Tupan and Surolf looked instantly about in interest, followed by the adult rats – white, camouflage, and gray. All four creatures joined the pony as he bent over a hollow between two titanic boulders – a hollow from which a pure white light bled.

The three adult rats talked softly, and then the gray female timidly slipped down into the open cavern and sniffed delicately about. She moved with care, as if frightened an enemy might return.

Watching thoughtfully from above, her heels tucked cross-legged into her rump, Tupan creased her brows in a frown. "Hey, she isn't like the other ones. They all have their fur painted in squares and stripes, but she's just plain. I wonder why?"

"Battle camouflage." Surolf sat hunched in the sand, wariness oozing from every pore. "The male is a war leader – the little ones are his kids."

"*Twelve* kids?"

"Sure. Why do you think the Shield Wall is there?" Surolf looked at the rats and shuddered. "They breed fast. Real fast.'

"Oh – *phtttttttb!*" The crude noise Tupan made with her tongue greatly interested the baby rats, who excitedly tried out the noise themselves. "Nothing breeds that fast! But hey – why has one rat got white-painted fur?"

"She's an albino, Tupan. Didn't you see her pink eyes?"

"An albino?" Tupan sucked at a canine tooth in thought. "What's an albino?"

"Freak of nature. No pigments in the hair and skin. They probably chased her out of her tribe."

"Poor thing!" Tupan instantly took the astonished white rat under her arm. "She's all skin and bone!"

"Hmmph – so are you."

"In my case, it's studied elegance." Tupan sat erect, filled with condescending dignity. "Coyotes are a rangy breed."

Surolf gave a snort. "And the longer the range, the better."

Their little *tête-à-tête* was interrupted by the gray rat, who had found something below. On a sandy floor covered with old footprints, she had discovered the obsidian surface underneath. A crack no broader than a finger had opened in the floor, and it was from here that the faint white light came.

The dogs and rats slipped into the cavern and cleared rubble aside to let Hern plod in beneath the door. The crowd gathered all about the crack in the obsidian, watching as the white rat and her sister began to avidly brush the sand away.

Overhead, the night wind whistled, and the broken pylon made an eerie sound. Hern lifted his ears, stared wonderingly, and swished his tail as vibrations trembled through the ground. "There's something strange coming."

The others ignored him, bent on their own discovery. Alive with pure fascination, they gathered about the crack and listened, hearing noises echoing in open spaces deep within.

"Look, the floor is made from blocks! It isn't solid!" Surolf stood, strikingly tall amid all the bustling rats. He craned his neck to study the natural vault of the space, composed of sloping blocks that had fallen this way and that. Stooping, he ran his hands across the sharp crack in the floor. "This whole area is made up of blocks. The broken tower's fallen sideways and levered them apart. See? This must lead beneath the pylon."

The large male rat had begun to clear sand from the crack, flicking it with sweeps of his camouflaged hands. The creature spoke a few cool words of its hissing language to Surolf, and the two creatures began to work side by side, wedging obsidian chips from the crack with the halves of Surolf's broken spear.

Sitting with the two grown female rats, Tupan placed an arm around each sister's neck and sat to watch the performance unfold. "Can we dig down?"

"Through two body lengths of solid volcanic glass?" Surolf gave a hard thump of his tail. "No."

"So, what are you doing?"

"I'm using my brain. If we can't dig through, we'll crack through." Surolf helped the male rat scoop rock chips onto the floor. "We clear the crack, caulk the bottom, and then fill it with fresh water. There's rainwater pools up among the metal shards." Surolf lay on his side to get a closer look into the crack. "At about dawn, if it gets cold enough, the water will freeze. Expanding ice should crack the block; then Hern can drag away the pieces with a rope."

"Crack the block?" Tupan stared into empty space, her tail wagging slowly from side to side, but then stiffening as she caught onto the idea. "Hey, that's really neat! How did you think of that?"

"You fix things – I *make* things," Surolf said as he worked side by side with the senior rat. "Didn't you ever wonder what I do?"

"Um, no." Tupan watched, fascinated by Surolf's work. "I thought you just kinda grumbled a lot and made really fragile pots."

"I do *not* make pots! I made a wheel for making pots and got paid off in trade!" Surolf shot the girl an irritated glance as he dug into the sand. "I make windmills. I make bellows. I show people how to get metal out of rock. I look at old machines and try to make them go!"

"Oh." Tupan bit her bottom lip. "Don't you guys all use oracles for that?"

"I'd rather do it for myself!"

"Hoopy." Tupan had opened a packet of dried apricots and began distributing them among the curious rats. "You know, I think we can make you a soul after all!" Surrounded by a gaggle of young rats, Tupan rose heavily to her feet. "Okay, you boys play. I'll have the rat patrol here help me get you something to caulk the crack. Something a bit soft, gummy and watertight, right?"

"Right." Surolf spared a moment from his excited excavations to peer at the rats. "You really think they'll be much help?"

"Sure!" Tupan planted her favorite tawny rat girl on Hern's back.

"Hey, kid – who's the best damned auntie in the whole wide world?"

"*Too-pan!*" The rat voice came garbled, high, and squeaking, but the intent was clear. "*Tupan!*"

Surolf gaped in shock. "She did *not* just say that!"

"Sure she did. Check it out." Tupan waved her arms at the rat and indicated objects all about the cave. The gold-furred baby rat pointed long fingers at each thing it identified, speaking in garbled Uruth tongue.

"Rocks, light, Tupan, up, down!"

"Great." Surolf lay down to join the male rat as it peered into the narrow crack, trying to see what lay below. "Teach it 'airhead' – then we'll know it can communicate with you. "

"No one likes you, Surolf. We did a survey." Tupan stuck out her tongue and departed, leaving the boys to be watched over by the white rat and her sister.

She and her entourage returned five minutes later, chattering and babbling excitedly in a dozen voices. With a rat riding on her shoulders and playing one of her bells, Tupan opened her arms and raised a joyous shout to the skies. "Hey, sourpuss, we're back!" The girl somehow managed to click all the fingers on each of her hands and end up pointing at the baby rats. "Hey, kids! Hit it!"

"*Surolf sucks rocks!*" The rats all squeaked together in their bright little voices, and Tupan folded hands in gratification against her heart.

"See? Aren't they great!" Tupan helped the rats unload strange pipes of black, evil-smelling goo from Hern's back. "Two more days, and we'll have them singing dirty limericks 'n' all! Hey, kids, try this; '*Old Surolf, he'd never have seen us, since he spent his days waggling his...*' "

"Tupan! Shut up!" Surolf irritably grabbed the black goo from nearby rats and shoveled the muck down into the floor. "What's this about two days from now?"

Tupan passed more muck to Surolf without bothering to watch what she was doing. "We're going to hang out together!" The girl happily spoke toward the little rats. "Hey, gang! *Tupan-ratties-pony*. All meet here – tomorrow. Tomorrow night – yes?"

The nestlings discussed things with the elder male, climbing over one another in their mad eagerness to be heard. For his part, the male rat tried to block his ears. He questioned the grave white rat and finally nodded to the children. Tupan's tiny proteges instantly began bouncing like mad fleas.

"*Tupan, ratties-ratties! Tomorrow night, dig rock!*"

Surolf slapped pulp down into the floor crack. "Why do we need the rats just to dig this stuff out?"

"Because *they* helped us find it!" Tupan spoke as if to an exasperating child. "Didn't your mother ever teach you how to play nice?"

Hern gave a smug swish of his tail. "Mine did."

"Hoopy! Hern, make Surolf behave." Tupan graciously took the white rat's hand and tied a bell around her throat. "Then, tomorrow night, we'll all go down into the treasure vault and see what we can see."

"Great." Surolf sniffed at the caulking material and made a face. "What the Howl's name is this stuff? It stinks!"

"It's squashed-up scorpion. See! I can invent things, too!" Tupan, her hands quite clean, sat on the freezing cold sand. "The rats chewed it for us."

This was all the information Surolf needed to feel sick. He let the male rat finish the caulking and walked outside into the bitter cold night air. Plunging his claws into a deep rainwater pool, he winced as his hands broke through the ice skin and dunked into the cold.

Something flickered across the surface of the ice water. Surolf froze stock still, his ears tingling as he tried to hear past the restless hiss of sand. He watched the reflections slowly ripple, and then jerked his head to stare up into the dark.

Something moved on the sand ridge above. Looking out over the tumbled bodies of dead scorpions, the dog saw a shadow slowly creep into view.

Frost outlined a sphere a dozen body spans wide – a silent, evil thing that slid purposefully across the sands. Tiny arcs of lightning chased outward from its skin, crackling and sizzling across the ice-cold sands.

"Guys?"

Tupan never heard; she was teaching more dirty ditties to the baby rats.

Surolf backed away as he saw the black sphere cross the sand pit's edge and tumble swiftly down toward the cave. *"Tupan! Get outside, all of you!"*

The sphere hissed and sizzled as it rolled, filling the air with a strange, unholy stink. Lightning struck the corpse of a scorpion, making the cadaver's legs twitch in the air. The sphere grazed the corpse and somehow sucked it inside. More lightning sizzled, filling the sand pit with a terrifying glare.

Rats scurried up from the rocks, three or four dangling from Hern's neck as the pony galloped hastily away. Tupan emerged from the cave and saw the Gur gate. She simply stared, her ears falling as the sphere trundled straight toward her.

The male rat moved quicker than a snake strike. He hit Tupan with a flying tackle that sent them both tumbling through the sand an instant before the sphere struck. Dragging the coyote woman by the bells, he pulled her up onto the broken pylon. They clambered up high above the sands. At their feet, the black sphere crashed against the pylon, and then somehow started to climb the metal tower.

Reaching the broken top of the tower and looking vainly for somewhere higher, Tupan and the rat stared down into the sphere. Showering sparks against the metal, the Gur gate inexorably crept toward the peak of the tower.

§

"Is the Giant there?" Teela ran behind her fleeing sister, heart hammering in fright. "Is it angry? Why is it after us?"

Running fast through the freezing sand, Oosha leapt high over a dead scorpion and slithered on a dune. "I don't know." Oosha ran along the tip of a rill, halting to rise on her hind feet and stare about. She panted, her mind spinning with fright as she tried to think what to do. "The gate's going to climb the pillar and get them! Look, it's already halfway up!"

Down in the sand pit, the Gur gate rolled inexorably up the broken pylon. The canine female had somehow managed to swarm onto a last tiny crest of the tower. She reached down just as Ra'hish slipped, caught his arm, and pulled him bodily to safety on her perch. Just below him, the Gur gate sizzled as it slowly climbed.

Weeping with fright, Teela headed after Oosha as she ran to another pylon a hundred body spans away. The two rats halted beneath the vast shadow of the metal rib. Teela and Oosha stared up at the black shape, their pulses hammering in their throats.

Teela looked to Oosha's bright pink eyes, her face shining with unquestioning, simple faith. "Call the lightning! You can close the gate and smash it!"

"Teela . . ." Oosha looked at the metal towers and quailed. "Teela, I don't know how!"

"You do! You just don't remember! Close your eyes and pray with me, like we did before!"

Oosha closed her eyes and murmured a prayer to spirits she could not believe in – to Giants she no longer thought were gods. She struggled to wrench upward with her mind. The very sands bucked and jerked beneath her feet. Sobbing, she opened her eyes and stared into a night that had gone mad.

Power blasted from the ground, snaking upward to the very crest of the new tower. The lightning shivered through the air, sheeting the landscape with brilliant violet light. Baby rats screamed, half blinded by the glare. The pony reared and kicked its hooves at the sky. All the world seemed transformed into stark black silhouettes – all except Teela, who sat curled into a ball, eyes closed in faithful prayer. The beautiful gray rat never wavered, and never opened her eyes. Oosha watched her sister, then stared dazedly out to see her handiwork.

The evil sphere had abandoned the broken metal tower. Moving ponderously, as though it weighed immeasurable tons, the Gur gate rolled over the dunes. Somehow dragged toward the lightning arc, it lumbered on its way, changing course as more blue-white jags lit a pylon a thousand spans away.

The sinister black sphere disappeared. The last lightning dazzle fled. The living were left sitting in pure darkness, purple afterimages crisscrossing their eyes.

Oosha had held her breath, her whole body tingling. Letting the air gradually from her lungs, she crept very slowly to her sister's side. "Teela?"

Her sister opened her eyes only slowly, already filled with an expression of calm. She sought Oosha's strange pink gaze, and then looked dazedly around. "You – you did it. You made it go away."

"Yes, I suppose I did." Oosha felt completely blank inside. "We should go back to the others now."

"Whatever you say, Oosha." Teela moved slowly, as though walking in a dream. "You'll know what to do."

Side by side, the sister rats walked off into the sand.

"What will we find beneath the cave, Oosha?"

"I don't know." The white rat suddenly felt the silver moonlight against her hide. "Maybe . . . maybe something beautiful."

"I hope so." Teela walked toward the watching rats and dogs. "It's strange. I don't feel very frightened anymore."

The moon rose. Cold sands blew. Surrounded by staring eyes, the two sisters walked back down into the sand pit and sat to gaze toward a glowing moon.

§

The huge ramparts of the Shield Wall stood stark against the graying sky as Tupan emerged from the weeds of Acomar. She saw the tower she had volunteered to guard – a mile from the Uruth village, it was unlikely to be checked by patrols before dawn. Tupan sniffed for danger with a long-practiced nose, then stood and shook sand from her fur.

Behind her lay the stark, deadly lands of Acomar. From all around, young rats materialized – their stealth so perfect they could scarcely be seen or heard. Their leader, Ra'hish, rose out of the dust, scanning the Shield Wall with his eyes and whiskers before allowing any of the young children to stand.

Plodding from the shadows with an ungainly lump of rusted iron on his back, Hern saw the palisade and gave a grateful sigh. "Good. Home soon. This stuff is heavy."

"We'll get it melted by breakfast time!" Tupan slapped the pony on the neck, starting up a cloud of dust and sand. "Hoopy! Surolf, you're as good as wed!"

The small rats crowded close as Tupan levered open the rotted tree trunk she had found in the mighty wall. It made a doorway, scarcely big enough for the pony to pass through. Hern reached back and peeled a sleeping nestling from his shoulders, depositing the little creature gently into the white rat's arms.

Tupan squatted on her heels, talking softly with the lean and terrifying Ra'hish. She slapped the creature on the shoulders and rose to head for home. "Hoopy! They'll meet us here tomorrow night. It's safer if they guide us through."

"Yeah?" Surolf cast a suspicious eye over the rats. "What are we paying them for this?"

"Food. They'll bring us some metal if we bring them some food. I think they're pretty hungry."

Seething with ill will, Surolf jammed the butt of his broken spear into the soil. "That's trading! Tupan, no one is allowed to deal with goblins! It's the law! No talking, no trading! These *things* are the enemy!"

Tupan clapped her hands, snapped her fingers, and whirled to point toward the rats. "Kids?"

"Surolf sucks rocks!"

"Thank you!" Tupan made a courtly gesture toward the open palisade. "After you, bridegroom to be. It's time to get your beauty sleep."

The baby rats crowded forward as Tupan made to leave, reluctant to let her go. With a bright wave, the strange, wild coyote girl bid the rats farewell and clambered up into the gloom. Moments later, the palisade seemed whole again, pegs and nails hammering the log back into place.

Standing with Oosha and her sister, Ra'hish gazed at the vast wall as it was touched by golden beams of sun. He patted Eeka on the head – ran fingers through Jez's soft, fine fur, and then turned his little tribe around and headed them softly back into the weeds.

Thistledown floated gently in the travelers' paths. Ra'hish caught one tiny gossamer seed and looked at it in his hand. He released the mote to watch it fly up into a perfect dawning sky.

Chapter 7

"Spinning tops! Grown warriors wasting their time with *games!*" Bridling with indignation, the old seer poked his stick toward an excited team of soldiers who were playing with new toys. "It's like a madness! All anyone will talk about is tops!"

The town's low hummock houses were all a-buzz with activity. Once the frost had hardened the muddy roads, midwinter became a good time for travel and trade. Miir-mice arrived from their nests, looking for dog-brewed beer and fresh-pressed paper. Cats came to view the excitement from afar, and with them came raccoons, bats and ponies from far-flung towns. Winter was a boom-time that brought life to the town of Sentinel.

This year, though, there was a disturbance. This year, wholesome trade was being muddled up by scruffy vagabonds selling toys. The town's high seer stamped along the central street and glared at the warriors and their spinning tops.

At the old seer's side strode the pride and joy of Sentinel's alpha clan – Koja, a powerful male dog, narrow muzzled, straight backed, and handsome as a dream. He guided his grandfather down the busy streets, protecting him from the worst of the traffic flow. As a file of soldiers marched toward the walls, the old man gave a snort and pointed to the toys hanging from the soldiers' belts.

His stick shaking in indignation, the seer gave a surly scowl. "More tops! They're going to be playing that stupid game on duty next, you mark my words! I'm having the guard sergeants double their rounds! Anyone caught playing games on watch will end up shoveling the garbage mounds for a month!"

"I'm sure no one will play on watch, Spirit-Father." Koja's voice rolled smooth and elegant – a man bred to lead his peers. "We are dogs, after all."

"Bah!" They had entered the little marketplace in front of the town tavern. Here, a spotted pony draped in rugs ran a stall that exclusively sold fighting tops. Soldiers and visitors milled about as someone demonstrated the new novelty to the crowd.

The old seer clumped his stick against the ground in indignation and walked steadily away. "Tops. Why aren't there any pots for sale? I could do with a few new pots."

"What happened to your old pots, Spirit-Father?"

"Someone broke them with a plague-damned top!" The seer made his way to the base of the town's gigantic howling mound. "Where did these damned things come from, anyway?"

"A foreign girl invented them – although the mason's guild is claiming that the invention was theirs." Koja bowed to a visitor as he helped the old man scale the wooden stairs that led to the crest of the mound. The visitor – the noble maiden from Kamla town, smiled at him with eyes that struck a shock clean through to his soul. Bewitched by images of slim curves and blood-red fur, Koja shook his head and helped the old man climb.

Leaning on his stick, the old seer climbed step by step until he was high above Sentinel's thatched roofs.

"A foreigner brought the tops, you say?" The seer cocked his head in interest. "What sort of foreigner?"

"A female rough-coat. Barbarian accent. Pointed nose, rather skinny. Tall ears, tawny fur, gray countershade."

"*Ah, ha!*" The old man crowed, raising his walking stick on high. "In my days, we had a name for those! We called them *coyotes*, and they were usually found rooting about in garbage!" The old seer gave a snarl of annoyance as a top skipped from its fighting arena and buzzed its way past the howling mound. "We drove 'em out! Nonproductive parasites, that's what they were. Philosophizing, idling, backwoods – living *parasites!*"

The old man finally reached the crown of the mound – a great flat arena with spirit posts placed at each point of the wind. Here the spirits of the ancestors – some from times so distant they had seen the giants rise and fall – were lifted by the howls of their descendants at the rising of the moon. From this high perch, the seer guided Koja to stare across the thatched roofs of the town. They stared at the frost-covered fields and little farms, and then at the town palisade and the mighty Shield Wall stretching off into the morning haze.

The seer dropped his eyes toward the populace, and slowly thrashed his tail. "Time should be spent practicing arms, raising families, tilling fields, contemplating spirits! Idleness is un-canine!" The old dog jabbed his stick toward a haughty pair of cats who rode a pony below. "Fads are for cats, for mice and their overstuffed little brains! But a dog labors! We make the world run. Without us, the sun stops, the plants die, and chaos begins!" The seer leaned on his stick. "We must not be weakened by female parasites."

Koja felt it his role to uphold justice and moderation:

"This coyote is not a parasite, Spirit-Father. She's the guide to a Howler"

"A Howler?" The old seer narrowed down his eyes. "The moon has been full for two nights running. I never heard a new voice raise a howl."

"He must be a true Howler, sir. The poor creature is spirit-touched." Koja tapped a finger to his skull. "He sees things you or I can never see. Our faith may still be wanting."

The seer slowly drew a breath of ice-cold air. "Faith? My faith is in the Shield Wall and a dozen dog towns to guard it. My faith is built on keeping *us* on the green side, and the goblins locked up beyond. Mark my words, boy – one moment of weakness, just one passel of goblins breaking out into these fields and streams, and the world you and I know is dead and done. They would strip the fields like locusts, eat the old men and the young, breed like maggots until the world drowns beneath a wave of flesh and claws.

"This is holy work we do. We are the chosen of the Giants, left as caretakers of the world." The old dog walked the edges of the mound, staring coldly out across the fortifications of the town. "If we fail, the Giants shall return – and we shall have to look them in the eye and confess we are unworthy children." The old man looked at his grandson, approval and raw power glinting in his eyes. "Honor is *loyalty*. Honor makes us strong with the spirits and raises us above the animals. One day, this town shall be yours – these fields, this market – and the responsibilities that go with the great wall. Know loyalty when you see it; find honor, and always hold onto it! That is the way to greatness."

"Yes, Spirit-Father. I will remember it always."

Behind the two nobles, a sharp face whirled and red fur shone. Arching her brows, Aela turned back to lay her offerings at the bottom of a spirit pole. Then she picked up her skirts to cruise serenely back down toward the streets.

§ § §

Long used to sleeping in the dirt, Tupan had decided to take advantage of her new-discovered bed. She slept curled around herself in a compact ball, her tail covering her face. With her stolen poncho as a cover, and growling occasionally with doggie dreams, she slept beside the tavern fire and was utterly at peace.

On a hook above the bed hung her one and only set of clothes – skirt, leggings, arm tubes, and bodice, all made from multicolored strips and bands. The bells stirred softly in the breeze as morning patrons opened the tavern door, and yet the girl refused to stir until the sun had climbed long past the point of noon.

The first thing to emerge from her nest was a wet black nose, sniffing and wriggling – followed by a length of golden muzzle and a pair of closed, long-lashed eyes. She emerged sleek and sleepy, clad only in tousled flaxen fur. Her whole scrawny being quivered as she sensed a delicious scent on the air. "Sausages!"

Hern had set the table nicely – if one excused the use of his lips as fingers. He deposited a great wooden platter of dandelions and sausages on the middle of the table, and then thoughtfully dropped a dandelion flower into his beer.

Sniffing the scent of sausages in total ecstasy, Tupan emerged from pleasant dreams, drew her poncho about her, and answered the magic call of lunch. "Sausages. . . ."

She ate slowly and sensuously, whimpering in careless delight as she slid sausages down her gullet. They were made of mutton and pine nuts, fried golden brown with crackling, crunchy skins. Lost in a daze of pure pleasure, Tupan chewed and swallowed until her middle swelled. She ate a dandelion, leaves, flower and all, before coming up for air and ordering herself a cup of turkey-berry tea.

The sound of fighting tops dominated the room. Tupan gave an immense yawn, well filled with sharp white teeth, and then watched her customers with approval as they noisily wound strings and took their places at the arena. Surolf came staggering through the doors, a great wooden tray loaded with cast-iron tops, still bright from the mold. He was instantly besieged by airborne bats, dog soldiers, and cats all clamoring for first pick of the new wares.

"He's been busy!" Tupan sprinkled salt on a dandelion root and passed it to Hern, who thoughtfully chomped the morsel. "The iron melted okay?"

"Okay." Hern helped himself to a bowl of oats thoughtfully left on the floor. "I think we're doing rather well."

"Hoopy!" Tupan scratched her flanks and stuffed her mouth with yet more food. She drew her leggings down from their perch and pulled them up over her feet. She had just begun slithering into her bodice when a fresh blast of icy air came shooting through the door. A gaggle of traveling mice – outlandishly dressed in robes covered with mathematical signs – squeaked in protest as the wind gusts blew their scrolls and diagrams across the floor.

Three heavyset dogs stamped the cold from their feet, ordered hot tea, and waved a loud hello to Tupan by the fire. The tallest, largest, and most horribly be-weaponed of the soldiers clanked over to Tupan's table mound and pounded one heavy hand on the boards.

"Hey, Lady!"

"Um – hey, ho!" Tupan kept a bright, welcoming face while her hind brain tried to find a face and attach a name. "How goes?"

"Cold!" The warrior wearily sat down, as if stating the damned obvious had worn out his mental energy. "We missed you at moon howl last night."

Howling! Tupan cleared her throat, trying to appear sufficiently grave and calm. "Aaah – my poor friend the Howler! Last night a message came upon him. He was wandering the woods, talking to trees for half the night." Tupan tried to look regretful while surreptitiously swallowing a mouthful of sausage. "Ah, me – the burdens the spirits place on us. . . ."

"He seems pretty lively now." The warriors turned to watch Surolf as he eagerly demonstrated fighting tops for a fresh pair of travelers from out of town. "Is he selling tops?"

"Yes! Yes, we try to give him simple things to keep his mind off . . . you know." Tupan tapped a finger to her skull and flicked a quick glance toward the rafters, where the spirit world might lie. "He's harmless."

"Well, we can use him! A great howl it's going to be night after tomorrow! A full moon – a *blue* moon. Yes, ma'am, a great howl indeed!" The soldier slapped Tupan between the shoulder blades, almost dislodging her eyeballs. "He'll be up to it by then?"

"Oh, yes! He'll be up to it! Never fear!" Tupan groped for beer as a tonic against concussion. "Right as rain."

The soldiers seemed cheered by the news. With a last wave to Tupan, they made their way over to the fighting tops, sparing a condescending pat on the head for Surolf, who ignored them with a clueless quirk of his brow.

Tupan watched the three men go and picked her front teeth with a straw.

"Who in the great flea demon's name was *that?*" Hern asked.

"He's the guard from the front gate, the one who let us into town – you know," Tupan replied offhandedly.

Hern had finished his oats, and so helped himself to stale bread from a nearby mound-table. "What did he mean by 'will he be up to it by then'?"

"What? Oh, I don't know. Whatever." Tupan had dismissed the conversation from memory, preferring to keep her thoughts on more interesting things. "I wonder if that water froze last night? Did it crack the stone?"

"Probably." Hern gave a shrug. "Will you do my pelt again? I think I've got some sand in it from last night."

"Sure. Hop outside, and we'll see what kind of morning we have."

"It's afternoon, Tupan."

"Eh – whatever." Tupan swatted the pony on the rump and let him precede her through the door. "Hope Surolf remembers to charge enough for those fighting tops; I still want soup with barley in it!"

The two creatures ambled side by side out into a glorious afternoon filled with chill and brilliant sun. Throwing open her arms, the girl drew in a great deep breath of freezing air. "Oooh! Cold! That's quite bracing."

"Yes." Hern thoughtfully chewed on oats. "You forgot to put your skirt on."

"Ah. That'll usually do it!" Tupan cheerfully wound her skirt about her middle. "There we go – at least it gave the livestock something new to see!"

"Livestock?" Hern wrinkled his snout as he walked down the crowded, happy street. "I didn't think fleas came out in winter?"

"I meant the locals!" Tupan paced merrily along, placing one pretty foot before the other in a funny little dance. "Dogs. Boring as tree mold unless you show them how life was mean to be lived."

"You're a kind of dog."

"Hey, every genus had its exceptions! Think of me as a humorous savant."

They walked past iron forges smelting metal, past anvils where carbon was noisily folded into steel, the hammers spitting sparks into the cold. About the towering howling mound were rings of hummock-shaped houses, each surrounded by squabbling pups and women gossiping, fletching arrows, and dressing game. Mice strolled past, their heads bent as they discussed history and philosophy. Tupan looked at everything at once, disparaging, adoring, loving the spectacle, and glad to be footloose and fancy-free.

At her side, Hern plucked a frozen grass stem from the verge and turned it noisily over in his teeth. "I pull a cart. Sometimes I turn a mill wheel in Surolf's village. They give me trade goods, and I use it to buy good things to eat."

Blacksmith's hammers far down the street sent sparks skidding out across the road. Tupan watched iron sparks jump and skitter, raising one ear toward Hern. "Oh? That's hoopy."

"Did you ever work on a cart, or walk with a wheel?"

"Me?" The coyote blinked, scandalized! "Spirits, no!"

"Yes . . ." Hern walked slowly as Tupan teetered atop a retaining wall, keeping her balance by waggling her hands. "Surolf makes things. Once he made a kite, and it flew very very high. I pulled on the string for him to make it go. It flew in the sky over the town. Everyone said he was clever." Hern stepped in a puddle and gave a little frown. "Did you ever make a kite?"

"Nope. Never had anything to make one with." Tupan deliberately slapped her hands together to change the subject. "How about this cold snap, huh?"

"Why? Why didn't you have anything to make a kite?"

They walked along beside the town ramparts, where the ever-vigilant dogs marched to and fro. Tupan folded her arms beneath her poncho, hunching with the sudden cold. "Because we're coyotes. We don't do what dogs do."

Hern watched her with deep brown eyes. With a cold wind bowing, Tupan sat herself on a tall tree stump and stared out across the mountains with their vast ramparts of snow.

"Up there. On the rim, where the villages are few. That's where my running group lived." The girl jerked her chin toward the mountains, keeping her eyes turned away from Hern. "We don't make towns, and we don't make houses. That's like being chained down to a stone. So, we wander. We carry everything we own, and we herd sheep and . . . and scavenge for stuff. People throw away a lot of good stuff, and we'd find it just lying around. Then the town dogs would throw rocks at us, like we weren't good enough to even use their garbage."

Sparks still slid across the frost, but Tupan's gaze was faraway. "I liked the towns. I sat there and I watched the lights – and I looked at my brothers and my sisters all fighting over rags, and I knew there had to be something brighter. There had to be a way to make life better. I make things better. That's what I do."

Ghost Mountain shimmered in the blue distance – a peak whose body never showed, an ice cap hanging in the sky. Hern turned his face toward it, a twitch flicking at his ears.

"Do you see the other coyotes at all?"

"Hmmm?" The girl stared abstractly at a muddy puddle. "No, I lost the pure way, you see. 'Make nothing, be nothing – live in the world and not on it'. That's the creed, you know. Like being a *scavenger* is some kind of noble thing." Tupan threw a rock at her own reflection and stood to go. "I'll see everything there is. I'll go everywhere in the whole wild world. I'll make things better. One day everyone's going to be glad there was a coyote in their lives."

Tupan wiped her eyes with her sleeves and stood, all business and bells once again. With a sharp draw of breath, she sealed memories away behind a brittle wall of cheer. "Marriage. Come on – lets go make Surolf into a happy man."

§ § §

She walked past as she had always walked – with a delicate, ladylike disdain.

Heart in his mouth, Surolf slipped from the shadows and made a frantic little wave, trying to attract the girl's attention without drawing notice from passersby.

Pausing beside a stall of fur tints, scents, and combs, the elegant young female frowned, swiveled . . . saw Surolf, and went stiff. Shooting panicked glances up the street, she snagged the greyhound's shirt and sped into a lane between two food stalls, dragging Surolf out of sight. *"Surolf!* What the Plague are you doing here?"

Tail wagging and sleek face innocent, Surolf stared at the girl with worship in his eyes. "I came! To – to do business." The scent of Aela almost made Surolf slide unconscious to the ground; a smell of warm musk, woolen blankets, and immaculately groomed fur. "I thought you were staying home!"

"I have business of my own." Aela stood, perfectly slim, ignoring the adoration in Surolf's gaze. "I can't be seen with you, Surolf. It would be very rude."

"I hope you're not put out. . . ."

Aela – who had handled her fair share of suitors without so much as a smile – raised one elegant, condescending brow. "Not *put out,* Surolf. Merely . . . alarmed. I hardly expected to see anyone from home. No one's due to come serve on the wall for three months or more!"

"Well, I had to. They think I'm no good! And they won't let me make a windmill – or even speak to you!" Surolf craned toward Aela, wishing she would just reach out to hold his hands. "So, I thought that if . . . if I made money . . . you know, I could bring it to your kin-group and show them . . ."

The attention was flattering. Aela paused, peered archly over her shoulder, and let a thought slip cool and delicious through her mind. "You came all this way, just to make a bride-price for me?"

"Um, well . . . yes."

"Oh, how *very*. . . " Aela clicked the claws of her hands together in secret delight. "Why Surolf, how sweet!"

"So – so, you'll speak to them! Let them know it's coming?"

"Oh, Surolf, do let's not spoil anything."

Thinking over her situation, Aela decided to let Surolf walk with her. He tripped along attentively at her side, unwilling to lose a moment of gazing at her face. "So, what business are you doing here?"

"Just business. Alpha kin-group things." Aela dismissed it with an elegant motion of her hand. "What do you think of Koja, by the way?"

"Koja?" Surolf blinked as he passed a sausage stall. "I've never tasted it."

"Neither have I." Aela gave a sly, condescending smile. "Koja is a person. The young alpha you perhaps have seen leading the old seer about town?" Surolf thought hard. Clearly the image rang no mental bells. Aela shrugged her red-furred shoulders. "No matter. I'm sure you will see him around."

"See him? Why?" Surolf felt a sudden sick twist of fear. "Who is he?"

"Just a pleasant person. Heir to the alpha kin-group here – I was sure you would have met." Aela knew perfectly well Surolf had not a sniff of status to his name. "I'm sure you'll get along splendidly!"

Surolf was suddenly certain of no such thing. A jealous stab of ice ran through his heart. "Is he why your family sent you here?"

"No! Oh, silly Surolf! No one sent me for any such thing!" Aela laid her poison bait with the greatest of ease. "I'm here for my *own* business – not the kin-group's!"

"Really?"

"Of course." Aela rolled an eye toward Surolf – allowing him to stop and buy her a pastry as they walked. "We're really a very small town, dear. Sentinel is so much larger – so much more important! Even when you're a noble, it's so hard to get them to take a small town girl seriously." Aela stepped primly over a puddle that Surolf blindly walked straight through. "Do be more careful, dear – you'll splash the two of us with mud."

They walked awhile, and Aela absently allowed Surolf to take her proffered arm. Adrift in a sea of bliss, the greyhound let her words drift through him as she steered him genially about the town.

"Loyalty . . . have you ever pondered loyalty, Surolf? A strange and insubstantial thing." The girl's scent worked on Surolf like a thousand sleepless nights, dragging him ever onward in a heart-thumping daze. "How do you even demonstrate it, do you think? It's hardly something you can pull out of a box."

Vague and thinking only of Aela's grace, Surolf tried to give an answer that made sense. "It's like love. When someone sees it, they know it was always there."

"Exactly! Yes, Surolf – that's it *exactly*." They had come to the central marketplace beside the gigantic howling mound.

Tupan the coyote came ambling happily along the street, Hern plodding at her side. For some reason, Tupan had begged, borrowed, or stolen a pile of old, dry mutton bones. She worked one with a knife point as she walked, drilling holes into the bone tube and showering the parings on anyone who walked by. She chattered to everyone who came near, swiping a carrot from a stall to stick into Hern's open mouth. They walked along simply basking in the day, as though they hadn't a worry in the world.

Aela watched the outlandish coyote go, lowering cool lashes across her eyes. "Yes. Just like love. Loyalty and love both have great rewards, Surolf."

The greyhound blinked. "They do?"

"Of course they do. . . ." She had Surolf standing in the shadows, hidden out of view. Suddenly Aela allowed the boy a kiss. Half-panicking, he opened his muzzle, tasting the impossible beauty of her. All his dreams and hopes and fantasies caught hold of his heart, and it took wing. He kissed her for as long as she allowed, releasing her reluctantly as she pulled away. "Surolf – say you'll always be here when I need you."

"Always!" Surolf swallowed, his senses reeling. "Always!"

"Good." Aela slowly slipped out of his grasp, winding herself like a snake through Surolf's mind. "Remember, Surolf. Rewards can be very sweet. . . ."

With a last flick of her tail, she left Surolf standing in the darkness and walked into the light. A moment later, she had fallen back in among her brothers and the local nobility. She greeted a tall young nobleman, flattering his parents and flashing her perfect smile.

All this, Surolf only half saw. He walked out to the marketplace, took a last adoring look toward Aela's perfect face, and heaved a grateful, dizzy sigh.

§ § §

Chill winter winds whipped sprays of sand from the crests of the dunes. Sitting like a black stone beside a corroded metal tower, G'kaa squinted against the breeze and watched intruders enter his lands. The interlopers were Itheem, perhaps a hundred warriors that surrounded a svelte, well-groomed female. This was no mere foraging party, nor was it an invasion.

Vast and furious, G'kaa thrashed the steel ball tied to his tail. "They're East Tunnel Clan. Sh'shoka – signal the fighters. If anyone moves without command, I'll strip them to their bones!"

The war band lay with its warriors concealed under every weed and stone. They lay in hidden scrapes inside the soil or even spread flat on the open ground. Two thousand warriors – invisible and vicious, ready to kill and die at the slightest command.

Walking confidently forward, the intruders strolled straight toward G'kaa's lair. The warlord took a long, hard look at the young female at the middle of her troops, and then slowly raised a finger to his shaman.

"It's *her*." The warlord bid his warriors rise from cover. "Let her see our numbers, and then see if she has the guts to go on."

The female showed no sign of interest as the hills suddenly turned black with G'kaa's emerging warriors. Two thousand Itheem closed in, watching and waiting as G'kaa let the matriarch make her way to him.

Her warriors parted to make a channel between the two leaders. The

East Tunnel fighters kept their arms very still, not daring to threaten, not even to meet an enemy's gaze. G'kaa scanned the creatures with his one red eye, and then settled himself down on the sands.

"A messenger said you wished to see me." The warlord watched the female and slowly thrashed his tail. "You are no clan mistress! Why do you need mercenaries?"

Meeting G'kaa face to face, the matriarch slyly appraised him. She let him lead her aside, toward a patch of open sand away from prying ears and eyes. The female glanced over his scars and formed a calculating smile. "G'kaa, you are larger even than legend makes you."

"Good." G'kaa knew that terror was the better part of reputation. "And my war band?"

"I would guess two thousand? A formidable force – particularly to be led by a male." The woman gave an emphatic lash of her tail. "Good. I am pleased."

"And who are you?"

"A mother, nothing more. A matriarch whose fate depends on her children." Scheming, ever scheming, Oosha's mother favored G'kaa with a carnivorous smile. "A junior female who seethes with an infinite. . . *potential.*"

She had brought gifts of bread for the war band. Her warriors opened the bundles and let G'kaa's troops lunge in and feed, anxiously keeping clear. G'kaa turned away and stalked to the crest of the dune. The female followed him.

The titanic black rat glared in scorn. "You did not answer my question. Why do you come seeking mercenaries?"

"I did not answer because I do not seek mercenaries." The female tilted her head to inspect G'kaa eye to eye. "I intend to make you into my ally."

"An ally?" The warlord sat with his mouth turned in a sneer. "I am the greatest warrior of the Itheem. Why tie myself to a powerless female?"

"Through me, you can have the East Tunnel Clan." The female suddenly dropped her simpering and mystery. "They say you seek a way to rule all of Acomar. I can give it to you – but you will make me your viceroy for the East Tunnel Clan! You will mate with me, and I will breed your future officers."

G'kaa looked at the female and slowly closed his eye. Finally he felt the machinery of his plans come clicking into place. "Speak."

"I am mother to the purest Hastaasi the Itheem race has ever seen." The female's cold face boiled with ambition. "With such a creature, the oracle will finally be controlled. With your troops, I can take over clan leadership, and give you control of the girl. "Control the oracle, and you control Acomar."

A pure Hastaasi; a creature capable of calling magic from the god-caves below the ruins – a creature that could bend an oracle to her will and bring forth weapons to destroy the barrier wall. G'kaa drew in a breath of winter air and slowly turned to gaze on the female at his side. "I will mate with you." The rat turned to take the female to his nest. "We shall mate. Then we'll plan how to seize this East Tunnel Clan."

§ § §

Evening darkened the sky, cloud streams began to take on colors of smoking purple-blue, and dark pine woods became walls of impenetrable black. Soldiers stood out as shadows on the walls.

Breath hanging in spectacular clouds of frosty air, Surolf tied a pack and saddle onto Hern's strong back. He pulled tight the straps, ignoring the pony's grumbling, and then began to hang him with rope and mattocks, picks and shovels. He had just begun to conceal the load beneath a chunk of cloth when a soft footfall sounded from the shadows behind him. Startled, Surolf snatched a spear from the wall. He moved with lightning speed – only to blink in shock.

Aela stood there, long cloak of soft gray wool drawn in about her slender form. "Did I frighten you, Surolf?"

The greyhound released his breath. Suddenly nervous, he let the spear rest back against the wall. "No! No, I was just . . . thinking about goblins. Makes me jumpy."

"Oh, well I'm sorry I make you think about goblins." Pouting, Aela turned, letting torchlight frame her figure with a golden glow. "Perhaps I should go. . . ."

Hern gave a snort.

Surolf elbowed him into silence as he came forward in a rush. "No, no! I was just . . ." The greyhound hid Hern's pack with a wild toss of sackcloth. "I was just helping to load this pony."

"And he tied the straps too tight." Hern grumbled in the dark. "He does it every time."

"Thank you, Hern." Surolf abandoned the pony and came to Aela, who stood waiting in the twilight. "It's just . . . I'm going out tonight. I'm on guard duty at Mile-Post Four."

"I'd heard." Aela posed prettily, managing to look a little wan. "Off out in the cold and so far from town? Why on earth would you want to do that?"

"It's . . . it's a soldier thing! You know – everyone serves." Surolf made a hopeful gesture toward his spear. "Just like back home, you know."

"Yes-yes, I know." Aela took a close look at the spear, arching one brow as she looked back across her shoulder at the greyhound. "Still, funny you should go off on guard duty. I heard tell you had become a Howler. . . ."

"I am *not* a Howler!" Surolf instantly scowled. "I trade. I make things. That's what I do – I make things to make life better!" Surolf angrily went back to fetching camp gear for the night.

Aela gingerly felt past his temper, seeking purchase on Surolf's heart. "And still they make you stand guard? Surely they won't send you very far. . . ."

Surolf gave a shrug. "We go waaaay out. Out to the midpoint between here and the first guard fort." It was a distance of almost a mile, a hard walk in the cold and dark. "If there's any sign of goblins, we just light the beacon and summon help."

"A cold, lonely job." Aela passed Hern without looking at his lumpy load. "But not too lonely? I suppose someone comes to inspect you, all the same."

"All taken care of!" Surolf wildly tried to evade the whole uncomfortable issue. Tupan had managed to muddle the instruction of the guard sergeants so that once again their watch would be undisturbed. "All handled. So, we'll be relieved at dawn."

"At dawn." Aela nodded, her eyes on the rooftops. "Quite." The girl turned, gazed at Surolf, and then reached out to trail a fingertip beneath his chin. "Keep your eyes open, my dear. I hope you know when it's the best time to retreat."

Aela departed, leaving Surolf staring after her, mind hypnotized by her scent but soul somehow prickling.

He was still staring after her when the tavern door flew open and Tupan staggered out into the night, bags and bundles teetering in her hands. "Hey, Spud-Puppy! You ready yet?" Tupan danced happily over from the tavern door to stand between her two friends. "We must have sold a hundred tops today. There's a merchant who wants some to take back home!"

"Oh?" Surolf blinked uncomfortably, feeling a vague impulse of alarm. Unable to pin it down, he shook the sensation away. "We really sold a hundred?"

"We ought to make enough to get your bride-price, easy!" Tupan began sorting out her packages – a bundle of mutton bones all now drilled with little holes, a length of tassel stolen from a passing sedan chair, and bag after bag of grain. "Hey, was that your girlie-girl right now?"

"No." Surolf felt a thrill of something cold and foul inside his soul. "Come on, let's go." The greyhound hastily prodded Hern and set the pony walking off into the dark.

Tupan tossed an apple to the pony, and then threw a length of sausage into Surolf's hand. Chatting happily to Hern, she led the way into the sunset as the evening sky turned an eerie deep sea-blue.

Walking behind, Surolf spared one last long glance to where Aela had disappeared. He backed away one step at a time – shook a vague blur from his mind, and ran off to join the others in the dark.

Chapter 8

Crashing on all fours through a tunnel, G'kaa left behind a choking stench of blood. He slaughtered sentries as he found them and stamped their bodies to the floor. The gigantic rat let his new mate's children guide him into the maze, past cunning traps.

G'kaa almost split the tunnel walls with his monstrous, knotted shoulders as he drove forward in the dark. Behind him stretched a packed column of warriors two hundred strong, whiskers feeling the way through lightless, airless spaces. War blades chinked as tubes struck the dirt, and tunnels echoed with the sound of hundreds of claws.

The warlord led the column, spearheading the drive into the East Tunnel Clan. Immediately behind him, a turncoat East Tunnel soldier whispered directions in his ear. The soldier was followed by one of G'kaa's most savage warriors, with orders to rip out the traitor's spine if they ran into the slightest trap. As the column came to intersections and new tunnel mouths, G'kaa's fighters peeled off to block them, guard details springing war blades and spreading the scent of sharpened steel.

"Slowly, Lord. The wind tunnel entrance is twenty spans to the right." The Easterner behind G'kaa whispered so hoarsely that his words were heard more in the mind than in the air. "Ten guards in a chamber – two sentries at the upper mouth beyond."

G'kaa turned into the wind tunnel, his whiskers stirring to the scent of damp earth, bones, and rain. Without slowing, the huge rat led his warriors up a sharply slanting passage that twisted into stony soil.

In the darkness ahead, a sentry suddenly jerked awake. "Who's there?"

G'kaa struck with vicious fury. His blades punched into the body ahead. The enemy rat fell choking on blood, the stink of death instantly filling the passageway. G'kaa's huge strength rammed the dead meat ahead of him as he burst in against a press of panicked, shouting warriors. He struck left, felt something stagger, and then ripped past the milling guards and up into the only other exit from the room. His own fighters flooded into the chamber at his tail.

A bitter fight began. In pure darkness, whiskers sensed shifting mass. On all fours, the combatants shoved forward, their weapons blurring in strike and parry. Steel sparked from steel. Flesh ripped and blood sprayed out onto the walls. G'kaa left the carnage behind and raced up the tunnel to where two guards stood framed in the half light of day. They peered down in astonishment.

G'kaa erupted from the tunnel with a roar, broke one guard's back with his blade-tube, and killed the other with a blow so powerful that his arm was elbow-deep in blood. He threw the bodies aside and turned to butcher a single East clansman who came fleeing up out of the dark. From below, the sounds of combat came suddenly to an end. Moments later, one of G'kaa's officers emerged from the passageway, blood making sticky footprints as he came to report.

"All ten guards are dead. We had three casualties, three others injured."

"We'll have the oracle heal the injured ones." G'kaa looked out across a bowl-shaped valley, in the center of which stood an oracle mound. "Clear the blood from the thoroughfare before you bring the warriors – I don't want the stink of battle giving us away. *Shaman!*"

The warlord licked his fur and weapons clean as he gazed out across the vale of bones. It was just as legends had reported – unfathomably deep in old dry skeletons. The valley floor was a carpet of rat skulls, vertebrae, and bones, packed deep until they had become solid soil.

The long battles for the oracle were beginning once again. G'kaa watched the bodies of the dead being cast down among the other bones, a new layer of death atop the old.

"Have one fighter go to the oracle caves and find the Hastaasi girl; her mother says she sits in the upper caves for days on end."

"Yes, sir." The officer selected one rat from behind him in the column. "Go to the oracle mound and capture a white female rat. She is to be left unharmed."

"We should have a fast scout for this. Someone who can snatch the girl and kill anything that tries to snatch her back." G'kaa wiped the blood frothing from his jaws. "Shaman! Where's that worthless parasite Ra'hish?"

A shaman came forward – G'kaa's spirit chaser, a creature with fur entirely matted with old dry blood and threaded with Itheem finger bones. The creature hissed through bared fangs as he sniffed the outside air.

"He could not be found, Lord."

"I'll have his throat out for this! No one deserts the war band of

G'kaa!"

Ra'hish had become an irritation. G'kaa regretted recruiting the creature instead of killing him. Still, the reputation of the savage, solitary rat had been impressive. Ra'hish had killed every hunting party that had ever tried to track him down. Such a creature had seemed a prize, but had turned out to be a claw scraping G'kaa's nerves raw. Ra'hish had never done homage, never lowered his tail. He'd tolerated orders only as they suited him, had hunted his own food, as though not needing G'kaa's bounty. G'kaa's empire was built on vision and fear. There was something decidedly un-Itheem about Ra'hish and his solitary ways.

Two hundred of G'kaa's picked warriors poured up out of the tunnel and into the valley of dry bones. Their East Tunnel allies pointed to positions by the path, and the warriors slid among the bones, making barely a rattle as they slipped from view. G'kaa looked over the scene as the last fighter vanished, breathing the stench of blood from the shaman at his side. "Are the spirits quiet, Shaman?"

"Quiet, Lord." The magician sniffed the air as though reading thick currents in the wind. "They're with you. They want the taste of Uruth blood."

"Then they shall have it." G'kaa thrashed his steel-tipped tail and crushed an ancient skull. "Come." The two rats walked down onto the thin path that threaded among the staring heaps of bones. As a chill wind blew through the distant sighing towers, G'kaa and his shaman stalked down onto the road.

From the tunnel mazes of the East Clan, a procession arose. It spilled over the valley lip and down across the road; warriors and breeding females escorting wagons of rust-laden soil. It was the daily visit to the oracle, the heart behind the power of the clan. Here metals would be made, the sick could be cured, and most importantly, the withered seed grains from the fields could be made healthy enough to plant and grow. Basket after basket of seed grains would be offered to the caves in the hope that one or two would be blessed instead of melted or consumed.

The oracle meant life. Grain and metal, bread and blades; the two things without which a rat could not survive. The East Tunnel Clan held a knife to the jugular of Acomar.

G'kaa sat with his tail curled at his feet, the winter light gleaming from countless foul scars. He sat and coldly watched as clan warriors flooded past him, surrounding him in a wall of blades.

The grand matriarch of the tunnel clans, here to oversee the offerings with all her senior daughters at her side, stopped before G'kaa and stared down her nose at him. "G'kaa! We have been waiting for your consignment. Where is your offering? Why do you come to see us alone?"

"I did not come for offerings." G'kaa tilted his head, inspecting the female rat. At eight years of age, she was a tribute to her own survival skills. "I came because I need your clan. The East Tunnel Clan and the Southerners must not go to war."

"*You* need our clan?" The matriarch flicked derisive glances to the sisters at her side. "The great Warlord G'kaa and his vagabonds will lead us in battle?"

"We'll lead, but we need more warriors." The warlord's blinded eye gleamed sickly white. "I need all the fangs and claws I can command."

Mocking and secure amid four hundred armed guards, the matriarch slowly waddled around G'kaa. "Ah? And who would you have us fight instead of the Southerners? The sky? The air? The sea?"

The warlord set his pitiless gaze on the warriors about him. "The Itheem will destroy the one true enemy. I will crush the Uruth and occupy their lands."

"The valley of Mornmist?" The matriarch had heard such dreams a thousand times before. What rat had never looked at the distant mountain peaks and dreamed about the rich green lands below? "A nestling's dream. The Uruth are the shield for the whole valley. They can hold us off with their walls until their armies can amass. No Itheem force can hold together long enough to defeat them in a siege!" Starved of supplies, rat armies would fall on each other for food. "There's no need for suicide. When the Southerners are dead, we shall have new lands."

G'kaa raised his savage, bloodstained head to meet the matriarch eye to eye. "The dogs can contain the attack of a few thousand Itheem." The warlord's powerful body swelled to the bunch and flow of muscles under his hide. "So, we shall not attack them with a few thousand. We shall assemble every single living Itheem. We will obliterate the valley forces with a single blow. I need Acomar's fifty thousand warriors. I will not allow you to destroy my plans with another of your useless wars!"

The matriarch stared at G'kaa as though he had gone mad. "The clans will never unite! While we attacked the wall, who would protect the oracle from interlopers? Other rats would leave scavengers behind to strip our fields!"

"Yes." G'kaa drew his claws slowly through the bones. "So, it means an end to clans – " G'kaa's rats struck instantly, blasting the bones apart with screams. The dead skeletons erupted into horrific life as fighters burst up from below. Rats launched themselves from the bones at the matriarch's feet, tearing into her guards, seers, and consorts. Blood sheeted across the dust as warriors fought in a blood-red savage haze.

Two hundred guards died in an instant, followed seconds later by two hundred more. Surprise and fury favored G'kaa's warrior – and the experience of a thousand vicious wars. Killing the matriarch with his own two blades, G'kaa let the battle run its course. He flicked the blood from his weapons and let the blades snap back into their tubes before walking coldly away.

At a tunnel mouth, Oosha's mother appeared, followed by a dozen armored sons. She bared her fangs in a snarl of joy as she saw the leader of her clan lying dead across the bones. "Victory!"

"Almost." G'kaa signaled to his men, who rounded up into squadrons and flitted off toward the valley pass. "We hold the oracle. Now I will summon the war leaders from the other clans." Vast, huge, and dark as night, G'kaa breathed in a deep draft of winter air. "Summon your daughter, and we shall make the oracle dance to our own tune."

Free access to a new, rejuvenated oracle, and a male warlord to break the cycle of endless civil wars – already on the path to immortality, the blood-spattered rat allowed himself the shadow of a smile. "Fifty thousand warriors . . ." Drawing his claws across an old, dry skull, G'kaa savored the glory of it in his veins.

Running breathless across the bones, a camouflaged rat came skidding to a halt before the warlord and lowered his tail in salute. "Lord! I've searched the oracle caves that were open. I found no white-furred girl."

"*What?*" G'kaa rounded on the warrior and sent him flying with one blow of his hand. "Idiot! I told you to search properly!"

"I searched, Lord! No white rat was found!"

The man fled back, leaving G'kaa snarling with rage. He signaled his shaman and officers. "*Idiot!* He was too frightened to actually go inside the caves!" The warlord summoned more warriors. "Search the mound again. Don't worry about attrition – *we need that girl!*"

"Unless the girl has gone." The shaman selected a thigh bone from the ground to use as a new spirit staff. "You will remember, Lord, rumors from days ago – a white rat seen on the plain of sighing towers?"

G'kaa froze. He gave a roar of rage. One sharp blow from his hand blasted down into a pile of brittle bones. "*Ra'hish!*"

Warriors turned to stare in shock.

G'kaa bellowed orders, sending his fighters streaking off into the dust. "Search the plains! Find her, kill anyone who tries to stop you! I want that white Hastaasi!"

Warriors dipped tails in salute and raced out of the valley, streaking past the incoming caravan of G'kaa's food supplies. G'kaa watched them go. He paced, seething with a hate so pure it almost made him blind.

The seer watched his warlord from the corner of his eye, stroking slowly at his brand new bone. "My lord?"

"Ra'hish has her! Why do you think he spent so much time out in the wilds? He thinks he can trade her like he trades his rusty baubles!"

"If he is on the plains, we shall find him. No one may cross the sands without leaving a trail." The shaman bowed. "I shall see to it personally. I will need a dozen men."

"Take them and go." G'kaa gave no threats; he merely settled down into a ghoulish nest of skeletons as his empire took solid form around him. The East Tunnel Clan was his, and he held the oracle. But now he needed the magic key to win the Southern clans; a pure Hastaasi priestess would be the heart of his lure.

"*Ra'hish...*"

G'kaa let the name seethe on his tongue. With the cold wind drying fresh blood on the vale of bones, the warlord sat to spin his thoughts of conquest and revenge.

§   §   §

The sound of little whistles echoed up and down the dunes. Sitting on obsidian blocks and wriggling their pretty feet, the nestlings tooted on Tupan's flutes, surprising themselves with every note. Cross-legged, scruffy, and irrepressible, Tupan the coyote sat beside her little students in the dust, showing them how to bring music out of hollow bones. She helped tiny little Rika spread her fingers wide, walking her through the scales until she could make them on her own.

Down in the cavern at the base of the broken tower, hammers chinked and stone chips flew.

Hern ignored a summons from below, instead choosing to show several nestlings a ponderous, complicated pony jig. His hooves thumped a convoluted beat to Tupan's twittering melody. The pony danced in due seriousness before an astonished crowd until the two grumbling workmen climbed from the cavern to discover what was causing all the noise.

Spectrally lean and gray, Surolf peered from the cave, sided by snakelike Ra'hish in his indelible camouflage. They irritably summoned Hern from his dance. With a last flourish and a bow, the pony dipped his ears to his cheering audience and went off to haul away another slice of broken stone.

Sitting with the moonlight on their backs, Oosha and Teela watched the scene and smiled. The nestlings were adorable. They had sung an eerie harmony to welcome the rising of the moon, and the sound of it made the fur stand all along Oosha's spine. She had reached out a thin pink hand, as if to feel the music in the air as it passed. Ever since that time, she had sat in thought, staring out across the shining nighttime dunes.

Shyly watching Oosha from the cave mouth, Ra'hish raised a timid hand and waved. Teela looked aside, smirking like an egret as her sister made a little move of welcome with her tail. Teela moved subtly aside, making room to coax Ra'hish onto the rock, and then sat exuding an insufferably self-satisfied glow. As the warrior climbed onto their little perch, she welcomed him with a smug flirt of her eyes. "Warrior Ra'hish! My sister was just talking of you!"

"Teela, I *never!*" Oosha jumped almost clean out of her fur. She blushed, ears bright red as she hid behind a wall of trivia. "You are being very silly tonight. I was merely remarking on how well the bone flutes sound. What a wonderful invention!"

"The golden dog-woman is very, very strange." Ra'hish watched the coyote with unfeigned admiration. "I believe she could talk the branches down from a tree."

"Or even the down from a thistle?" Teela had spent a rich day tweaking gossip from the baby rats. She wriggled happily as Ra'hish's ears actually blushed. "I think we'll all get on well!"

Rapidly grooming whiskers to hide his embarrassment, Ra'hish tried to move on to nice, safe ordinary business. Rats rarely spoke about the weather; instead, they spoke about food. "The dogs brought some bread – and some sort of meat made into solid tubes. Did you try some?" The male rat tried to hurry on lest Teela take advantage while his tongue was tied. "I'm sorry I was away during the day. There's little food here. Were you safe?"

"We'll always be safe now! Oosha can make the sky-fires come." Teela looked at her sister in love and awe. "She's in touch with the old ones! She can hear the Giants talking in her dreams."

"Perhaps I can." Oosha hunched, uncomfortable with Teela's unswerving faith. "I just don't know."

"I can hear them now – and so it's all because of you." Teela beamed. All was right with her world. "And tonight we'll find a treasure! We've finally escaped the ugliness."

A cold wind blew in from the sea, making sand crystals tinkle delicately against the sighing towers. Far off in the distance, a pylon gave a mournful boom – a deep, eerie sound that made fur rise in awe.

Whiskers straining to catch the heat of Oosha's skin, Ra'hish blushed and rapidly began to groom. Sensing Teela's smirking eye, he coughed, craned about, and looked down across the dunes from his high perch. "We already have two lookouts. What are you doing up here so high?"

Oosha let the night wind stir her fur. Her pink eyes watched the empty silver sand. "I'm waiting for something."

"Something?"

"Something I know will come. Tonight I'll be ready."

Ra'hish caught the abstract, drifting tone in Oosha's voice. His ears rose, and he found himself looking at her. The girl still stared out across the empty wilds. The towers boomed and sighed out in the dark.

Her voice seemed strangely strong and clear. "I used to dream about commanding oracles and making all the ancient ones rise again. But now I'm not so sure. I look at little moments of beauty and wonder how to change things so that they can somehow fill our lives." The white rat gripped the rock beneath her with fine pink toes and hands. "There must be a way! There has to be!"

Teela looked at her sister in puzzlement. "How?"

"For that, we need wisdom. We need to steal *time*."

From below, a cheer arose as Hern plodded from the cavern, dragging a big wedge of shattered obsidian. Surolf stalked out of the cavern to take a drink and a bite to eat. Watching him, Ra'hish gave a little sneer.

"Now this one is more like a *real* dog. He has a rotten temper."

"But you like him." Oosha indulgently raised one brow. "It's no crime to admit that you get on with a dog."

Ra'hish watched Surolf glaring at Tupan and the baby rats. "See the way he looks at Tupan and the children? He's shocked that the children can talk at all."

"Why? They've learned dog-speak well!" Teela's own time of rapid learning had almost gone, but even so, dog speech was easy enough to pick up. The young rat gave a lofty sniff of disdain. "Don't they learn things on the far side of the wall?"

Oosha tilted her head and watched the dogs in thought. "No – not as fast as we. Remember – they change more slowly. We are the result of generations of war." Oosha's intelligence was pure and crisp as morning dew. She was a creature of eminent common sense. "We learn quickly because we need it to survive. But a dog? A dog just . . . lives. Tupan will still be playing flutes and watching clouds long after we are all killed."

"But we're talking to the dogs now!" Teela let the thought fill her with hope and pride. "We don't have to be enemies! We can show the dogs the children's music! We can show them the moon over the sighing towers – or the dances you and I invented by the quiet caves!"

"Yes . . ." Moonlight struck red sparks from Oosha's eyes. "What would they do to us, if they knew we were more than hostile animals? Itheem are dangerous. We are a plague – make no mistake. The Giants placed us inside a cage and hid the key. Because of this, there can be mountains, and green fields – and lovely Tupans watching clouds."

"What do you mean?" Teela and Ra'hish felt a touch of cold in their hearts. "Surely you'd like to walk out there in the green, soft world?"

Oosha shook her head and closed her eyes. "We would destroy the world. Breeding as we do – how long would the beauty last? We would turn the whole world into another Acomar. . . ." The white rat stared blankly off to a horizon filled with stars. "We need time. Somehow we need a chance to change."

Shivering, she shook away the mood. With a wan smile, Oosha sought Ra'hish's eyes. "The little ones adore you." She noticed the warrior's instant blush. "You really care for them, don't you? I wonder why."

Ra'hish blushed and muttered down into his claws. "They needed someone to show them how to survive. Someone had to do it."

"Yes, but no one else stepped in." Oosha nodded her chin down toward the sand. "They're waving to you. I think we might have reached the final piece of stone."

Down on the sands, Tupan uncoiled herself from where she had been showing young rats how to shape an old rag to look like a plucked chicken. Eeka had climbed onto Tupan's head, and the little rat was chittering excitedly in her ear.

"Lady, lady, pretty lady! Hern pulls stone!"

"The *last* stone!" Tupan avidly rose to her feet and walked, nestlings clinging to every limb and tooting flutes. "Hoopy!"

"*Hoopy!*" The nestlings echoed Tupan's favorite cry as they bounced down onto the sand and scampered off toward the chamber.

Scowling irritably, Surolf tried to keep the little creatures back as Hern trudged past, dragging a cable that sank through a hole in the floor. "Tupan! Keep the little buggers back! There could be anything down here!"

"Ha! Well, if there's a monster down there, it starved to death back when the moon was born." Tupan tried to wheedle past the workers and peek into the hole. "But I'll tell them to keep away."

The last hunk of rock was rising from the shaft. Stone grated on stone as Surolf heaved at a heavy crowbar. The chunk of obsidian rose slowly, easing inch by inch behind the straining pony. Hern's hooves sank deep into soft sand as he struggled to plod out into the open air.

Bouncing down from the hill, Teela tried to help wield a crowbar. Tupan clicked her tongue and held the young girl back, lounging comfortably as she watched the males struggle. "Don't, honey. It's a boy thing!" The coyote patted the rock behind which she sheltered and leaned on it with her elbows. "Hang out with me and watch them strain! Surolf's mean as a snake – but I still say he has a cute little tush."

"Tush?" Teela spoke the unfamiliar word in wonder. "Whaaaat eees toosh?"

"Sit upon! Front of the tail! The squeezy bits!" Tupan slapped her skinny backside by way of demonstration. "Tush – you see?"

"Tush! Yes!" Teela hissed and clicked something in her own tongue.

"Surolf haaaas cute tush."

Struggling with a pry bar, Surolf shot a dark glance Tupan's way.

"They speak pretty damned well after only a day of practice!"

"So, they have a gift for languages!"

"Yeah – and a gift for music, too. There's something weird going on here."

Tupan gave an airy wave of her hand. "Go on, admit it! You think Ra'hish is cool!"

"I do not!"

"Do too! I saw you trying to practice with those pointy knife things of his!" The girl propped her chin on her hand and happily watched Surolf work. "Hey, is this treasure hole open yet or what?"

"What!" Surolf gave a mighty heave with Ra'hish at his side. Both creatures squawked as the stone slid free into the air. Brilliant, white-blue light instantly flooded into the cave, blinding everyone and sending the delvers wincing back from the hole.

Hern unharnessed himself by pulling at a bow knot with his lips. Beside the shaft in the floor, Ra'hish and Surolf tried to hide their eyes from the painful glare, at the same time peering cautiously across the lip. The light hissed and struck the cave roof with all the pressure of a raging wind.

"We're through! The hole's big enough to climb down!" Surolf fought to peer inside. "It's two body lengths deep, but I can't see the bottom!"

Everyone retreated from the hole. The light crashed against the ceiling in a brilliant, living stream, striking harsh reflections from the obsidian walls.

Tupan crowded happily forward, stuck her head into the hole, and wagged her tail. "This is hoopy!"

"Keep away from it!" Surolf dragged the coyote back. "We might have undermined it – the floor could fall in or something!"

The greyhound signaled to Ra'hish, who gathered the rope from the puddle of rainwater where it had fallen. A jutting shard from the metal tower made a perfect anchor point, and the two males made fast the rope, took up the slack, and made to drop the line down into the hole.

Teela's whiskers jangled, and she suddenly snatched the rope away. "*Wait!*"

Surolf angrily swiped at the rope again, only to be held back by the female rat.

Teela wrung her hands as she tried to grapple with the unwieldy Uruth tongue. "No touch! Wait!"

The rat motioned everybody back. She tossed the sopping rope down into the hole and lunged back.

A sizzling stream of lightning blasted up out of the ground, along the rope, and into the broken metal tower. The energy spat and twisted like a maddened snake, lighting the cavern a stark, mad white.

Ra'hish and Surolf cringed back. Tupan stared in stunned fascination. Hern reared in fright, hooves thudding the sand as nestlings squeaked and fled madly aside. The baby rats buried themselves in the sand, only their little tails sticking out.

The lightning crackled away, though the bright torrent of wind continued. The rope smoked with heat.

Teela's panting breath was the loudest sound in the cave. She swallowed hard, staring with dazed eyes at Ra'hish. "Safe now. No more lightning."

Surolf uncoiled from the sand and blinked half-blinded eyes. "Good call, Lady!" Surolf sighed raggedly in shock, staring first at the ropes and then back to the apologetic little rat. He swallowed hard and nodded in gratitude. "Damned good call . . ."

Moving as though the ground were somehow fragile beneath her feet, Teela tiptoed to the center of the cave. The rat girl drew closer to the hole and peered down into the clear blue space beyond. Light waves made ripples in her soft gray fur. It was a wonderful pretense of courage.

Ra'hish came to her side and ran a hand across her spine, feeling her lean into him in fright. "It's all right. It missed us." Teela nodded, frightened, and Ra'hish looked at her thin little face in amazement. "How did you know it was there?"

"I just . . ." The girl shrugged bony shoulders hooded with soft gray fur. "I just *knew.*"

"And it's safe now?"

"There's no more sparks – not for a while. But we should hurry."

Ra'hish went to make himself understood by the male dog – a process involving much mime and hand waving. Teela meanwhile stuck her head out of the cave and called toward the lonely figure perched on the rocks above. "Oosha! We're going down into the ground. Are you coming to see?"

"No." Oosha remained on her pedestal amid the sands. "I'll stand guard up here. You be careful!"

"Is something coming?"

"No. Not yet." Oosha's pure white fur rippled in the freezing wind. "But it will soon."

Inside the cavern, Ra'hish and Surolf mustered the baby rats and checked their equipment. The nestlings' war blades were checked for fit while Surolf passed a second rope about the anchor and let it down the hole beside the first. The adults brought out torches, tinderboxes, mapping sheets, drawing sticks, and even gloves for handling fragile, sensitive artifacts. Pleased with themselves, Surolf, Ra'hish and Teela looked over their affairs. Suddenly a bright voice pealed out of the hole.

"Ooooh, *hoopy!*"

"*Tupan!*" Surolf dived over to the hole in the floor and shouted into the blinding glare. "Tupan – you get out of there at once!"

"No way! This place is wild!" The girl positively bubbled with glee. "There's this sort of sphere thing here!"

"Well, don't touch anything."

From the hole came a little *clunk*, followed by the sound of breaking glass. "Oh." The girl seemed annoyed. "Drat!"

Surolf stared aghast into the hole. "What?"

"I think I broke it. No, wait – maybe I can stick it back on!"

"*Tupan!*"

"Oh, wow! All its guts are coming out!" Tupan's efforts made a noise like crockery falling from a shelf – or a cart load of valuable pots smashing straight into a tree. "Do you think it's really supposed to do that?"

Surolf sought out the male rat – the only reasonable soul in a thousand miles. "I'm going to kill her!" The greyhound passed a turn of the rope about himself, and the rat helped him negotiate the ragged glass edges of the hole. "No – first I'm going to bury her to her neck in a pit of soapy frogs, and *then* I'm going to kill her!" The light hissed, battering Surolf's fur like a sizzling wind. He crammed his eyes shut against the blinding glare and dropped down the rope. He slid through a thundering barrier of wind and into sudden, blissful peace.

Eyes closed, Surolf hung in an empty space that rippled to the sounds of quiet streams. He smelled green growing things and rich brown soil. A breeze stirred his fur with gentle fingers of warmth. Taut and wincing, Surolf relaxed bit by bit and hung, swinging blindly in an alien world.

"Just drop, you big dill weed! It's only half a span!"

Cursing, Surolf braced himself and let go of the rope. Muscles tensed and legs spread to take the impact of a fall into a vast, deep cave. He fell almost two hand spans, landing with less of a thump than if he had stepped from a chair. Tupan's hooting laughter made the greyhound blush as he opened his eyes – and stared into absolute infinity.

On an island made of summer herbs, Surolf was adrift on a sea of stars.

He stood on a square platform rimmed with polished wood – a platform planted with plush, cool moss. Another island stood nearby – and another, and another until hundreds and thousands of them lay in orderly rows, forming vast corridors afloat on a silent sea. Glowing motes of light drifted through the air, leaving behind them a sound of laughter and the faintest smell of spice. The islands floated on a surface that was almost water, but instead seemed a thin, cool skin stretched across an infinite depth of stars.

Something stirred inside the water – a shape like a turtle with six flippers growing from its shell. The creature showed only where it broke the magic water skin, leaving ripples in the sheer black space in which it swam. Surolf stared at the numbing images of the dreamscape, his ears falling and his tail hanging between his knees.

On an island nearby stood a flowering tree – and in the crown of the tree sat Tupan. Like a mad magician in a cave of wonders, Tupan perched cross-legged on a clear sphere of light, floating in midair amid a swirling current of ribbons, skirts, and bells. Clearly, she was having the time of her life. She ran drifting motes of light between her fingertips, her whole being shining with delight. The girl grinned at Surolf and spread her hands. "So, is this hoopy, or what? This place is so neat, I may have to change my underwear!"

It was a sea of stars, a long chain of perfectly spaced islands diminishing into impossible distance. It could not possibly fit beneath the metal pylon – beneath the plain of sighing towers, or even beneath Acomar.

Surolf sagged and slowly sat down on the warm, soft ground. Just above him, a square of utter blackness simply hung in the air, a trapdoor into empty sky. Two rope ends dangled from the square, but above it was nothing but open, empty space.

From her perch in the neighboring tree, Tupan made a crow's caw of delight. "Isn't that wild? Just starts and ends nowhere, hey?" The girl reclined effortlessly on her transparent sphere. "Remind you of anything?"

Surolf stared. The trapdoor looked a little like the Gur gate – the same insubstantial black window into another place. Tupan seethed with delight as she watched Surolf the engineer confront the impossible. She leapt from the top of her tree perch, sprang onto Surolf's island, and pranced to his side.

She rapturously took Surolf by the arm, turning with him as they stared into the magic land side by side. She felt warm and wonderful, impossibly alive. Starlight glittered in her eyes.

Tingling with awe, Surolf scarcely even dared breath. "Is this Gur? Is this where the giants dwell?"

"No. It smells . . . peaceful." Tupan clung to Surolf's arm and sensed that he shared her joy. The girl stared at the stars, the islands, and the ripples in the stellar sea. She and Surolf were utterly alone in a private, magic world. "Surolf?"

"Yes?"

"I'm glad we were here together. . . ."

Ever so slightly, the girl leaned her head against Surolf's neck. A moment later, a loud Itheem shout came from above.

"*Too'pan! Soo'holf! Iss danger you in?*"

"No – it's okay!" Tupan broke back from Surolf to look up into the gate above. "Hey! Come on down! You have to see this to believe it!"

The rope jiggled, and then a long camouflaged rat tail appeared. An instant later, Ra'hish hit the moss upon all fours, twin blades flicking out. The rat dived and rolled – looked about himself for enemies . . . and simply sagged as the sea of stars took hold on his mind.

Tupan watched the rat's face and gave a hoot of joy. "Hoo hoo! I like that look!"

She danced over to stand beneath the ropes and catch nestlings and they flooded into her arms. The little creatures looked about in astonishment, rushing to the island's edges and hanging their heads down to watch the stars. Whiskers twiddling, they leapt from one island to the next. Teela slid down the rope and landed in their midst. She simply sat on her rump and made a noise of wonder, allowing Tupan to take her by the hands and show her the reflections in the starry sea.

Not all the islands were the same. Some had trees, some had flowers, others had a single large rock, and more still were made from pure bare soil. Keen to explore, Surolf pulled on Eeka's tail and stopped her from reaching out to touch the water skin. He chivvied the nestlings across to the neighboring island, and the party crowded admiringly all about Tupan's tree.

The tree had flowers – each of them identical and about the size of an open hand. Amid the flowers hung metallic fruit – golden spheres of uniform shape and size.

Tupan pointed to a broken sphere and stirred inside the split shells with a stick. A gray dust clung on the twig in Tupan's hand. "It broke off when I climbed the tree. I thought it was fruit – but it looks like fungus spores."

Ra'hish leaned forward, his fantastic spray of whiskers quivering as he sniffed above the fruit. He spoke a few words to Eeka, who sat back on her rump and chittered to the canines in her funny little voice. "Not fruit! Not toadie-stool!"

Tupan continued poking with the stick, fascinated by the process as though she had discovered a wild new toy. "Wow! Hey, check it out! The dust moves! It spreads up the stick all by itself – see?"

"*Crap!*" Surolf instantly slapped the stick from Tupan's hand and jerked her back from the fruit. The adventurers all gazed at the dust in new suspicion, shuffling their feet and keeping elaborately far away.

Teela inspected another twig broken off by Tupan's climb. "Not live tree. Dead tree." The rat girl lifted her face to gaze into the leaves. "Machine."

"The tree's a machine?" Surolf looked at the tree in shock. "Are you sure?"

"Teela *knows*." The rat's voice seemed dazed. She looked down into her own hands. "Teela knows."

Excited, Surolf drew in a deep, full breath of air. "If it's a machine, it has a purpose! It can be replicated. I could make a machine tree of our own!" He looked about the islands – some in the distance seemed to have different greenery, or to be covered in dancing fireflies. "We could find a Giant and discover how it's done!"

Tupan stood, clapped her hands, and rubbed her knuckles into Surolf's skull. "*Hooookay!* Surolf's on a wee trip to ga-ga land! He'll be back right after he invents perpetual motion and flying without wings!" The girl looked about and breathed a sigh. "Well, maybe we can live here or something? You know – plant some crops on the islands and sell them to the rats upstairs? I mean – it's warm here. I think it would be really neat!"

From the black gateway above the next island, Hern's voice drifted down into the void. "I think you should know that these ropes are starting to give off smoke."

Everyone instantly whipped about to stare at the two rope ends – both of which seemed perfectly hale and hearty. One by one, the rats and dogs jumped the star sea and landed on the island. All clustered about the gate and stared up in puzzlement.

The rope shook. Oosha came sliding down headfirst, her pink tail and feet braking her as she popped into view. The girl took one wild, astonished look about. Agitated and in haste, she flipped about without setting foot on the ground. "Get up fast! It's coming."

Teela instantly shot up the rope after her sister, followed by an chain of little rats, each one gripping its brother or sister's tail. As each rat climbed into the square black gate, they disappeared from view. Ra'hish hurried the last of his charges aloft, then swarmed nimbly up after them, his prehensile feet giving him an easy climb.

Blinking, Tupan felt herself being hoisted onto the rope by Surolf, who lifted her as though she weighed no more than a feather. "Wait! we can't go!"

"Oh, yes we can! The rats are scared of something." Surolf used one hand to boost Tupan's thrashing tail. "That's good enough for me! Up!"

He chased the girl aloft, smacking her backside to force her to climb. Passing through the gate felt like piercing a crisp, cold skin, and Surolf found himself in a jagged channel of obsidian, blue light leaking upward from the gate about his waist. Swarming up a damp rope that suddenly seemed smoking hot, the greyhound felt Hern's muzzle grab him by the neck and haul him out of the hole. The pony shoved the two canines with his forehead, propelling them in panicked exodus among the last few scurrying rats.

Oosha – vigilant and strangely beautiful – stood guard on a rock outcrop at the cave's side. She waved the dogs and pony past, speaking in a wonderful, pure voice. "Go. Go to sand and hide."

The sound of sizzling power hovered in the air. A sudden wind seemed to have hit the sands even though scarcely a dust mote stirred. Behind a ridge of sand, rats, dogs, and pony flung themselves into cover.

Surolf pointed off across the plain of towers. In a flash of opening moonlight, a darker patch of nighttime slid across the ground. "The Gur gate!"

The black sphere rolled against the sands as it moved, luxuriating in the desert's soft caress. Spitting sparks and coils of light, the sphere smoked and hissed its way across the ground, consuming the few small weeds lying in its path.

Shrinking flat, Tupan stared into the shape and felt her tail turn stiff with amazement. "I can see inside it." Tupan's whisper barely drifted above the sound of raging winds. "That's not the sea of stars. . . ."

The vast black sphere held a venomous landscape – a place that smoked and seethed, where skeletal creatures hunted prey. Mindlessly drawn by the scent of power, the sphere rolled across the sands and moved into the glow of light seeping from the cave.

Suddenly, the sphere flashed with light and became a questing mind. The Gur gate swam with colors, a fantastic, evil eyeball smoking on the sand. It was as though a hungry god had suddenly awakened from its sleep. Inside the sphere, something stirred – a presence colder than glaciers, a chill of terror deep in mortal bones. For an instant, an alien shape appeared, massive and frightening. The image lasted for a heartbeat, and then disappeared, leaving after-ghosts of terror in the mind's eye. Mysteriously filled with *purpose*, the Gur gate swiveled slowly about, taking in a view of the living world.

The nestlings gave a whimper. The adults could only stare and feel their skins go cold.

Only Teela moved. Her mouth hanging, she rose from cover, fear gleaming in her eyes. "Oosha!"

The white rat remained in the sand crater at the base of the shattered pylon. The Gur gate moved crisply toward the little cave beneath the tower, and *something* seemed to leave the gate and go delving deep within.

Her fur lit by the flickering lights of the sphere, Oosha sat on the sands by the cave, pink eyes fixed and calm.

In a daze, Teela stared down at her sister's quiet shape. "She knew it was coming. It's drawn to power. When the lightning flashed, she knew it had to come. . . ."

"Oh, Sweet Spirits!" Ra'hish stared at the tiny white rat sitting so courageously below. "Doesn't she know what that thing is?"

"Oosha knows." Helpless to act, Teela's breath sobbed with fear. "This is what she wanted to do."

The rats were frozen.

Wiping her nose, Tupan hitched one leg beneath herself to make a sprinter's start. "Okay – I'll grab her! If the gate moves, run!"

Surolf stared at the girl in fright. "You're mad! What if the gate attacks you?"

"So, we'll dodge into the cave and hide!" Tupan made ready to launch herself into a charge. "Here we go!"

Surolf kicked the girl's legs out from underneath her in a sudden surge of fear. *"Don't!* Don't go near it!"

"But the rat!"

"It's too late!"

The blue light from the cave shut off as though a hidden door had slammed. After a long, painful minute, the lights inside the Gur gate suddenly came to life again. The gate surged – swiveled – and moved slowly away from the little cave.

§

"Stop." Oosha came from the shadows to place herself in the gate's path. She felt strangely calm, skin tingling, senses bright and clear. It was almost as though she watched herself from far away. "Stop. I want to speak with you."

The gate swayed and moved to place the little rat beneath its terrifying gaze. Oosha could feel an icy mind rake across her soul.

"You want those spheres, don't you? You need them." Oosha moved as the gate tried to pass her by. "We led you to them. I want you to answer a question in return." Walking slowly toward the gate, Oosha made quiet little footsteps in the sand. "Did you deliberately curse us as you made us? Do you have any idea what we've become?" Oosha's pink eyes sparked pure bitterness. "You are old. Tell me how to live a long life without breeding! How can we grow old enough to be wise?" The little rat paused. Her fur rippled in the drifting wind.

The sinister black Gur gate hung like an avalanche above her – an insensate *thing* restrained by a careless, brooding power. It was cold. The gate's skin smoked where the air touched it, dripping water in little runnels that quickly froze to ice. Something dark stirred in its heart. The gate turned and moved aside, scoring a hissing path across the sand. It became a dark, mindless thing once more – a behemoth blundering through the dark and off into the empty plains.

Behind it, the gate had left a single tiny prize – a bauble glittering in the sickly light. It was a silver apple – its skin beaded with dew and reflecting images of Oosha's staring eyes.

The girl reached down to take the object in her hands and turn it slowly around. Oosha swayed in terror – and then quickly closed her eyes and cracked the apple's shell with a single, frightened bite.

"Oosha – *NO!*" Teela's wild cry ripped through the ice-cold air. Oosha scarcely heard the shout as the apple's innards foamed up into her mouth. Choking, she felt dry dust pour across her tongue. She tried to swallow, coughed in pain, and felt the dust claw its way into her body like a living stream of lice.

Dust pierced her, spread into her stomach, crawled into her lungs and through her bloodstream. The rat dropped the empty shell and clamped hands against her skull as she felt the motes writhing in her brain. She made a low moan of terror, jerking as her limbs twitched of their own accord.

Horrified, the white rat looked up at the retreating gate. She suddenly seemed to understand. Her body spun stiffly, shuddering as something blasted at her from within. She threw back her head and howled out a tortured scream.

Teela shouted from above – a cry of pure fright.

Oosha lay curled on her side, convulsing in agony. She moaned, a sound that began low and desolate but built to a maddening, tortured squeal.

Racing to her sister's side, Teela wrapped the girl in her arms and saw a silver powder disappearing into Oosha's lips. "*Ra'hish! Do something!*"

Ra'hish slithered down the sand, landing in a rush and dragging Oosha into his arms. He tried to wrench the girl's mouth open, only to retreat from her deadly fangs. Oosha neither foamed nor drooled – signs of poison.

Maddened by the fruit, Oosha fought with all her might, curling inward and flailing her claws. The girl ripped a savage wound into her own chest. Teela gave a cry – and then stared in shock as silver motes poured from the wound, knitting flesh together in the blink of an eye. Oosha laughed wildly as the wound simply disappeared – until another wave of pain swept over her and she jerked frenziedly in her sister's arms.

Ra'hish wept, folding Oosha in his grasp and trying to hold her down.

The coyote girl arrived beside him, touched Oosha, and jerked her hand back with a cry.

Grabbing Tupan's hands with pleading little fingers Eeka tried to drag the coyote down to Oosha's side. "Tupan! You fix! Put you hands

Oosha! Fix! Fix good!"

Tupan tried in vain. Helping was simply a thing of instinct, but here, all instinct failed. Something crawled through every fiber of Oosha's blood and bone, bringing agony to every drop of blood and speck of hair. The white rat rolled mad eyes and squealed in pain. . . .

For hour after hour after hour.

Midnight came and passed. The still hours of early morning brought with them an icy chill. Hern searched the dunes for weeds and brought them in his mouth, piling them high to make Oosha a little fire. The cavern was now devoid of magic light. The passage down to the sea of stars was gone, replaced by a shallow hole dug part way into the obsidian. The nestlings brought blankets to keep Oosha warm, and then left her to Tupan and Ra'hish. Surolf found himself sitting with frightened little rats crowded beneath this arms, his hand resting on Teela's skull as she stared back toward the cave. They sat there through the midnight hours and scarcely dared say a word.

With the fire fading to warm embers and silence lying on the sands, Tupan finally climbed from the obsidian chamber, running tired fingers through her smoky fur. She came and sat amid the nestlings at Hern's feet, taking a weary grip on Surolf's hand. "It's passed. Whatever it is, it's finished. I helped as much as I could."

"Bad. Very bad." Hern's tall ears twitched. "Rats eat insects, don't they? I found her three beetles and a caterpillar."

"Thank you, Hern. I'll keep them for her for later on."

Surrounded by rats, Surolf scarcely noticed that he cradled a tearful little Rika in his arms. "She was nice!" Surolf stared at the silver sand. "She was so nice. Why did this happen to her?"

Tupan wiped her eyes and gave a tired sigh. "She wanted it. Oosha's braver than I am."

Staring forlornly at the cavern mouth, Ra'hish tried to keep tears from his eyes. He spoke sadly to the wind, and Eeka translated his words for canine ears. "Oosha wants time. Oosha wants to make things better for the Itheem – no more wars." Eeka softly reached out to touch Ra'hish's fur. "He says we must protect her until we know if she has won."

It would be dawn in two hours – time for the guard to change on the Shield Wall. Tupan rose and dusted herself free of sand. "What now?"

"Home." Surolf stood, hitched a nestling between his shoulder blades, and searched for his spear. "You go home. I'll stay and look after the white rat."

The coyote blinked in shock. "Why you? Ra'hish can stay! And me – maybe I can help her when she wakes."

"No. We can't reach the Shield Wall without Ra'hish as a guide, and we can't just leave the nestlings here as guards. It's deadly out here, and they're only kids." Surolf found took a waterskin, a stick of bread, and a blanket from Hern's back. "I can protect her, and Ra'hish can protect you. Have him guide you to the wall before roll call."

Tupan anxiously looked at Surolf. "But why don't we all just stay here?"

"We'd starve. One of us has to get back and trade for food. There are some iron chunks. They should buy a few sacks of grain. Get the rats to bring you safely home, and then come back tomorrow night with food. They'll meet you at the wall."

Sitting unhappily in the entrance to the cave, Ra'hish tried to follow the language of the dogs. Eeka whispered a translation. Reluctantly, Ra'hish gathered the nestlings, left Teela to give Surolf extra aid, and trudged heavily away. As he passed Surolf, the dog raised a hand. Ra'hish looked the canine in the eye, nodded, and clapped Tupan on the flank. He led Hern out onto the sands.

A sack of rusted junk on his spine, the pony lumbered past Surolf. "I'll bring you oats. Then we can all have porridge."

"Thanks, Hern." The greyhound patted at his old friend's neck. "See you tomorrow."

Hanging back, Tupan shuffled her feet in the sand and refused to look Surolf in the eye. "Hey – be careful."

"Yeah. I will."

"And we'll make more money. Lots of it. Hern has it in a bag!"

"Money?" Surolf looked at the girl in bewilderment.

She tilted her head and stared at him in shock. "For the bride-price! You know. It's. . . it's what you wanted."

"Oh." Surolf wavered, feeling strangely numb and confused. "Yes, I suppose. . . ." The greyhound heaved a troubled sigh. "See you tomorrow?"

Tupan kissed him. She stared at Surolf, as though seeing an art piece she alone had long admired, and then chucked him beneath the snout and walked away. Like a sorceress, she spread her bell-laden arms, summoning the nestlings, who swarmed about, chattering and wanting news of Oosha.

Ra'hish spared a last reluctant stare toward Oosha's cave and ushered his charges off into the dunes. With a slither of tails, they faded clean from view, leaving Surolf alone beneath the broken metal tower.

The Gur gate had gone, but it's presence remained – a stab of ice in the wind. Teela stood watching from the entrance to the cave, hands wringing as her sister whimpered in pain. Gathering his spear, Surolf wandered back inside to feed the fire and keep warm through the dawn.

On the dunes above, sand shifted in a quiet cascade. A long shape rose on its haunches to sniff the quiet breeze – saw the firelight glowing inside the cave, and gave a cruel hiss of glee. The figure instantly turned and sped off to the East, leaving no hint of its passing except a rattle of dry bones.

§

The empty plain gave way to weeds and folded outcrops of stone, all aglow with the weird light of nighttime Acomar. Tupan walked along in unaccustomed silence, hand resting on the strong muscles under Hern's braided mane. All about her, rats flitted and went to ground – halted and conferred, required sudden and constant course changes. Once Ra'hish charged a bare patch of open earth, blades wicked and fangs snarling in rage. Three half-seen figures burst from the soil and fled, chased by nestlings until Ra'hish ordered the creatures back to his side.

On the coastal flatlands far away, fires bloomed and shadows danced. There, Acomar was thoroughly alive. tunnels were dug and wars fought, spirits were summoned and iron dug. Tupan looked out across the strangely powerful scene and wondered if the town dogs had ever really seen their enemy.

"He'll be all right." Hern had found a thistle tip and munched the sugary purple flower. "Better there than in the town."

"Hmm?" Tupan kept looking back toward the plain of towers. "What was that?"

"Surolf. He's much better away from town." Hern chewed and swallowed. He spied another thistle and changed his path toward it. "Keeps him away from that Aela girl."

"Why is that good?" Suddenly despondent, Tupan kept her eyes fixed on the way ahead. "Aren't they in love?"

"Surolf is Surolf. Aela is Aela." Hern's lofty expression seethed with equine disapproval. "Better Surolf stays in the sand. Might give him time to think."

Overhead, the dark mass of the Shield Wall blotted out the stars. As the wall came in sight, Ra'hish pulled in closer to Tupan and carefully scanned the open ground.

"Safe iss?"

"Oh, yeah – all clear. We told the town sergeant the fort sergeant was inspecting us, and the fort sergeant the other thing around. No one missed us!" Tupan heaved a wretched sigh as she thought of the white rat lying somewhere in pain. "Okay, so I'll get this lot of metal melted down, trade it for grain, peas, and bacon, and bring it here tomorrow night."

Ra'hish tilted his head. "Half you, half we?"

"Naaah, this load's all for you guys. You need it." Tupan patted Hern on the back as the wall spread its huge black shadow overhead. "Thanks, guys. I'll see if I can find any medicine or anything for Oosha. You guys fade – Hern and I can take it from here."

Koopa, one of the largest nestlings, rose from a weed clump, a puzzled look on his face. He sniffed at the night air with frown. "Ra'hish? Ra'hish!"

Something hissed through the air. Suddenly the nestling boy was down, kicking in agony as an arrow jutted through his back. More arrows flew – invisible flickers in the dark. The nestlings rose from hiding to call out to one another in a surge of fright.

Ra'hish hissed a squealing challenge, drawing arrow fire from somewhere high above. He dived and rolled aside, arrows stabbing home behind him. "Run! Hide!"

From the ramparts above, dog soldiers roared in hate and launched themselves onto the ground. A dozen armored dogs bayed for blood and charged Tupan and the rats.

Koopa squealed as he tried to reach his arrow wound.

Without thinking, Tupan scooped him up and threw the injured nestling across Hern's back. "*Run! Back to the towers! Ra'hish – go!*" The coyote smacked Hern's rump, and the pony lumbered off into the darkness with the wounded rat.

Nestlings fearlessly made to charge the onrushing dogs, but Tupan and Ra'hish herded the little creatures back into the weeds. Tupan picked herself up out of cover, intercepted Eeka who had begun her own attack run, and turned her around. In her long-practiced lope, the coyote ran off into the dark.

Suddenly, she spun sideways and fell. Eeka went whirling from her grasp to crash into a thistle. Down danced madly in the air. Tupan blinked and looked down at her thigh to see an arrow sticking clean through. The coyote blinked, lightheaded and wondering why the world was wrong. She slid sideways and stared blankly, numbly at the weeds.

"*Tupan!*" Eeka started forward, but saw a wall of vast, huge creatures charging her. The little rat got to her feet, clicked open her war blades, and made to save her friend – only to feel a hand jerk her backward as an arrow sliced a whisker's breadth before her face.

"Run! Go!" Ra'hish thrust Eeka back and took one last hopeless look toward the Shield Wall. The dog soldiers had surrounded Tupan. Hissing, Ra'hish fled into the dark.

The Uruth gave a victory roar and gathered to collect their spoils. Lolling limply, Tupan was dragged off toward Sentinel town. A hundred torches came to light the cold gray sky.

Chapter 9

Straining his old eyes into the dark, the ancient seer spied the returning heroes long before the town wall's guards. Standing on the battlements, the old man cracked his stick against a soldier's helmet and gave a wild howl of joy, baying at the ebbing moon with his strong old lungs. All along the palisades, the night watch jerked about and stared. They crowded to the western walls as more noise came from below.

Dawn erupted into chaos as the soldiers raised a scream of victory. Doors opened and children sleepily spilled outside. Fathers lunged out, armed with spears and expecting an alarm, only to find their neighbors dancing in the streets. The gates were opened and the returning warriors inched their way through the enthusiastic crowd.

A thousand citizens packed the streets around the conquering heroes. Whacking a path into the surging crowds, the foul tempered seer beat a last few cheering females from his path and fought his way toward Koja, joining his grandson at the head of his troops. Together, they marched toward the howling mound.

"Koja! Grandson, be welcome!"

"Spirit-Father!" The handsome young soldier hunched as cheers battered at him like a storm. "You knew we were returning?"

"A spirit came to give me a taste of your victory!" The old man changed course to lead the way up the steep steps of the mound. "How many goblins were slain?"

"Maybe three or four, Spirit-Father. They fled the moment we appeared!"

"No stomach for an honest fight. That's why we beat them so easily." The old man took the stairs like a youth of seventeen, striding up two at a time. "No honesty in them – no mettle. As spineless as a damned coyote!"

A landing at the middle of the steps gave grandfather and grandson a place to join with the prime family of the town. The alpha clan – Koja's mother, father, brothers, and uncles – had gathered with noble guests from far-flung towns to greet the returning heroes. The seer let them have their moment of reunion as the soldiers filed past – a dozen bowmen, a dozen fighters, and a dozen elite from the corps of scouts. He gave a wild cackle of delight as he saw the captive lolling bloodily in the grasp of the men, and then lunged forward to clap his grandson hard upon the arm.

"*Up!* Come up! Time for family later – now the Uruth race must be served!" The old man swatted relatives with a stick, chasing some uphill and others down like a shepherd chivvying his flock. "Only the most important few can come right now. Father – Mother – and one more! One more who's place is nobly earned!"

The seer took his two favorite young folk by the arms – his grandson and the girl Aela, the new bright star in his eyes. He watched the captive coyote being slung up onto the open howling platform and regretfully felt dawn's light striking sparks from frosty roofs.

"Night's the time to put the final touch on this. Night – when we can raise the ancestors to see! We'll call canines in from near and far – bring in the farmers and the traders. Even those damned mice and cats will want to see." The seer stared down at the prisoner, now pegged and chained to the ground. The coyote stirred, delirious with shock, an arrow still transfixing her thigh. Watching her, the seer could only give a bloodthirsty smile. "So – consorting with goblins; a traitor to the Uruth race." The old man turned to favor the beautiful girl beside him with a stroke of his knotted hand. "Daughter, you have served us well tonight. We have neglected our eastern cousins shamefully these past few years. You have the right stuff; the kind of intuition and vigilance that Sentinel needs. Wouldn't you say so, Koja?"

"Yes, Spirit-Father." Timid in the presence of Aela's perfect allure, the young warrior felt his senses swirl. His grandfather firmly placed the girl's hand in his own. Warmed beneath his cloak, they wandered together, male and female, toward his family as soldiers praised the ancestors with the wild ritual howl.

Gazing out across the town roofs, Aela took a firm grip on Koja's hand and peered up at her catch through artful eyes. Around her, hundreds of warriors roared out her name in praise. The most powerful alpha family in the region welcomed her into its arms. And it had all come from a single whisper of betrayal. The coyote girl would die, Surolf would fade away, and Aela would become Sentinel's power behind the throne.

The girl spared a last cold glance toward the prisoner dying in the frost, and then turned about to bathe her new-won audience with a perfect smile. . . .

§   §   §

An eerie silence had fallen over Acomar. The planted lands among the weeds were devoid of their hidden life. No rats guarded the crops. No parties fought in harvest wars, buying each mouthful of grain with Itheem blood. No battle cries, no scouts, no ambushes. . . .

Staggering through the dawn haze, Ra'hish could only blink and wonder why the whole world had suddenly drifted far away. Dazed, the other rats felt cold sand beneath their feet and looked up to see that they had brought themselves home. Hern staggered as he walked, blinking and shivering, his ears hanging low. As the party came across the dunes, the towers began to softly sigh, sparking with the rose-gold colors of dawn.

As they reached a dune crest beside the broken metal tower, Ra'hish's little party dwindled to a halt. There was something odd about the scene below. Countless footprints were trampled in the sand and the stink of Itheem bodies lay thick on the air. Koopa whimpered with the pain of his wound. Ra'hish stumbled forward toward the shelter of the obsidian cave.

"*Ra'hish! Look out!*" A nestling shouted as the sand erupted at Ra'hish's feet.

Faster than thought, the warrior streaked sideways, parried, and snapped his blades out of their tubes. Steel slashed at his eyes. He ducked under and ripped open a stinking belly with his weapon, filling the morning's calm with a sudden frenzy of screams.

More rats burst from the soil. Hern reared and plunged hooves down to almost smash an ambusher's skull. He turned as if to run, drawing an enemy to leap for his back, and delivered a lethal double kick that sent the rat cartwheeling through the sky.

A second figure leapt for Ra'hish's throat, only to spill sideways as nestlings leapt to the attack. A blade punctured the enemy's hide. He lunged at Eeka only to have another nestling stab him in the thigh. The warrior reared and fell. The nestlings pounced on him like an army of ants. The creature thrashed in agony before falling suddenly, awfully still.

A last survivor sped away across the sands. Flicking his weapons clean and sliding the blades into their tubes, Ra'hish turned slowly around to find the nestlings staring at him, perched on the body of their prey. There was blood on little paws and whiskers, and shock in young eyes. The nestlings panted, wanting to be proud of what they'd done.

Ra'hish reached out to touch their faces one by one, and then glanced down at the corpse. "You shouldn't have had to do that."

"He was going to kill you." Rika, seeming tiny as a grasshopper, looked up at him with frightened eyes. "We attacked, just like you said!"

"You should never have had to do that. It's wrong." Ra'hish sadly sank into the sand, crushed and forlorn. "Just flutes and songs, and little tails by the shore. That's what it should always be. . . ."

The little rats gathered quietly around their hero. "It's all right Ra'hish. You showed us what to do. We want to be like you."

Ra'hish stared down toward the bloodstained sands. "I know."

The dead were from G'kaa's band. He always used smoke-blue camouflage bands instead of black or gray. Ra'hish peered into the empty cavern, its roof still scarred with soot, and found a few white hairs from Oosha's pelt. The nestlings fanned out to sniff and scan the ground, even helping one another climb the metal pylon to look out across the hissing sands.

They picked up Koopa – still whimpering from his arrow wound – and took him to the obsidian cave to lay him down. Inside the cavern, Ra'hish sniffed the floors. He found a lump of rock with a bloody patch on one side – a patch in which there were fine gray hairs. He hunted his way across the sands to find the deep pit that he had helped carve into the obsidian. The hole's bottom had been filled with chips of stone.

Ra'hish smelled a familiar smell, and peered down into the narrow hole. "Eeka?"

"Yes, Ra'hish?"

"Surolf is in there. He's covered with bits of rock." Ra'hish grabbed the girl by the tail and lowered her down the hole. She sank down, her pink feet splayed wide. "Pull the rocks off him and pass them here."

The little nestling pulled at chips of heavy obsidian, tugging them free and passing them upward to Ra'hish. Grunting as she worked, she emptied the hole piece by piece, finding Surolf lying under a shallow layer of rock and weeds.

"He's alive, Ra'hish! He's breathing!"

"Good. Lets lift him on a rope."

Hern came trudging in and looked down into the hole – grumbling lest the rats see a tear in his eye. With the nestlings gathering, Eeka, Hern, and Ra'hish managed to put a rope about the dog and slowly drag him up into the light. They laid him on a bed of weeds and gently dabbed rainwater on his fur.

The nestlings worked on Surolf, licking gently at a thousand scrapes and cuts and wounds. The dog had taken a bash across the skull and then fallen headlong into a pit chipped from volcanic glass. He was otherwise unscathed. Satisfied that his friend would live, Hern surrendered his blankets to make a bed for the injured and busied himself in the world outside.

Koopa's arrow wound was light. The weapon had passed through his back under the shoulders, missing muscle but tearing skin. Ra'hish nipped off the arrowhead with his teeth and pulled the weapon back through the wound, and then used his mouth to squirt salt water through the hole. Koopa squealed in pain, but he would live. Rats always did; anything that failed to kill outright always healed.

The same could not be said for Surolf. A blow to the skull should have been easy to heal, but after an hour, the dog still remained asleep. Ra'hish sat to look after his patients while Hern took nestlings on his back and roamed the local dunes. They came back after a while, and the pony spoke in his beautiful, slow voice.

Eeka listened and translated for the warrior rat. "They've looked all around. Rat tracks lead off to a place covered in footprints. The boys say twelve rats came here – and they joined a hundred, which joined two thousand. A whole war band or more went past in the last few hours."

"A whole war band?" Ra'hish felt tired. He sat and tried to think, hearing somewhere a distant stir of drums. "G'kaa has Oosha."

"Did G'kaa hit Surolf?"

"No – Surolf's still alive. G'kaa would have killed him and eaten him." Surolf stood and brushed the fur from his rear. "I think Teela must have done it, and hid him in the hole when G'kaa came. She saved his life."

Itheem nursing was always rough and ready; Ra'hish prodded Surolf with a fingertip. He tried his foully accented Uruth language skills on Hern. "Dog sleeps. Rat ways no good for dog. You know thing to make dog awake?"

"Oh, yes. I know a special treatment." The pony clip-clopped his way unhurriedly out the door. "Hang on – I just need a few things. . . ."

After a pregnant pause, Hern duly returned. Hern had drawn a mouthful of ice water from the rain pools. Walking past the rats, he paused above Surolf and carefully poured the water onto his face. The dog moaned and tried to escape, feebly working his closed eyes and waving his hands.

Eeka crinkled her nose with a frown. "Well, anybody could have done that!"

The pony bent down to begin licking the dog with his gigantic spotted tongue. He diligently worked Surolf up and down, churning his coat with a rough, sticky massage. Finally Surolf opened one sickly eye and managed to focus on Hern's face.

"Hern – stop that."

"Gets the circulation going." Hern kept on licking, quite content with his work. "You're salty."

"I think I'm going to be sick."

"I suppose so." Hern busied himself with Surolf's feet. "Good morning."

"Good morning."

The dog rolled over – was copiously sick – and then found a nestling trying to put a cold compress on his skull. He nodded thanks to the little creature and managed to sit up, drinking from a cup as fine and white as snow.

Hern watched as the head cloth was wrung out and dipped in a puddle once again. "Do you feel better?"

"I feel awful." The dog closed his eyes and drew a long, slow breath. "Oooooh, my head! What's that noise? It sounds like someone banging with a rock!"

"It's someone banging with a rock." The pony shrugged. "They're using a knife and flint to start a fire. I think it's all going rather well."

Hern sat down – a difficult process since he seemed to be entirely made of knees. With a heavy sigh, he folded his hooves. "They got Tupan."

The words simply made no sense. Sick and reeling, Surolf closed his eyes and held the ice-cold cloth against his skull. "What?" Surolf forced his eyes wide open, hoping the world would somehow make better sense. "Who got Tupan?"

"The dogs. The town dogs. They hurt a nestling and captured Tupan. They tried to kill us all."

Surolf let his gaze wander until he found himself staring at a blank patch of wall. His whole body had instantly turned chill. "Is she dead?"

"I think she's alive. The dogs picked her up and took her away."

The greyhound touched the back of his head and found a patch of blood. He stared at it, and then looked dazedly around to see little Koopa lying by the fire at his side. "What happened to the little guy?"

"He was shot." The pony frowned. "I told you he was shot. And then they captured Tupan."

"We have to get her back." Surolf looked up at the sky. "Is that dawn or dusk up there?"

"Dawn."

"Then we have the daylight hours." Leaning on the pony, Surolf tried to stand. "But once the moon rises – they'll kill her."

Ra'hish came into the cave, carrying an armful of dried weeds for the fire. He took Surolf's cup – a rat's dried skull – and refilled it with water, offering it to the nestling and helping him drink. "Koopa. Are you all right?"

"It hurts." The little rat was miserable. He lay beside the fire, two sisters holding him in their arms. "It really hurts."

"Stay warm. It will heal in about four days."

"Where's Tupan?"

"I don't know, Little One. I'll go find out."

With a trail of nestlings close behind him, Ra'hish flowed past the fire and sat down, confronting Surolf. The two creatures were from alien worlds; trust did not come easily. Ra'hish and Surolf inspected one another through reddened, tired eyes, each seeing a mirror image of their own concern. Surolf finally looked away into the fire.

"I'm sorry. I tried to guard them, and I failed."

The rat spread thin, expressive hands tattooed with camouflage. "Dog is better?"

"Dog feels better. Teela hit me on the head." Surolf spoke to Ra'hish face to face for the first time, and found the creature's alien expressions troubling. "There were rats – hundreds of rats. I picked up my spear, but Teela hit me."

"Teela save Surolf. Hide him from G'kaa." The rat wiped a hand across his face, trying to decide just what to do. "Teela and Oosha are taken by G'kaa. Big war band! G'kaa is powerful – needs Hastaasi to make all rats follow him. He will make war with dogs – kill them all."

"Make war with the valley?" Surolf leaned forward to the rat, speaking slowly and clearly. "You mean just Sentinel town?"

"Valley." The rat made a chopping motion of his hand. "All dog, all cat, all four legger – dead. G'kaa kill everything."

The dog and pony swapped a chilled stare. Surolf half hoped he had failed to understand. "So this G'kaa wants to attack once he has all the rats on his side?" The greyhound opened his hands in confusion. "How can he do this? How many warriors does G'kaa have?"

Ra'hish consulted with his nestlings, his language skills coached by Eeka. Frustrated, the rat held up his hand and spread five fingers out before the fire. He counted his fingertips in his hissing Itheem tongue, making sure the dogs would understand.

"Ten more times of this. Then ten more times, then ten more times – yes?"

Surolf blinked.

"Five times ten times ten times ten? He has five thousand warriors?" Sentinel had two thousand citizens; with the town walls to hide behind, the odds were not so bad. "That's quite a few rats. That's bad."

Eeka and Jez both frowned, and then whispered in Ra'hish's ear. Jez did quick calculations, using his fingertips as an abacus. Ra'hish bit his lip and tried again.

"No. Five – yes?" He held up fingers making sure the dog followed every word. "Ten more times. Then times ten, times ten, and times ten, yes?"

Hern let his ears droop. "Fifty thousand. Oh, dear."

Appalled, Surolf felt the fur along his spine stand clean on end. "Fifty *thousand* warriors! G'kaa has fifty thousand?"

The rats consulted, and then gave an idle nod. "He will take a day to gather Itheem clans. Tomorrow, G'kaa will attack."

Surolf could only sit, stunned into silence, and try to picture the seething life outside the cavern walls. Previously, the rats had been a piecemeal menace – a few thousand at most, attacking haphazardly at the wall as the mood struck them. But they were a people who measured fighting strength in tens of thousands – who replaced entire populations in the blink of an eye.

The local towns might muster five thousand adult fighting dogs in all, with perhaps half as many cats and bats and mice – none of whom were truly fighting stock. Unless G'kaa was somehow stopped, Sentinel town and the whole Mornmist Valley was doomed.

Running fearlessly from the door, tiny Rika began tugging frantically at Ra'hish's leg. "We can't leave Tupan with the dogs! They'll kill her with a knife when it gets dark!"

"We must find her before G'kaa attacks." Ra'hish sat up and drew a long, deep breath, and spoke in the tongue or Itheem. "Tupan is smart. Tupan fixes things! When we get her back, she'll help us figure out how to rescue Oosha and Teela from G'kaa."

The nestlings looked at Ra'hish in awe. "Are we going to fight G'kaa, now?"

"Oosha said that the Itheem needed time. She said that G'kaa's plans would only bring more suffering." Ra'hish sprung his war blades from their tubes, checked the fittings, and slid them back out of view. "So, we fight him. We give Oosha her time. Take Oosha away, and G'kaa has nothing to hold the clans together. He won't have the numbers he needs to attack the dogs." The rat warrior jerked his chin toward Surolf and Hern. "Eeka? Ask the dog how much time we have to rescue Tupan."

The little nestling sat on her haunches before Surolf and politely spoke, then turned anxiously to Ra'hish.

"They'll put her on trial tonight at moonrise, and try to kill her once they can raise the spirits with a howl."

"Now ask him if he knows how she can be rescued."

The greyhound heard the question and walked away to think it through. He saw the town in his mind's eye – the howling mound, the battlements, the catapults. He imagined the trial-speeches made and seers howling, spirits being summoned in the dark. The greyhound held the image, turned it this way and that, and simply stared across the sand.

Spirits. An idea slowly dawned. He would defeat superstition with honest engineering! The dog's eyes sparkled, energy blazing through him as he whirled toward his friends.

"Ra'hish – we need bones. Lots of bones."

"This is Acomar." Ra'hish shrugged. The vale of bones spilled clean out into the ruins. "There are bones."

"Hern!" Surolf leapt to his feet and threw the cold compress from his skull. "Hern, go shopping. Ra'hish will show you where to find a load of skulls and bones!"

The pony came plodding over from the fire, his ears lifting in joy. "Are we rescuing Tupan?"

"Yes! First Tupan, and then that white rat and Teela!"

"Won't the kidnappers object?"

"Tupan will figure something out we get her back. She always fixes things." The greyhound began frenziedly rooting through collections of camping gear. "We'll need all the rope, and sacks. . . . Eeka! Tell Ra'hish I need body paint – black and white, like that stuff you guys put on your fur!"

The dog strode amid the little nestlings, chasing them out onto the open sand. The little creatures leapt and bounded over him like fleas. *"Tupan! Save Tupan, save Teela, save Oosha!"*

"That's the stuff!"

Surolf gathered Ra'hish beside him and began rapidly sketching a map of Sentinel town in the sand.

"Go bring the bones, and we'll get started." Once he began moving, Surolf became a font of energy. The dog had finished drawing a strange shape on the sand. He picked half a dozen nestlings and sat them in a row. "You guys are good at learning things. Who wants to learn basic ballistics?"

Ra'hish and Hern simply shrugged at one another, made a travois from two long poles, and gathered a few nestlings at their side. They trotted past Surolf and his studious little group, and Hern called across his shoulder with a frown. "How many bones did you want, actually?"

"Oh – two sacks full. Skulls are good." The greyhound paid little attention to the interruption. "Come on! You have half an hour, and then we have to go!"

Hern clopped onward through the sand, a nestling perched on his rump and a confused, concerned Ra'hish at his side. As they passed over the dunes and left Surolf behind, the pony turned toward Ra'hish and nodded very slowly with closed eyes.

"Don't worry about Surolf. He's quite a nice chap once you engage his enthusiasm. Very good with engineering and machines." The pony creased his brows in thought. "Very bad with pots, though. Very bad. . ." Quite content, Hern wandered on into the sand.

Beside him, Ra'hish listened to the beat of distant drums, hastening his pace as thunder seemed to shiver on the air.

§ § §

Shaman drums were rare; made from vast spans of sewn rat skin stretched across hoops of bones. They were filthy black with the blood of slaughtered enemies. A hundred drums all in a line were being beaten by young warriors, the drumsticks blurring as the beat became a deafening storm of noise.

Surrounded by a vast, churning ocean of rats, G'kaa basked in the savage noise and opened his arms. "Magnificent!" The rat shouted to his nearby "guests," his huge voice easily heard even above the drums. "We are summoning envoys from every Itheem clan."

Tethered to a peg by a steel chain, Teela cradled Oosha in her arms. "The dogs will still win! Even if you break the wall, they still have other lands beyond. Their army will slow you down until other dogs can arrive."

"I think not. We have a weapon at long last." Yellow fangs gaping in a sneer, the warlord looked down at the shivering Hastaasi at his feet. "A pure Hastaasi – white as snow. A Hastaasi who can control the Gur gate's path."

Teela took a tighter grip on her sister as a sudden thrill of fear rushed into her soul.

G'kaa saw her terror and gave a vicious, filthy laugh. "Yes, girl! We saw it happen! You were watched as you went digging in the dunes!" G'kaa savored Oosha's scent, sniffing it as though it were the very scent of victory. "This is far, far better than I had even dreamed."

The voice broke into Oosha's tortured dreams. The girl blinked and opened her eyes, dazed and confused. She somehow found Teela's face and focused her eyes. She stared for long, blank minutes as though trying to sift through pictures scattered in her mind. "Teela . . ." The white rat gave a sudden cry of pain, her body hunching as she clamped her head between her claws. Fighting for breath, she began to struggle to her feet.

Teela anxiously tried to help her sister stand, feeling Oosha's thin body shaking in her grasp. "Oosha? Are you better?"

"I . . . I can bear it." The fine white rat squeezed her eyes shut and took a deep breath to shut back the pain. Her voice danced with banter – alarmingly light and drained of care. "G'kaa found us, didn't he."

"He came for *you*, Oosha."

"Then he's more an idiot than we thought." Oosha reeled, almost laughing. She gave a jerk of pain and straightened. This time when she spoke, her old seriousness had returned. "It's spread everywhere now. I... I can feel it. Like – " The girl bit back vomit, shaking with pain. " – like ants crawling in my mind."

Teela stared at her sister in pity. "Ants?"

"They rebuilt it all. Everything's... changed. Inside me, it all feels... *wrong.*" Oosha panted, sickened, her fingers exploring the fur of her abdomen. "Teela? I think I'm sterile. Something's gone. I don't even know if I'm Itheem anymore. . ."

"Oosha?" Teela tried to prop her sister up and force her to awaken. "Oosha – Oosha, we need a way to escape!"

"No, no, I think perhaps we need a way to stay." Oosha looked down at her own fine hand – thin fingered, skin as pink as a winter sunrise. "That was always the problem, you see. We can't leave until it's safe for us to stay."

"Oosha?" Teela felt a chill strike her heart as Oosha babbled. "Oosha – help me!"

"Ironic, isn't it?" Oosha hunched, trembling. She gave a tired laugh. "Poor ratties. Poor, poor ratties. We cannot leave until we no longer need to leave."

Oosha wiped a hand across her face, sat up, and blinked suddenly lucid eyes. Terrific and intelligent, she looked about herself at the gathering army of G'kaa. "Teela?"

"Yes? Yes, Oosha?"

"G'kaa captured us. Why?"

"He wants you as a weapon." Teela looked out across the plains with frightened eyes. Warriors from far-flung clans and war bands had begun to arrive, and the land was a dense, seething mass of flesh and fur. "He says we can destroy the dogs."

"We can, but we must not." Oosha licked her lips, breathing heavily to keep the insanity at bay.

"Teela – do you know what would happen if we were to break out into the valley? We would breed like a plague. As the Itheem now stand, we would breed twelve by twelve and strip the world, spreading outward like a locust swarm."

Teela stared, mesmerized, across the black tide of rats. "But maybe that's what we were meant to do?"

"There is no 'meant' – no greater plan. Gods are something we invent to give us excuses for resignation. We are what we make ourselves to be."

The army gathered – fifty thousand warriors aflame with the bloodlust supplied by G'kaa. They had come to see Oosha perform the miracle that would bind them to G'kaa. The girl stiffened and slowly drew herself out of Teela's arms.

"The future is made by little people who know they can do something for the best." Oosha sat perfectly erect, as though controlling her pain with difficulty. "I believe I shall have to . . . to do what's best. Teela –

I'm sorry."

Oosha turned and called out toward G'kaa. The massive black rat sat on a cairn of rocks, proud and violent as he gave passionate speeches to the matriarchs and chiefs. His pose triggered something in Oosha, and she began giggling like a child. She looked at the warlord and wept, staring at him, teeth chattering in a manic grin.

The bitter, awful laughter drew G'kaa's attention. He gazed at the thin, beautiful white rat and gave a predatory smile. "Excellent. You have returned to us at last!"

Oosha choked like a child hiding an especially funny secret. Fighting laughter, she tried to straighten her face and save her aching cheeks. "Um, wh-why am I so special, G'kaa?"

"Because I need a demonstration from you. You will summon the lightning to the towers and make the Gur gate appear."

Oosha looked up at the gigantic black rat and waggled her ears as she replied.

> *"Poor old G'kaa made a mistake,*
> *When the little rat sisters he did take!*
> *No real Hastaasi did he find!*
> *No oracle listens to her mind!"*

Shocked, Teela watched her sister, seeing the tick in Oosha's cheek and the mad-bright twinkle in her eyes.

G'kaa merely hissed, hunching low, his fangs almost as long as war blades. "What do you mean 'no oracle'? Don't you hear the voices?"

Oosha jerked as though shocked. The girl sobbed, looking at him in quiet desperation as though hoping he meant to make a joke. "They won't go away. Like – like a plague crawling in my blood!"

"Good. Then you can speak to the Giants and the old ones. It is better than your mother ever promised." G'kaa turned to look across his chanting shamans, the drummers, and the tens of thousands of Itheem, ravenous for victory. "Hastaasi, you shall be the opener of the way! Through you, we control the Gur gate. Through the Gur gate, we have the means to destroy the other races, and take the world for ourselves."

Oosha looked up at G'kaa with strange, sad innocence.

Teela felt a weird sensation of warning, and tried to reach her sister from the end of her chain leash. "Oosha?"

The white rat walked slowly toward G'kaa, and the warlord suddenly flicked open his war blades in deadly threat. "Hastaasi, you will obey me!"

Small and perfect against the scarred, vicious shape before her, Oosha wandered softly across the sands. Her eyes grew deep and pink and clear.

"For so long, I have wondered – how can I make a difference? What will make it worthwhile having had an Oosha in the world?" The little rat rose onto her rear legs, gazing toward the warlord as she spoke in her beautiful, calm voice. "If you are lucky, there comes a time in life when you may choose between love of self and love of world. In the end, perhaps your only worth is based on how you choose." The white rat stared into G'kaa's single evil eye.

"I love you, Teela. And I'm sorry. Now you will have to find your miracles all alone."

G'kaa began to move just as Teela opened her mouth to make a horrified little cry.

Too late.

Oosha lunged and snatched G'kaa's blade. With a wild scream, she rammed herself onto the needle point, impaled cleanly through the heart.

"*Oosha!*" Teela lunged to the end of her tether, shrieking as Oosha killed herself.

With a blade jutting from her back, the white rat somehow found the strength to raise her head. "No . . . miracles!" She clutched the baton as though it were her savior – and then her little limp white body simply hung and dripped bright blood onto the ground.

Shamans stared in shock – the warriors looked to see the Hastaasi sliding slowly from G'kaa's blade. A shocked silence spread as G'kaa's promised secret weapon simply bled and died.

The warlord gaped at the dead girl – at the pool of blood spreading to lap at a shaman's feet and the stains dripping from his wicked blade.

Teela screamed a desolate, hopeless scream and tore at her leash, frantic to reach her sister's side. "*Oosha!*"

Oosha's blood spread about her little corpse – blood laced with an eerie silver sheen that glittered in the sun. The blood spread across obsidian rock and soaked into the sand. G'kaa stared at the corpse in shock, and then leaned closer and gave a grunt of alarm.

Something was happening. It started slowly, but soon progressed too quickly to see. Silver dust crawled within Oosha's flesh and writhed in her blood. The edges of the wound closed, light glittering on silver particles that shimmered in the sun. The staring pink eyes were glazed in madness, not in death.

Oosha breathed slowly and steadily, and her hand managed to grasp a fistful of dust. "Not . . . funny . . ." Laughing weakly, Oosha stared off into the dust. Her voice whispered as quietly as thistledown upon a summer breeze. "My mentor . . . has a sense of humor." Oosha laughed at herself in bitterness. "It seems I will grow old enough to be wise."

The white rat crawled painfully to her feet before the eyes of fifty thousand warriors – still dripping blood from mortal wound. Dazed, she lifted a hand and stared at the silver motes swarming in her flesh. "Yes. I see now why it wanted the fruit."

Standing stiff and chill, Teela watched her sister and swayed in shock. "Oosha? Are you all right?"

"I am . . . alive." The white rat looked blankly at her hand. "Feel them, Teela. Can't you feel what they are?"

"Machines." Teela could *feel* them – sense them with some strange part of her mind. She looked in horror at her sister. "Like . . . like ants. Rebuilding you."

G'kaa edged away from the patch of blood. With tens of thousands of warriors behind him, he stared toward the girl. "Immortal!"

"Close enough." The madness and the pain came again; Oosha's face twitched until she somehow regained control. "The price is . . . is far too high."

Whirling suddenly to face the warriors, G'kaa let his voice roll out across the plains. "Do you see? Immortal, *and* Hastaasi! Mistress of the Gur gate! She pledges me her power!"

The rats took a breath and instantly gave a wild roar. Fifty thousand Itheem screamed in triumph, their war cries thundering across the ruined land. Blades leapt up in a deadly forest and pumped up and down as the rats chanted G'kaa's name. The warlord turned slowly around, blades spread wide, and drew power from the crashing sound. With warriors shrieking out his name, he slowly sank toward Oosha, his voice low against the yelling crowd.

"Call your lightning, white maggot. Bring the Gur gate and make it stop at my command."

"And what will you do to me if I say no? Kill me?" Oosha bitterly giggled – found the joke funnier, and laughed brightly, tears running down her eyes. "Perhaps you could tear me apart!"

"Don't test me, maggot, or I will!"

"To make a dozen Ooshas – each part growing like a bloody child spawned in pain." Oosha stared at the ground as though seeing her severed organs slowly rising. "Yes. That must be how I'll have to breed now."

G'kaa raised a claw, and his shaman snatched Teela, a blade shooting out into his hand. "If you disobey me – if the lightning doesn't come, I shall kill your sister! Strip by strip, I'll peel her to the bone."

At this, Oosha froze. Her face lost its insanity and became sharp and cold. "If you were truly intelligent, you might realize you have made a worthless threat."

"Your silver ants cannot save her." G'kaa made a signal, and the knife point ground into Teela's side, making the girl give a terrified squeal. "Don't imagine I won't kill her."

"Fool." Oosha turned away, drawing breath as something tore into her mind. "Have your Gur gate, for all I care."

The white rat kept her head bowed until she sensed her sister being lowered to the ground. Eyes closed, Oosha heaved a sorry sigh. "Teela?"

"Yes, Oosha?" Teela wept, shocked by Oosha's death and rebirth – terrified by the knife at her own throat. "I'm here, Oosha."

"You know that I can bring the lightning, don't you?"

"Yes, Oosha." Teela's voice shook with fright – and with a pure, trusting love. "You are the one, the speaker to the magic."

"Then believe it now. Pray, and the lightning will come."

Teela closed her eyes and clasped her hands, praying fervently to she-knew-not-what, straining to make unseen powers heed her sister's call.

A silence fell. Vast hordes of rats stared toward the sisters as the metal towers moaned beneath the breeze.

The power came with sudden violence, sound crashing out to terrify the Itheem. Lightning seethed up from the ground and crawled along a metal spire, lashing upward to dance inside the sky. The lightning spat again and again, crashing out to sheet the land with brilliant, painful light. The call shot above the ruins of ancient Acomar as fifty thousand warriors stared in amazement.

The outer edges of the rat army stirred in fright. A black presence crept onto the nearby dunes. The Gur gate had finally appeared. It smoked with frost, the vortex sucking scraps of litter into its heart. Wide enough to swallow thirty Itheem side by side, the hideous globe rolled down a dune, changed direction as a lightning leapt from a nearby tower, and wavered to a halt between two crackling arcs of power.

Teela stared, watching the Gur gate as it moved. "You did it, Oosha! The lightning came!"

"Yes, I did it." Oosha seemed strangely sorry, and spared a sad gaze toward her sister. "Where power strikes, the gate comes."

The white rat sank down, shivering and clutching at her skull while the surrounding warriors stared at the gate and gave a mighty roar. G'kaa posed in triumph and bellowed for the matriarchs and war chiefs to assemble. The plain boiled with leaping shapes as the Itheem prepared themselves for war.

Shivering, Oosha hunched down to fight the voices whispering in her head, scarcely noticing as the seers quietly led Teela away.

Chapter 10

As night spread across the peninsular skies, Sentinel town lit its streets with brands of burning pine. Torches sputtered from the doors of the pit houses and from staves set in the streets. The long stair leading up the howling mound rose between two solid walls of lights. On the great flat platform at the center of the mound, a ring of torches made a wall against the night as winter winds whipped across the battlements.

The howling platform held twenty nobles, the seer, and his prisoner. Two picked soldiers pinned Tupan to the ground at spear point, the shackles on her leg clamped tightly to a wooden stake. Hung with hunting trophies, the old seer gazed toward the assembled town. Countless faces staring up toward the howling mound. Fur streaming with the smoke of sacred fires, the seer whipped about to scream a challenge to the stars.

The dogs responded, howling in a chorus that split the sky. Hundreds of voices bayed, making Lammada spit and Amiir flee into the night. Voices echoing across the forests, the dogs called for their ancestors, and the seer bathed in the crashing waves of power.

As the moon arose, ancient spirits stirred – the guardians and ancestors of the Uruth race. They came flooding from the forests and swirling from the stars – shapes seen only by the faithful as they shot past the howling mound. The seer yelled in triumph, opening arms to let a wolf-ghost thunder through his flesh and out into the sky beyond. Other warriors whirled about to watch the spirits loop and dance, shouting acclamation as ancestors flashed past their eyes.

Standing under Koja's arm, Aela saw nothing of the spirits, but she had long practice in pretending to watch unseen images in awe. She shrank back as though frightened by a ghost, and Koja sheltered her in the warmth of his coat.

Slumped, sick and dazed, on the ground, Tupan retched. She slowly raised her head. The arrow remained in her leg. She had been left staked to the cold hilltop throughout the winter's day, while the wind hissed across the mound. Her head swirled. She shivered. Her skin was tight with pain, illness, and the merciless cold. With only the vaguest idea where she was, the girl sat up. She found the arrow sticking through her thigh and wondered just why such a thing had been put there.

A ghostly swirl of starlight came to roar and hiss before her eyes. Tupan waved the spirit irritably away, still trying to make sense of events. "S-scram! I gave at the tavern!"

Weak and dizzy, Tupan heard a speech roar out across the snow. The girl found the arrow point in her thigh and, with shaking claws, stripped the fletching from the shaft. Scarcely feeling a twinge, Tupan drew the arrow cleanly out. She looked at the bloody shaft and frowned. It had a bone point instead of metal, and the once-broken shaft had been repaired with twine and glue.

"Cr-crap, I've been shot by a cut-price arrow." Tupan pitched the bloody weapon at a passing ghost, and the spirit swerved frantically away. "You people are *unbelievable. . . .*"

The spirits were getting thicker and thicker on the mound. The howling that had awoken Tupan grew louder and more savage. Lifting her head, Tupan saw the ring of torches and the screaming seer – the old man shrieking hate down into the crowds. Spirits swirled and ghosts burst from the ground. An armed mob gathered about the howling mound.

Tupan heaved a depressed and sickly sigh. "Not one of my better days…"

Coyotes had no gods except for the spirit of the Trickster, who kept a few chosen children in his heart. Tupan sensed something lean and hidden skulking out there in the night. With a nod and a weary wave of her hand, she flicked the thing away.

" 'Sallright. I'll fix it." It was time to get talking. Finding a spear point at her throat, Tupan grabbed the thing and used it to drag herself to her feet. "Thanks, ugly. By the way – you got a bit of rust here, right on the end."

The girl yanked a pennant from the spear and used it as a bandage for her thigh. She clapped a hand to either side of her injury; muttering as the numbness faded and real pain set in. She "fixed it," light spilling from her hands and making the injury close.

The howling subsided in shock as the light of magic shone across the howling mound. Tupan gingerly tested her stance – found the leg too weak to take her weight – and hopped forward to the end of her chain.

"Now, was there a problem I can help you guys with?"

§

"All right – there it is. Keep low and watch for guards." Surolf crouched in the bushes, talking in a whisper to Ra'hish's rats. They had already disappeared into Hern's saddlebags. Even when they had been out, their camouflage made the creatures as invisible as ghosts.

Tugging his huge sackcloth cloak about his face and fur, Surolf hissed to Hern, who staggered out from the bushes and headed toward the road. The town of Sentinel loomed overhead, the howling mound stark against the stars. Torchlight made the huge palisades and sharpened stakes gleam with blood-red flickers.

Hern spared a glance toward the dancing shadows of Uruth soldiers and gave a disapproving grunt, folding his ears back because of the deafening howls. The pony had four small, lumpy sacks hanging across his withers.

Surolf spared a glance toward the town walls, backlit by fires and looming like cliffs in the dark. He trudged across the frozen grass and down toward the beaten path.

Swathed in long coats and cloaks against the cold, two Uruth soldiers stood guard beside the town gateway. Almost invisible in the nighttime shadows, they stirred reluctantly from shelter as Hern and Surolf came plodding down the road. One dog leveled his spear while the other shouted halt – his voice lost against the frenzy of noise from inside the town. "You two! What do you want?"

"Bed." Hern grumbled, shivering beneath his blankets. "I want soup with barley in it, too."

"Traders – bringing in candles and candlesticks." Surolf used his spear shaft to whack one of Hern's bulging bags. "Got delayed on the road awhile. Here's the entry tax."

The sound of another dog's voice was instantly comforting. The two soldiers accepted coins from Surolf, tipped thick-gloved fingers to their helmets in good-bye, and knocked on the gates. The double doors swung apart, opening into the zigzag earthwork designed to slow a charging Itheem horde.

Hern began to plod his way into the town, only to halt as a guard suddenly turned on his heel and frowned. "Hey! Let's have a look in one of those bags."

Hern raised one tall ear and disapprovingly sucked a tooth. For his part, Surolf merely hid deeper in his great flapping robes and plucked at the opening of the nearest bag. Nervous fingers worked at the knots, at last managing to get the bow untied. "Sure."

"Not that one. *This* one." The guards suddenly came close, reaching for one of the sacks closer by. "Open it."

Surolf, his face hidden in his hood, quickly began to unlace the indicated sack.

He had undone half of the laces when the second guard stared at Hern and scowled. "Hey – the first bag just moved!"

"It's . . . um – fish bait." Surolf had undone his sack and noisily rattled the bits of metallic junk inside. "That's. . . that's my trade. Fish bait and candles!"

Hern gave a snort. "And candlesticks."

"All right – and candlesticks, too." Surolf gave the pony a hard jab with his elbow. "Down south it's a very common trade."

A guard gave Surolf a searching glance. "But you came from the north road."

"I . . . got lost!" Surolf helpfully jangled his sack of metal shards. "So, can we go?"

One of the guards suddenly reached toward the first sack.

Surolf gave a heavy sigh and pulled away the cowl of his robes. Where his head should have been, there was now nothing but a naked, staring skull. "*Boo!*"

The first guard froze in fright, and Hern duly kicked him, thumping the guard in his armored belly and slamming him back against a wall. The second guard gave a shout of alarm – a noise totally lost against the howling on the town mound. He lunged with his spear at Surolf, only to drop the weapon and claw frantically at his head as a bag of rats exploded in his face.

Bursting from Hern's cargo sacks, three little nestlings leapt onto the canine guard. The creatures kept the man staggering blind until Surolf could kick him in the groin. The rats sprang free as the guard sank to the ground. Surolf hit the man on the head with a chunk of scrap metal.

He wiped his face, and then cursed as white fur-paint smeared onto his hand. Pulling his robes in about himself, he hid his made-up features beneath the sackcloth hood.

Hern looked at the unconscious guards and gave a scowl. "Why did you start to open a sack that had a rat in it? You should have started with the sack of junk."

"*Tupan.*" Surolf signaled the three baby rats to lie flat in the gutter, and then began to drag away the unconscious dogs. "You ever watch Tupan in action? She always starts to show you whatever you *want* to see, knowing you'll be suspicious enough to outsmart her and look in another place."

"Hmm, perhaps it's just the way she says it." Hern nudged his nose at the gates. "Oh, well. I'll wait outside the walls now. Don't get killed."

"Yeah, great – I'll bear that in mind." Surolf winced as a howl thundered from the streets ahead. "Go wait with Ra'hish."

Surolf closed the town gates behind Hern, leaving them unbolted, just in case he needed a route of speedy escape. He looked about, seeing no sign of the little rats, and ran stealthily toward the ladders to the gateway towers. As he reached the rungs, three shadows appeared at his side.

The little rats sat on their haunches, their silly long whiskers eagerly testing the breeze. "We jumped on his face! It was keen!"

"Great, guys! You did great," Surolf yelled. He wanted to whisper, but nothing less than a shout would have been heard above the howling noise. The three little male rats soaked up the praise like sponges, swelling their chests with pride, and Surolf waved them down into the shadows. "Okay, now, just be careful – um. . . ." The greyhound looked at the three near-identical faces, and chose one at random. "You! What's your name?"

"We told you! It's Eeka, Rika, Shika, Oota, Goota, Koopa, Marta, Barta, Loopi, Hoopi, Shoopi and Jez!" The nestling made a blink of surprise. "The one we left outside is Jez!"

"Right – so that would make you. . . ?"

"Loopi, Hoopi and Shoopi!"

Surolf hitched up his itchy sackcloth robes. "All right, Shoopi, you're in charge. I'll go up the stairs. You guys be ready to help if I need you."

Spear in hand, Surolf took the rungs two at a time until he reached the battlements. The thick earthen wall with its log palisade overlooked a vast stretch of defenses. A ditch and a thick row of felled trees with sharpened branches pointed out toward the pure black night. Above the gates, two log towers overlooked the city roofs. Surolf started up the ladder, only to have two canine faces peer down at him through the trapdoor.

The guards squinted, trying to pierce the dark. "Who is it?"

"It's me!" Surolf's talent for dissembling was a little on the scanty side. "I'm just coming up!"

The dogs above shrugged and let him come. As Surolf's head appeared through the trapdoor, the torchlight caught the skull pattern on his fur. The two guards gasped. One screamed in fright. The other bailed out of the firing platform and slid down the tower's legs onto the battlements – whereupon three baby rats jumped him, beat him silly, and tied him up in several hundred spans of hairy string.

Left alone in the catapult tower with a large, heavily armored, panicked adversary, Surolf blinked and wondered what to do. What would Tupan have done? Surolf snatched up an empty barrel and upended it over the guardsman, knocking him cold and trapping him in a wooden prison. He piled heavy catapult stones atop the barrel and removed the bung so the fellow inside would have a way to breathe.

A second tower stood on the far side of the gate; Surolf could see a single guard on the firing platform beside a sinister ballista. The guard watched the howling mound, where the shouting and capering rose to a frenzy. Time was running out. Leaning from the tower, Surolf signaled the three rats below, who climbed the other tower's stilts and swarmed the guard.

Surolf meanwhile checked the catapult in his own tower. The huge weapon was well greased and protected by a canvas tarpaulin. Surolf stripped the cover away, found a pry bar, and began to laboriously turn the heavy engine around to face the town. After a few minutes of backbreaking work, he had the howling mound in his sights and began cranking back the weapon's throwing arm.

A rat head popped through the trapdoor and looked about. The three little rats came trooping up the ladder. "We tied him up – but I had to bite him in the foot and on the ear. Is that all right?"

"That's fine." Surolf tried not to think of Tupan with an arrow in her flesh. "As long as he's alive, I don't mind."

"Hoopi hit him in the wobbly bits, but that was because he hit Hoopi in the tooth. Hoopi gets cross sometimes."

"Good for Hoopi – here, keep working this winch." Surolf showed the three rats how to cock the catapult. "Did you find any thread?"

"Only hairy string."

Down on the battlements, Surolf took a careful look along the town's defenses. In the darkness, any activity on the walls would be utterly invisible. He saw no sign of alarm, and every animal in the town seemed to have congregated at the howling mound. The greyhound gave a whistle and lowered a length of hairy string into the dark. Moments later, he felt a tug and drew in the string, followed by the scorched, ragged rope that had accompanied him on his adventure into the sea of stars. Surolf made one end tight about the leg of a tower, looked up to the howling mound, judged the angles of approach, and felt the rope vibrate as rats began swarming up from the darkness.

Ra'hish appeared. He gazed over the battlements, tested the air with long whiskers, and flowed soft as gray silk onto the walls. Behind him came the other nestlings in quick succession, popping up like beads on a string. Surolf sent some up into each tower, and the rope disappeared hurriedly from view.

The greyhound took Ra'hish up into the second tower, where the rat warrior began to inspect the ballista. The giant crossbow fired spears longer than a dog was tall, capable of impaling several victims at once. The greyhound gathered Eeka and her sisters and had them watch as he hauled the heavy weapon around.

"This one's the ballista. The spears it fires are by the wall." Surolf watched the nestlings swarm the machine, excitedly touching and testing. "I'll crank it back and aim it. Don't touch the trigger until Ra'hish says!"

Rats tied one end of the rope to one of the spears. Ra'hish joined

Surolf in squinting down the sights toward the howling mound. . . .

. . . where the shouts and cries suddenly had ceased.

Small in the distant firelight, Tupan dragged herself upright to face a phalanx of her accusers. The coyote swayed and almost fell.

Surolf dumped his robes and stripped off his clothes. Standing in the freezing cold, he was tall, thin, and fearsome – his fur painted black with fat and charcoal and bones painted on with pure white chalk. Ribs and skull, hips and spine all shone against the night. He seemed a walking demon. Surolf turned his coal-black eyes to Ra'hish and touched him nose to nose in the oldest greeting of them all.

"Run, run. Be spook." The rat's whiskers jiggled as he whispered. "Itheem take care of things from here."

"Have you got the bones?"

"Got bones. Surolf go." The rat warrior thoughtfully inspected Surolf, and then nodded and let him go.

The naked dog hurried down the ladder and moved off, the painted bones shocking in the dark.

§

Eeka sat upon the ballista and gave Ra'hish a strange little salute. "We put the spear in! I think it will shoot now."

"Good. Now bring me the bags of skulls."

As Eeka shinnied down the ladder, the howling began again on the mound behind her. Ignoring the blood-red torchlight dancing on the rungs, Eeka reached the bottom of the ladder. There, Rika and her sisters had nicely laid out coils and coils of rope.

Eeka tugged at parts of the old burnt cord, and looked very disappointed. "I say, Rika! This rope is all thin and hairy."

"Hmm." Rika pulled at a particularly frayed looking piece, and suddenly found that it had come apart in her hands. "We ought to knot it. Do you know how to tie a knot?"

"I can do a bow!" Eeka sat up on her haunches looking pleased with herself. "Tupan showed me how!"

"Well, we'd better do that then – and maybe another one over here." The sisters busily went about their repairs. "There – as good as new! Surolf will be ever so pleased!"

The whole plan seemed to be going splendidly. As Rika one by one retrieved the bags of skulls and shuttled them to Ra'hish, the other nestlings swarmed happily to their posts. They faded into the shadows and lay upon their little pink bellies, settling in to watch the fun.

§

The seer screamed and ranted, shook his staff and brought savage spirits swirling about his ears. He pointed a damning finger at Tupan and spat her name.

Still wearily healing her leg, Tupan blurted, "What the frot is *your* problem?"

The seer reacted with an incoherent scream of rage. He stormed back and forth across the howling mound, bellowing at his warriors. "Do you see? Do you see what we have here before us! This is a parasite upon the very hide of all Uruth!"

"A parasite?" Tupan raised one eyebrow. "Hoopy! So, do I get piercing, sucking mouth parts now?"

The seer slammed his staff against the mound. "A liar, a cheat, a charlatan!"

"But I *do* have a very cute tail." Tupan rubbed her skull, trying to keep her spirits up and her gorge down. "Lighten up! So some rats helped us get some metal – metal for a game? Big deal! It's you dogs who ended up playing the game!"

"She consorts with goblins, with the enemy!" The seer instantly knew he had won his audience across. "She is a *race traitor!*" Those two words made every dog in a hundred spans scream in rage. Weapons shook, torches waved, and the crowd surged up toward the crest of the mound. The seer crowed in triumph.

Tupan sneered, losing patience at long last. "You people are a bunch of dolts! Did any of you ever even talk to a rat?"

"You don't talk to goblins! You kill them! They're animals!" The seer spoke for the crowd, parading himself around and around as the howling died away. "We can thank the spirits that we had one female among us who saw through your plans! One female worthy of all that is Uruth!" The seer laid one possessive hand on Aela, who simpered sickeningly at Koja's side. "I say death to the race traitor! Death before the spirits of the canine tribes! Let the rat ghosts defend her if they can! Let dog spirits save her if she is innocent!"

The seer had primed his warriors to surge into the attack, whirling spears to run Tupan through. The coyote swayed as she saw them come.

The night split apart to a horrific, feral yell. The howl came from the far edge of the mound, where the torches had abruptly gone dark. With a voice that bayed wild and deep, a savage presence appeared in the night. A prancing skeleton leapt from the night and sent spirits flying madly out across the mound. Bones showered down from above – rat skulls with long teeth and staring eyes. They whistled as they fell, smashing dogs from the mound to send them tumbling onto the streets.

Warriors cursed and ran for cover. Nobles covered the screaming, protesting seer and dragged him to the ground.

A second storm of skulls came raining down upon the mound. Striding amid the bones, the dog skeleton continued its dreadful racking scream, and advanced toward a staring Tupan. Its keening cry broke to a croak, and it had a minor coughing fit.

Tupan looked at the skeleton and blinked in surprise. "Bless you. Like some water?"

"Nope." Surolf wrenched the girl's stake free from the ground and advanced bellowing to drive back a few warriors who thought to surge in close. "Can you hold onto me?"

"Okay." Tupan dazedly took the whole thing as her due, scarcely understanding a thing. "Nice paint job. You know, I think we might have finally found your look." She put her hands about Surolf's neck and clung to him from behind.

A massive spear came winging through the night sky and smacked deep into the wooden stairs leading up the mound. Surolf screamed and ran straight for the spear, grabbing a length of Tupan's chain in his hands. A rope stretched taut from the spear butt to the town gates far below; Surolf flung a loop of chain across the rope and took a running leap from the stairs, sliding swiftly down the chain.

Warriors below came to their senses as Surolf and the escaping prisoner whizzed high overhead. Here and there a spear arced up into the dark, only to reach the top of their flight and curve back down into the crowds, who instantly fled in fright.

Tupan clung to Surolf's greasy back as he whizzed down above the thatched roofs of the town. She looked slowly about herself, realizing the beauty of the idea. "Hoo-hoo! Hey, Surolf – good rescue, man!"

"Thanks!"

With an almighty jerk, Surolf's downward flight suddenly came to a halt. The chain loop had suddenly hit a big knot in the rope. Surolf and Tupan swung like puppets, dangling a dozen spans above the ground. Below them, figures grabbed torches and shouted orders as archers came running from the town's far walls.

"Crap!" Surolf tried to bounce the chain across the knot, but the rope merely jounced and swayed.

Tupan looked the problem over with a critical eye – then took one trailing strand of the bow knot in her teeth and gave a gentle pull. The rope parted. Gravity took hold. The two fugitives began to gracefully fall.

"*Tupaaaaan!*" Surolf squealed like a weasel as he plunged through the air. He hit the thick straw of a well-thatched roof, burst through someone's ceiling, and landed on a rather messy bed. Tupan contrived to somehow alight on Surolf's face, spat straw from her snout, and looked dazedly about as a scream of terror jangled her ears.

A young girl lay in bed trying frantically to cram herself into a corner and hide behind a sheet. The young warrior she had been entertaining lay somewhere under a dusty pile of fallen straw.

Tupan lurched painfully to her feet – idly stuck an apple in the mouth of the screaming girl, and staggered about the place trying to find a door. "Surolf?"

Surolf lunged up from the bed, treading on a semi-conscious warrior and opening an escape route to the rear. With an arm about Tupan, he helped her out into the night, toppling torches to plunge the streets into gloom. "This way! Can you walk?"

Tupan tried to put weight on her leg and heard her own voice cry out in pain. Surolf wrapped an arm about her and half-carried her down a sloping street, helping her hobble span by span toward the safety of the gates.

"*There they are!*" A dog caught sight of the fugitives and raised his voice in a baying hunting call. A dozen soldiers came on the run, pounding down the streets to kill their enemy with spears.

One warrior at the rear suddenly fell, and then another and another. Something small and savage blurred in the dark. Steel sparked, and a dog fell shrieking, trying to stop the blood flow from his arm. Ra'hish parried a spear aside, stabbed a man clean through the thigh, leapt onto another's face, and knocked him to the ground. He poised his blade to punch into the dog soldier's throat. . . .

"*No!* Don't kill! Ra'hish – don't kill!" Surolf bellowed in fright.

Ra'hish snarled but obeyed. He abandoned his victims, and flung torches up onto the thatch. Straw immediately began to burn. Dog soldiers hung back to fight the flames or protect the injured. The rat hissed, whipped about, and suddenly ran away.

Tupan and Surolf had reached the gate. Surolf levered the heavy doorway open, only to see three dog soldiers charging straight toward him along an alley.

With an almighty squeal, nestlings launched themselves from the walls above. Rats crashed onto soldier's helmets, smashing the dogs to the ground. The little creatures cracked their weapons against men's shins and brought them toppling down.

Surolf managed to carry Tupan past the battle and through the open gates. He was already off into the night as the nestlings came rushing past him to escape into the trees.

Hern the pony ran briskly out from behind a bush and crouched to let Tupan flop, stomach first, across his back.

Two dog crossbowmen kicked their way through the town gates, saw Hern, and gave a wild cry. They lifted their weapons, took aim, and fell screaming as a shadow tore into them from behind.

Ra'hish punched one man across the neck and felled him, ducked beneath a crossbow, and broke the other man's shin. He remained behind, facing onrushing soldiers as Hern and Surolf took Tupan carefully away. A dog soldier burst through the gates and made a lunge. Ra'hish clawed under the weapon and ripped bright wounds beneath the soldier's arms, sending the canine reeling aside. Only when the other fugitives had gone did the rat back away, pace by pace. He gave a final foul hiss of defiance and sank into the dark.

Splashing through a freezing stream, Ra'hish caught up to the others as they ran. Hern paused on the edge of the stream, and nestlings gathered anxiously about. Tupan slipped from his back. Shaking and exhausted, the coyote was lowered to the ground and immediately buried under solicitous little nestlings – each one anxious to explain their vital part in her escape.

Hern peeled a warm blanket off his own back with his mouth, and clumsily draped it about Tupan's back. The girl leaned her head against the pony and fixed her fingers in his mane as Surolf quickly wrapped her up from head to tail.

Eeka swarmed her way up a pine tree – marveling at the smell and feel of it beneath her hands. The pine cones were strange new delights – rusting needles seemed like pure magic. Ostensibly keeping look-out, she wrapped her tail three times about a branch and blinked off toward the town. The place was now well and truly aflame, with sparks flying between the thatched roofs. Eeka's toothy jaw hung open in amazement and dismay. "Tupan! Tupan – place iss burning!"

"Let it." Tupan huddled inside a blanket, licked steadily on the head by Hern and hugged tight in Surolf's arms. "I hope it burns the lot of them."

Surolf stared dully at the fires, seeing figures outlined against the light as they beat at flames with wet blankets. With a heavy sigh, he shook Tupan and tried to stir. "We'd better move on. They'll be coming for water from the stream."

"It was all *her*." Tupan slowly shook her head, talking to no one in particular and amazed at the turnings of the world. "It was Aela. She turned us all in. I've never even met her."

Hern gave a slow raise of one brow. "Aela?"

"She doesn't know what she's talking about. She's in shock!" Surolf wrapped another blanked about Tupan's shoulders. "Come on, now – let's go somewhere and hide."

"*Oheeee!*" From above, Eeka leaned dangerously far from her perch using her long tail as a tether. "Ra'hish! G'kaa *ch'ish chik-k'ho maa!*"

The two dogs and the pony looked up in amusement as Ra'hish swarmed up the pine tree and stared off toward the black shadows of

Acomar. Ra'hish froze, framed perfectly in the light. He slid swiftly down the trunk, chasing Eeka before him. "G'kaa comes. Many warriors. Move into the trees and let him pass."

"G'kaa? G'kaa is here?" Surolf's skull mask hung its jaw open in shock. What's he doing here?"

Tupan listened, but didn't understand. She gazed toward the town, and then to the Shield Wall with its endless lines of battlements. The Shield Wall flickered in the night. Tupan blinked, tried to clear her eyes, and then dazedly watched the darkness move against the stars.

Hern lifted his ears and stamped one rear hoof in alarm. All talk instantly stopped.

For hundreds of spans, the battlements of the great wall rippled. A black shadow spread across it, down the earthwork ramparts and palisades, through the defensive ditches, and out onto the roads. Within the shadow, firelight flickered from countless thousands of gleaming blades and eyes.

Rats. Tens of thousands of rats.

They were coming across the wall in a silent, stealthy wave – not a cattle raid, but an entire invasion army tens of thousands strong. The wooden palisade began to collapse from the sheer mass of bodies climbing over it, and the noise of tumbling logs finally drew the attention of nearby guards on the watchtowers.

An Uruth lookout ran toward the town, only to be pulled down by rats like a grasshopper caught by an army of ants. In a high tower, a catapult twanged. A rock thumped into the churning mass of rodents below, the dead swept beneath the unstoppable tide. The rats broke into a sudden screeching charge.

On the town walls, one or two soldiers turned to stare at the tidal wave of Itheem thundering toward them.

Safe and sound in the woods high above, Tupan listlessly watched G'kaa's warriors sweep past and rested her face upon Surolf's fur. "Well – there goes the neighborhood."

§ § §

"RATS! *RAAAAATS!*" The scream echoed as the town walls shook to a deadly blow. Dog soldiers looked up from their fire fighting and scrabbled for bows and spears. Soldiers raced frantically for ladders. A sudden chittering hiss rose to shudder through the night.

Thousands of Itheem were already pouring up across the walls. Here and there, the wall guards tried to hold them back, only to disappear beneath a tide of blades and claws. Rat officers waved banners topped with skins and skulls, directing savage torrents of Itheem into the streets.

Dogs halfway up the ladders hesitated and died, or leapt down into the streets to find brothers and make a hopeless stand.

The Itheem came like a nightmare – an endless onrushing carpet of screaming fangs. Their charge blasted through the dogs' defenses and smashed townsfolk aside. Rats raged down streets, leaping and rebounding off walls like a locust swarm. They poured over rooftops and spilled from eaves. Rat warriors armed with forearm tubes swarmed on all fours into the streets and attacked at a dead run. In the confined spaces, they were invincible.

Dogs chopped with swords, only to have the blows blocked and their enemies leap onto their chests, war blades punching in a frenzied blur of hate. Rats fought so they could smell an enemy's breath and taste his blood, launching themselves at their foes with berserkers' rage. Phalanxes of dogs were blasted apart by rats smashing into them from all sides. Dog archers fired hopeless shots into the onrushing tide, and then broke and ran.

Their walls buried under a flow of rats, the dogs retreated in panic to the howling mound and began to fight a bloody, slow retreat to the summit. With space at last to use their blades, the Uruth finally began to hold their own – but too little and too late. The town was already lost.

Protected by a shrinking ring of fighters, Aela saw the rats closing in. Quick as thought, the girl jumped down the steep, lightless far slope of the mound, slithering on her backside straight down into houses below. Hurt and stinging, Aela sped into the shadows, abandoning the town to its doom.

Fires spread from roof to roof. Uruth civilians screamed as rats burst into their homes.

With fires raging all about, Aela found a deep rainwater gutter. Slithering like a snake, the girl sped to safety on her belly, wincing once as a body crashed lifelessly onto her back. Rats overleapt her ditch in their hundreds, and rampaged into the town streets to clash weapons with town guards; Aela followed the ditch to the town walls, where it ended in a steel grate. She frantically kicked the bars until the grate gave way, fighting clear into a frosty field lit by fires and ripped by screams. The girl wiped her face, spared one brief glance behind herself, and ran on all fours, swift and silent off into the dark.

§ § §

High on the mound, the seer raised his arms and brought storm winds whirling about his staff. In the center of the Itheem horde, G'kaa's shamans screeched with glee and cast bones into burning houses, bringing a swarm of plague spirits up from the flames. Spell countered spell. Spirits bit and screeched high above. Shamans laughed. Unseen forces shook the night with their cries.

Atop a tower, looming like a vast, scarred demon, G'kaa watched his warriors killing every living thing in their path. A pony with a cat clinging to its back raced through the streets, scattered rats with its hooves. It somehow made it through the gates. Amiir rose and fled, squeaking with fright into the dark. Some swooped to rescue their mouse masters, who ran in terror below. One small knot of canines hurtled iron weights wound with strings, whipping the missiles with incredible force into the onrushing Itheem. Most of the dogs scattered and fled, leaping from the palisade in a desperate attempt to escape.

G'kaa watched his warriors fight their way up the howling mound, toward the town's ruling elite above. He bared his yellow fangs in a smile. "Don't surround them! I want an escape route left."

"Yes. Lord." The Itheem officers watched their troops, occasionally dashing down into the fight to bring the frenzied warriors to heel. Rats danced amid the flames and tossed their booty in the air, stripping houses of tools and blankets, cloth and food. The corpses of the dogs were a long-awaited feast. Behind the battle lines, utter chaos reigned.

On the high summit of the mount, the last knot of dog soldiers bore their leaders slowly backward before a screeching, leaping wall of rats. Sword met war batons in showers of sparks. Here and there, the dead fell and were instantly consumed. The dogs held their own – wavered – and were suddenly fleeing down the dark side of the hill. Half a dozen survivors made their way along a ditch

G'kaa bellowed orders to an officer below. "Guard those fugitives! I want at least five nobles to escape!" G'kaa wanted dogs to flee all across the Mornmist valley. He wanted his enemies to raise armies – to gather forces such as the Itheem had never seen. "I'll eat any rat alive who harms them!"

Below the warlord, hundreds of houses burned while rats raised a scream of victory to the stars. The walls were down,. The guards had fled. The Itheem's long imprisonment was finally at an end.

§ § §

Bleeding from a cruel puncture wound to his shoulder, Koja dragged his grandfather along beneath his arm. He draped them in a black cloak, hoping to hide in the shadows of the burning town. One uncle, a sister, and two visiting nobles from Kamla town were still alive – their swords red and notched to tatters by the frantic attacks of Itheem blades. The little group dragged itself onto the town palisades and looked back into the hideous pit that their home had become.

The seer struggled under Koja's arm and tried to head back into the flames. "Let me go! I can raise the spirits! We can hurl them back!"

"We are lost, Spirit-Father!" Koja dragged the old man forcibly backward, blood sheeting his fur. "Run, Grandfather! We have to leave!"

The towers had begun to burn. In the light, a monstrous rat could be seen. Black and foul with knotted scars, the creature seemed bigger than a horse as it shrieked its triumph into the night. The old seer stared at the apparition – felt his own ancestral spirits beating a retreat, and let himself be slowly dragged away.

"To Kamla town, boy! Get there fast. The Itheem are out. We need every spear, every bow, every blade." The old man stared at the vast tide of Itheem that had come to drown their town. "Every blade . . ." He stared at the sheer number of Itheem, stunned that so much horror could so quickly fall. "We slept too long. We should have exterminated them, but instead we built a wall. We turned back raids, and all the while, they were fashioning an army!"

Uruth, Lammada, Miir, and Amiir were still dying in the ruined town. Itheem feasted on their enemies, and even on the bodies of their own dead.

The dogs backed away into the darkness, panting as they gazed for the first time on the true horror of their enemy.

The old seer watched the death of his town and tightened hard old fists about his staff. "Where is Aela?"

"Gone, Spirit-Father! She must have been separated from us in the attack."

"We shall avenge her! We shall avenge them all." The seer slowly straightened his back. "Metal weapons. The Itheem have an oracle! A working oracle! We must obliterate their army, and then destroy the oracle itself. We must reduce them to the mere animals they are – or they will destroy everything good and beautiful."

From dense black banks of pine by the road, something crashed and spilled through the undergrowth. Koja's family sprang forward, swords raised, only to see a slim, red-furred figure thrash helplessly on the ground. Fighting free of the bracken, Aela looked up in shock at the Uruth soldiers, brushed her forelock from her face, and let her eyes flood bright with tears. She made a cry of joy and flung herself into Koja's arms.

"Koja! Thank the spirits you're alive!" The girl somehow made herself seem small and brave, sobbing with the shock of her ordeal. "I-I fell down the mound, and they were everywhere! I killed two with a spear – but there were too many! I couldn't hold them back!" The girl fought for breath, holding herself as though injured in a fight. "We have to go back! We have to save the poor town!"

"It's too late." Koja tried to break the news gently, sheltering the brave young girl beneath his cloak. "We have to go now, Aela. But we'll come back to fight again. I promise you."

Aela made a broken little noise, theatrically strained to reach the town, and let herself be held back. She buried her face against Koja's neck, weeping, and allowed them to take her into the safety of the dark.

The seer clapped an old hand on the shoulders of the young couple as they embraced. "Rebuild. We can rebuild. Hope is with us." The old man turned and led the tiny group of survivors down the road into the dark. "But first, we have work to do."

Chapter 11

The Itheem spread out into green pastures and farmlands, stripping pines of their cones, farms of seed stock, livestock, crops, and tools. They ate the wildlife in the fields and the weeds beside the roads. Every scrap of food disappeared into the insatiable belly of G'kaa's massive army. In this new green land, survival was an easy affair. Warriors used to fighting for each tiny mouthful of food gorged themselves on a dazzling new bounty. Farms and settlements were burning – hamlets, villages, and towns. G'kaa's army had scattered in a rampage of destruction and savagery, killing everything in sight.

From a distant section of the Great Shield Wall, Tupan, Ra'hish, Surolf, and Hern stood watching plumes of filthy smoke rising to meet the dawn. An earthen ramp gave access to the top of the wall, where Tupan's secret gate to Acomar had been found by her captors two nights before. Leaning on the guardrail to keep the weight off her bandaged leg, the coyote wanly surveyed the smoky sky. "They're spreading out into the fertile lands. The valley is done for!" Tupan simply shrugged the disaster away. "End of civilization as you guys know it. Ah, well, you win some, you lose some!"

Sitting miserably on the wall, fingers gripped into Hern's braided mane, Surolf wiped soot and ashes from his painted fur. "Are we safe up here?"

Tupan shrugged. "When you spend life on the run, you get a kinda instinct." Tupan leaned on Hern's neck, gently scratching between his ears. "The rats have all gone out into the fields."

"Bad. Very bad." Hern swished his tail emphatically as he stared across the frosty green fields. "Long war – years and years long. Everything will be changed."

Watching it all with his sharp, intelligent eyes, the rat Ra'hish let his whiskers test the air, and then went back to sharpening his blades. "This raid only. When rats conquer, they dig tunnels for breeding. G'kaa brings no females; he will not stay." His Uruth speech had slowly improved; the other creatures pondered his words.

Surolf looked back out at the landscape with a puzzled frown. "Yes, if it was really an invasion, they'd bring their females." He looked at the stain of smoke spreading out across the world. "They're just destroying, burning, killing. . . . Why?"

"Oosha." Ra'hish pitched a scrap of bark toward the ground, but it was caught by the winds and carried far away.

Tupan looked at the rat and shifted stance, favoring her wounded thigh. "Yeah, Oosha. I smell a scam." The coyote girl leaned her muzzle on one hand and gazed across the Shield Wall into Acomar. "No *way* does G'kaa want to stand out in the open fields and be attacked by dogs. They might outnumber you guys five to one, but face it – dogs are pretty hot stuff with pikes and swords."

"So, why are they here?" Surolf waved an embittered hand to show the destruction of his world. "This is just a food raid?"

"Sort of." The coyote rolled droll, expressive eyes toward Surolf. "What are your stubborn, block-headed dogs going to do about all of this?"

"Raise an army!" Surolf swelled, utterly incensed. "There's ten thousand dog soldiers ready to march the moment they hear the word! And the cats will join us – and the mice, the other races will all join forces! We'll drive the rodents right back into their lairs!"

Tupan leaned on the guard rail and twirled one finger in the air. "Not just to the border?"

"After killing children? Pregnant women in their beds? Never! They'll burn the creatures right out of their nests. . . ." The greyhound blinked, then turned to stare into Acomar. With the coming of the sun's heat, the towers had just begun their haunting song. "The plain of sighing towers. "

Clicking his blades back into the hollow tubes of his batons, Ra'hish settled onto all fours and unhappily fluffed his fur. "G'kaa will use Oosha to summon Gur gate. Roll it over dogs as they make battle. Kill..." how many close-packed soldiers would such a weapon destroy? "...*thousands.*"

G'kaa intended to draw the dogs and their allies into a gigantic trap. Rather than fight a long, hard war, G'kaa had a way to smash the only army that could stop him. With the local army destroyed, the whole valley would be utterly at G'kaa's mercy.

Ra'hish whispered something to the little male nestlings who lined the wall nearby. The creatures bustled off to gather their brothers and sisters. The rat settled his blades on his forearms and made ready to return to Acomar. "We go now. G'kaa's warriors come soon."

Tupan jumped up, her injured leg forgotten, and eagerly dusted off her hands. "Go? Too right! Let's sod off and find somewhere really, *really* far away. Somewhere with beaches!" Tupan had long, long practice in bugging out when things got tough. "Well, time to run like screaming weasels! Last one to an island paradise is a rotten egg!"

Surolf and Hern turned to stare at Tupan in shock. Hern gave a grumpy noise, then stolidly dug his hooves into the ground. "I don't think we should go away. I think we should help."

"Well, that's very nice, Dear." Tupan hobbled, overdramatizing her injury. "Hey, these people were planning on killing me – and now they're *rat chow!* I think that's enough of a demonstration of my cosmic powers for one day! I say we leave while I'm on a roll!"

"*Tupan!*"

All injuries forgotten, Tupan gave an eager wave of her hands. "We can bog off and find a really neat new home! The little rats can sing,. We can make stuff and have a good time – explore places, find hoopy things!" The girl brightened as she warmed to her vision. "Hey, we could become ruin hunters! We were pretty good at that! Maybe we can find that place with the islands in the sea of stars again! Now that's a place I'd like to live!" Tupan grabbed the rat, dog, and pony and tried to hustle them away. "Hey, got your bags packed? Off we go!"

Hern stubbornly stayed in place. "I think we should go stop the war. We should be able to do that."

"Well, let's just have a quick look and see!" Tupan shaded her eyes with her hands and gazed off toward the smoke-shot horizon. "Nope! The war's taller than we are, and has more teeth. Well, looks like we'll just have to make an idyllic life in a distant land! Come on, time to go!"

The girl tried to drag her friends on their way, only to have them resist and scowl.

Surolf stayed beside Ra'hish. "What about Ra'hish, hey? I promised you'd help rescue Teela and Oosha from G'kaa!"

"You did? Well that was really sweet of you!" Tupan clasped her hands on her cheeks and fluttered her eyelashes. "Did anyone notice his girlfriend is possessed by otherworldly forces and *happens* to be held hostage by about a million starved, cannibal warriors? No? Well, those are details *probably* worth taking into the equation!" Tupan pushed Hern's backside from behind. "Come on, come on, come on! Idyllic life with beaches, cakes with that crystallized fruity stuff on top – all of it *just* over there! Better get going!" Tupan planted her back against Hern's rump and tried to heave him into motion.

While she strained and labored, Ra'hish whispered into Surolf's ear, and Surolf gave a cunning smile. Innocently preening himself, the greyhound studied his nails. "Yeah – well, I suppose there're just some things that can't be fixed after all. No real shame on you, I guess."

"*What?*" Tupan had begun using Surolf's spear as a lever, trying to budge Hern. "Fixed? What are you on about now?"

"Fixing things. I guess you just weren't good enough to handle it. . ."

The coyote froze. She dropped the spear in disgust. "Oh, *no!* No no no no no!" Tupan walked away, waving one finger in the air. "That's your idea of fast talk, is it? You're leading pigs now? You are just *so* transparent!"

The greyhound merely gave a shrug. "Hey – I just thought that Tupan fixes things – you know."

"You're trying to appeal to my ego, and I just happen not to *have* an ego." The girl poked out her tongue. "So there." There was an instant of silence. Tupan couldn't help herself. "BUT – if I *did* have an ego, it wouldn't be. . . be swayed by clumsy guilt trips about rescuing rats and stopping major wars!"

Surolf took Hern by the ear and led him back down the ramp. "Hey – it's fine! It was too difficult for you – you just drew a total blank on ideas. It's okay. Maybe we should go look for someone a little brighter."

"Excuse me! *Brighter?*" Tupan stared, agog, and then followed hastily after the other three, planting her hands on her chest. "Am I not the gal who invented fighting tops out of nothing! Am I not the gal who made you *personally* enough cash to go off and marry that traitor scum Queen Aela?"

"Look, if it's too hard, it's too hard." Surolf led the way back down the ramp. "No one's blaming you. . . ."

Tupan raced around her companions to bar their way. "Okay, okay – let's just *say* for one minute that we can divert the lightning and make the Gur gate go away! I mean – how does that really help us?"

Surolf looked at Ra'hish in dawning astonishment. "Divert the lightning . . . ?"

"Yeah, but it's not gonna happen." Tupan waved a hand at the rat. "Because diverting the lightning and rescuing the rat gals loses G'kaa the battle, and losing the battle hurts the rats; and our pal Ra'hish here is a *big* enthusiast of freedom for his little friends! So, it just isn't going to happen. So, there!"

The rat warrior looked quietly out across the burning lands. "Oosha tell Ra'hish Itheem not ready to walk the world. She find a way – but Oosha need time to make it so. We save your world, we give Oosha time to make it so."

Tupan seethed in ill humor, fur disheveled and ears laid flat. With an annoyed sigh, she tramped back up the ramp and began knocking down the secret door that led into Acomar. "All right, all right! So, we divert the lightning and shift the gate. We rescue Oosha and Teela in the confusion. We save the world and everyone's happy." The coyote girl spread wide her arms in appeal. "So, when that's done, can we maybe *then* go off somewhere really nice and have some fun?"

Trooping up the ramp from the frosty fields below, the twelve little nestlings perched in a line before the adults. Fur shining nut-brown in the sun, Eeka sat on her tail and addressed the adults in her perfect little voice. "Ra'hish – are we going off to save Oosha yet, or should we make breakfast first?"

Tupan used Hern as a perching post for baby rats and straightened her ragged clothes. "Don't worry, kids – auntie Tupan's here to save the whole damned world again. We'll head into Acomar, blow up G'kaa, and save your friends."

"I hope Oosha's all right." Eeka waved her funny skinny tail. "We found a bag of flour – and some red things frozen onto bushes. Shall we eat before we go?"

"Red things?" Tupan raised an eyebrow and peeked into a bag held open by a nestling. "Oh, strawberries! Hey – I'll make you guys strawberry pancakes the special coyote way when we get back to Acomar!" Tupan slapped Surolf curtly on the back of the skull. "Don't look so worried! Tupan fixes things!" The girl levered open the hole in the palisade and led the way down into the empty wastes. "Strawberry pancakes for breakfast – rescue the world by tomorrow night. Hey – it's just another average day."

Hern gave a rich, expressive snort and swirled his long white tail. He tramped past a protesting Tupan and made his way off into dusty Acomar, bright-eyed nestlings perched comfortably on his back. Tupan shrugged, chased the other travelers through the gate one by one, and bustled off to work the magic that would save a waiting world.

§ § §

On the fourth day of their captivity, Oosha and Teela sat on a carpet of frost-dusted pine needles and stared across the valley floor. Eyes accustomed to the infinite subtleties of the Acomar wastes simply stared in stunned amazement here. The world was a riot of white, rust-brown, and green. Amid cold fields, vast thickets of pine soared. Little streams foamed crisp and icy between the trees. Fences zigzagged about verdant fields. Burned-down farm huts formed startling black star shapes on the ground. In the clear blue sky above floated the Ghost Mountain, white with snow.

Shivering to the smell of wood smoke on the sharp winter air, Oosha blinked and caught a tentative hold on her*self*. Swallowing, she kept her eyes on the distant mountain peak and spoke a few words to the presences nearby. "I'm better now."

Extending one thin pink hand, the rat took up a fistful of pine needles and felt them crackling in her grasp. Beside her, Teela quietly touched the fur between her shoulder blades.

Oosha's sickness came and went in waves – spiritual, lucid moments interspersed with dazed rantings or cries of pain. Her madness had left her thin and tragically beautiful, habitually examining every tiny thing about her with amazed, new eyes.

Teela stroked her sister's back and carefully kept her eyes on the scenery. "Oosha?" The girl spared a fearful glance at the guards and tried to pitch her whisper to Oosha's ears. "Oosha! I overheard guards talking. They're taking us back into Acomar today."

"Acomar . . ." Oosha drew in the word like a breath of half-remembered fragrance. "Yes. Yes, I suppose it's time."

"But I thought they were invading the valley!"

"By roundabout means. Oh, G'kaa is clever." Oosha slowly stretched, as though she had fought a long, hard fight and was testing herself for injuries. "He wants the final battle on the plain of sighing towers – so he can use his *secret weapon.*"

"But there's been so much fighting!" Teela looked out over the plains. "Itheem have been fighting battles for days! You mean G'kaa is letting his warriors lose?"

"He's sacrificing them. Losing the lives of his warriors just to give the canines a belief in their own superiority." Oosha turned toward a column of rats – perhaps eight thousand warriors – that swarmed across the pretty valley like a hideous plague. "He only uses a few of his fighters so as not to demoralize his army. He keeps up morale by letting his fighters butcher little settlements by the score. Oh, yes. He . . ." The white rat blinked – the sure sign of her reason struggling against the haze. ". . . he is . . ."   Oosha choked and swayed sideways.

Teela hissed and supported her sister's weight.

Dragging in a breath to fight away the agony, Oosha buried her face against her sister's side. "Oh, Teela – I have . . . matured you. But I'm thin – stretched thin as a spiderweb, strands parting piece by piece. . . ."

"Don't talk nonsense!" Teela held the other girl up and tried to redirect her meandering thoughts with simple common sense. "I'm your sister, I love you – and we need you to survive!"

"Do we? I suppose we do. . . " Oosha jerked and shivered as pain rippled through her spine. "Only in the long term. I . . . I can only help you if I'm given time."

"Long life and invulnerability." Teela gazed sadly at her sister, in constant pain. "But will you be wise?"

"By default – maybe one day." The white rat threw off her spasm, eyes opening and gaze beautified by pain. "Wise enough. . . to know that the Itheem must not yet break free. . . "

"We'll find a magic spell when G'kaa is overturned. You'll make it all better – just you see!" Teela turned her sister about and headed her back toward the guards in the trees. "You'll do something wonderful – make the ancient powers kill G'kaa! Then we can find Tupan and Ra'hish and the pony and the little rats! We can go wandering! We can go looking for your magic spell to make the Itheem whole. Just think of it, Oosha! With you beside us, we found a whole hidden cave of wonders – an ocean of stars! We'll find another – new trees, new magic! Something to make all the wars go away!"

"The wars come from mouths, Teela." Oosha limped back toward the circle of shamans and guards that ever surrounded them. "They come from little rats popping out of mothers, twelve by twelve. . . "

G'kaa appeared in the valley below, surrounded by his shamans and officers. The inner elite of the Itheem were filthy from feasting on dog flesh and striding through the soot of burning homes. As the forerunners of the Uruth army appeared at the far end of the field, the black warlord gave a triumphant snarl and ordered his army into the retreat.

Knowing exactly what they did and why, and seething with the pure cunning of it, the rats grinned and sped off toward the ruins of the old Shield Wall. G'kaa deliberately left a scattering of items behind – a child's half-gnawed doll, a string of severed tails, staved and stripped dog skulls – things designed to whip the canines on into Acomar. When the last rat had passed, G'kaa turned his back on the swelling ranks of dogs and simply walked back toward the Itheem's home. A single spell winged after him – a spirit-driven ball of flame that sputtered out and died before it reached him. G'kaa turned, rose, and reared in mocking triumph before his enemies. He then wandered back across the broken wall.

Marching along amid a unit of G'kaa's elite, Oosha and Teela could only pause briefly in the broken Shield Wall and stare out across the lands of Acomar. An army of dogs had gathered behind the Itheem – dense ranks glittering with armored hides and shining steel. There were Uruth running swiftly on all fours, spear-carriers marching shoulder to shoulder, and Miir sorcerers riding wagon back. The dogs had found allies in the cats of the river towns and the raccoons of the forest. Ponies trudged in their midst, dragging catapults mounted on little carts. All the forces of the valley had come to crush the rat attack. After weeks of fighting, the fields at last had been swept free of Itheem hordes. Now the Uruth wanted to sweep the whole world clean.

Stumbling as a guard pushed her down the slope into Acomar, Teela fell against a tall thistle stalk and startled as she heard the thing jingle gaily in reply. The girl looked up to see a ribbon tied about the thistle – a ribbon from which hung a funny little brass bell. Another bell and ribbon hung from a old dead tree limb by the breech – ribbons bright and beautiful and utterly unnoticed by the Itheem warriors. Teela nudged Oosha and pointed, exchanging a sudden glance of hope, and then she was separated from her sister, dragged onward into Acomar.

Above the track, the bell tinkled in the wind – a sound fine enough to carry above the sound of scrabbling feet. Teela gave a smile and began to furtively scan the weeds beside the marching warriors, finally feeling a little joy rekindle in her heart.

§   §   §

Scouts loped swiftly on all fours, arrows rattling in bow cases as they coursed down a road violated by Itheem. Amid a knot of long, lean soldiers, Koja rose onto his hind legs to scan the road. He held up one hand to make the scouts fall into cover at his side. Koja scanned the nearby forest eaves for sign of rats, and crept closer to a patch of road littered with broken toys. "The ground has been disturbed."

Another pit trap; a scout edged close and poked at it with a spear, dislodging the cover from a deep hole lined with sharpened stakes. The rats had left traps both big and small to slow the canine advance – yet it could never turn aside the irrevocable retribution. The armies of light had come to destroy the darkness. The evil of the Itheem would be exterminated at long last.

A scout screamed as a rat erupted from the pine needles beneath his feet and stabbed him through the breast. The rat sped off through the woods. A dozen scouts bayed in rage and raced after its trail.

Koja snatched one man back and roared orders out toward the other scouts. "Stop!"

The shout made dogs halt – all but one who had almost caught hold of his prey. The dog snapped his jaws at the rat, who ducked and ran beneath a trip line. The dog parted the line. A spring-loaded branch whipped a whisker's edge above the rat's head and buried spikes into the dog's chest. The corpse was flung back into the trees where it slid slowly down the hill, blood spreading steam above the frosty grass.

"Spirits curse it! I've told you to remain in ranks!" Koja released the one dog in his hands and bellowed at the others. "If you see a rat, shoot, don't chase!" The young nobleman could see the crest of the Great Shield Wall now – the palisades had been pulled down and the rock face littered with gnawed corpses and things even more unspeakably foul. Koja broke forward, circled the obvious route, and labored up the earthen embankment until he stood at last inside the breech. The first dog into

Acomar, he put foot on enemy soil and glared out across a dead, defiled land.

In the front ranks of the allied army, surrounded by Lammada sorcerers and Miir carefully consulting their books and scrolls of spells, Aela perched in a wagon, paralyzed with fear. All around her sat seers cradling baskets of bones, singing to ancestral spirits and summoning their aid. Trying not to see the destruction and carnage left by the Itheem, the girl bit her knuckles and let her ears hang low.

At her side, the old seer laid a hand upon her shoulder and gave a laugh of glee. "Victory, girl! Victory! I knew we had to share it with you!" The old man seemed not to see the gnawed corpses of valley folk, instead looking toward Koja, framed against the sky. "Victory! Yes, girl – you'll need a taste of victory before we marry you to Koja. He'll be a hero after this – the leader of the alliance! We'll make him the greatest general of all time – destroyer of the Itheem, protector of the valley! With loyalty and example like yours at his side, there's no heights the two of you cannot reach!"

Anxiously trying to think of such heights, Aela closed her eyes as the wagons rumbled past a butchered family and its farm. Holding a cloth against her sensitive nose, the girl tried hard not to be sick.

At the Shield Wall, engineers widened the breech, making ramps that led from the green world into hideous Acomar. With evening leeching sunlight from the skies, the poisonous lights began to gather, pinprick by pinprick, in the shadows of the rocks. Miir knelt to examine the effect, digging out the soil to discover tiny glowing organisms writhing in the dirt. Specimens were tagged and bottled, and the Miir were bundled back onto their wagons as the army of the valley swept onward in a relentless tide.

The rats retreated, but the Uruth brought all they needed to besiege the creatures in their holes. They would lock the Itheem in their lairs and starve them to death. The rats' oracle would be captured and put to worthy ends, or destroyed to make Acomar safe at last. It was a plan that should have been enacted many years ago. The Itheem retreated, and the dogs snarled to realize they had so long feared such an unworthy a foe.

With nightfall coming to shut the short winter's day, the army slowed its advance. Turning back from the troop columns, the allied officers rode to council with their sorcerers and seers. Dressed in armor of bronze and silver scales, the lord of the Chelth Valley came to consult with Koja, Aela, and the council of war.

"My lords, the rats continue to pull back." The old nobleman looked tall and lordly in his armored suit. The gray streaks on his muzzle shone like burnished steel. "Should we withdraw to the wall, or shall we camp here for the night?"

At Aela's side, the old seer drew in a breath of Acomar's foul air, and then released it in slow, cold thought. "The rats fight in the dark as well as they do in the day. They'd love for us to camp and stack our arms!" The seer stood on the wagon to gaze about the plains. "Where are the Itheem?"

"In the sands, Lord! The sands among the towers." The tall nobleman climbed onto the wheel of the wagon and lifted a hand to point. "They must know we cannot drag the artillery through the dunes."

"It will be useless in a night engagement anyway. Send it back and have it plug the breach in the Shield Wall." The seer shrugged away mere machines as unimportant. "The army has marched only four hours, and the rats have their backs to the sea. I say make the kill now, before the rats can filter away in the night and rob us of a clean victory!"

A Lammada uncoiled from beside a little can filled with glowing coals and reluctantly came out into the cold. Tail shivering and arcing, the creature delicately walked on all fours along a wagon's rim. "How does my honored colleague intend to fight an enemy he cannot see?" The cat sat, curling its tail elegantly about its feet. "It's unwise to fight shadows."

"My colleague forgets we are dogs. We are used to practicalities." The old seer's voice brimmed with contempt, and he refused to even spare the cat a glance. "In the moonlight, the white sand dunes will be bright as day."

Undecided, the lord of the Chelth Valley stroked his muzzle in thought.

Seeing the hesitation, the old seer raked the lord with contempt. "Do you forget the sights we have seen along the road? Families dead – whole towns destroyed! Children eaten, their bodies gnawed like mutton bones!" The old seer leaned forward, and other dogs flattened their ears and glared. "You are a weak instrument, my lord. Falter in this purpose, and the spirits of the ancestors will abandon you!"

Dogs stirred, their killing fever whipped up. Whirling away, the lord of the lower valley ordered the troops to advance, packing the ranks tightly as protection against ambushes in the dark. The wagons were abandoned, and the magicians climbed down into the dust.

The old seer kept a firm hand on Aela's arm. "You see, my dear, what weak things lead us?"

"But he is the lord!" Aela looked unhappily after the departing nobleman, half wondering if the man's fears had been justified. "Shouldn't we do as he says?"

"You shall replace him, my dear. It is time the Chelth Valley came under a stronger political order." The old man propelled the girl forward into a land of rolling silver dunes – a place where a dimming purple sky held the silhouettes of titanic metal towers. "Walk, my dear. Walk with me and watch a new age being born. Tonight will see the valley change forever more. . . "

§   §   §

At the head of her busy digging teams, Tupan shouted orders, pranced about, and tried to look useful while she made other people sweat. Standing atop the broken metal tower, a chill wind breezing through her fur, she looked down upon her handiwork and threw open her hands in a delighted cry. *"Hey, Surolf! Surolf – I'm a genius!"*

Struggling to unload armfuls of dripping, stinking kelp from Hern's back, Surolf looked irritably up from his slimy, freezing work. "Great, you're a genius!" Nestlings happily twittered about, laying the kelp down into long troughs dug in the sand and pouring water across the strands, freezing them to ice. "This had better work, Tupan, or we'll be stuffed!"

The coyote girl slipped backward down a long, smooth curve of pylon, landing with a smile. "I told you – the kelp is wet, and wet stuff acts like a path for lightning! It's just like when I made sparks in the tavern to attack the cat!" The girl airily breezed over her plan, twiddling mere details away with her fingertips. "So, Oosha calls the lightning because G'kaa makes her do it – and the kelp hijacks the lightning to another tower! Sooooo simple! We just guide the Gur gate to where *we* want it to be!"

Hern walked on, shaking his back to dislodge dripping kelp onto the ground. Surolf slapped his hand down onto a pile of the stinking muck and spread it in a line toward the broken metal tower.

"We've finished linking only three towers! How do we know which tower Oosha will call the lightning to first?"

"No idea!" Tupan gave a happy little wave. "Be kinda hoopy to find out!"

Dragging a sack of kelp and weeds behind him, Ra'hish worked toward Surolf from the base of the tower. "We must keep watch." Ra'hish found a small dead crab amid the kelp and threw the tidbit to Rika, who sat upon a stone washing her whiskers. "We hide one nestling near each pathway. We blow Tupan's bone whistles to signal – path one, two, three, four, and so on! Nestlings cut the paths that are not to be used, then run!"

"It sounds dangerous." Surolf helped Rika step down from her stone. "I don't want them hurt."

"We'll be careful."

The kelp trails were laid in deep troughs of sand. Eeka and her sisters covered the seaweed with sand and drew thistle wands over the surface to make it rough. By the time they had finished, the trails were utterly invisible – except at the bases of the pylons, where high-piled kelp had been crammed against the metal towers. Here, nestlings burrowed into the sand, holding long sticks with which they were to knock away the kelp from the unneeded trails.

From their perch at the broken tower, Tupan and Surolf oversaw the final preparations, watching Ra'hish direct his little charges into perfect hiding places. Below the couple, Hern nibbled a piece of kelp, made a sharp noise of disgust, and climbed a dune to watch for the army of G'kaa.

Tupan looked across the plain of towers, drinking in the panorama. The rat hordes were approaching fast, units crowding forward in one vast black mass of hate. The silver-armored Uruth trailed behind them, filling the horizon. Sunset sent streamers of purple through the clouds as the metal towers somberly began their evensong.

Faced with the fragile, precious moment, Tupan ate a bug, and then clapped a loving arm about Surolf's shoulder. "Hoopy! Let's go save the world!" The girl clambered onto the topmost stub of the tower and lay flat on her belly to survey the view. Taking a mutton-bone pipe out of her belt, she tooted it once or twice to test the level of noise. "Okay – I'll do the signal stuff. This should do."

Surolf looked at the girl and slowly shook his head in dismay. "They are going to see your scrawny butt up here and swarm this tower like lice!"

"No way!" The girl held aloft a little bag. "Fish fat! We boiled it last night. I'll spread it on the handholds!"

"And when the dogs win, they'll still find you." Surolf grumbled, slung his spear, and climbed to join the girl aloft. "This is a really dumb idea."

"Those are always the best kind!" Tupan made space for Surolf to lie beside her, and spread her blanket above them both as he settled at her side. She felt herself fit against his hip with ease, and moved to bump him. They lay side by side, high and warm, watching the army of G'kaa flood across the dunes below. Tupan rolled onto her back to stare at the sky. Her usual smile fell from her face. "Hey, Surolf?"

"Yes?"

"Thanks – you know – for coming into the town and saving me." The girl turned her flute over in her fingertips. "I was doing okay, though. I had an escape plan of my own."

Surolf fixed the girl with a smug eye. "You did not."

"I didn't say it was a *good* escape plan." With a sidewise glance toward Surolf, Tupan rested her snout on her folded arms. "Hey, Surolf?"

"Yes?"

"We may get eaten by rats or hunted down by rabid killer dogs. I've been shot and frozen, and run a really, really long way." Tupan suddenly reached out to run thin fingertips across Surolf's ruffled fur. "I'm glad I bumped into you." Her hazel eyes glittered with a warm innocence that brimmed with life.

Surolf stared for a long moment, and then gently reached forward to kiss the girl. "I'm glad, too."

"Sorry about breaking your pots – you know, back when we first met."

"That's okay." Surolf tucked the blanket coat in about Tupan's skinny neck. "I can't imagine why I'd ever wanted them."

§   §   §

"*Ready, Lord!*" G'kaa's shaman tightly gripped Teela's neck, a blade in hand. Guards surrounded Oosha in a ring, watching her every move.

The army spread about G'kaa like vast black wings, rustling and screeching as the rats sharpened their appetite for blood. Here and there, fights broke out in the ranks. The warriors chafed in eagerness to hack into the enemy. G'kaa bellowed an order and felt the army ripple to a halt and turned about, perfectly attuned to the force of his own mind.

G'kaa stood with his back to their enemy. The first beams of moonlight traced his scars and chased back and forth along his hide. The rats fell silent and stared toward their warlord, crouching and waiting for their victory.

"The Uruth towns, and then the Chelth Valley, the mountains, and the world beyond! We shall plunder their plenty and be free at last!" The warlord raised his voice into a savage bellow that echoed out across the sands. "*The fit survive! The Itheem will walk the Giants' paths!*"

Fifty thousand voices answered with a roar. Blades flicked out in a forest of steel. Moonlight shattered on the knife points to scatter in a hundred thousand sparks.

On the opposite dunes, the Uruth and their allies had seen the Itheem turn about. Faced with the set-piece battle that their seers craved, the dogs packed their spear formations tight and settled their skirmishers on the wings. Their seers summoned spirits in swirling, howling clouds. Miir-mice chanted in little circles, spreading their hands to begin weaving battle spells.

G'kaa saw their preparations and laughed as he felt the Itheem's triumph in the wind. "Hastaasi, start your spell! Make the Gur gate consume our enemies."

Surrounded by G'kaa's guards, Oosha sat – small, white, thin, and luminously beautiful. She looked about the dense-packed mass of rats, and then glanced up to where the broken pylon stood, stark against the stars. Bells fluttered from a ribbon tied near the tower's base. Oosha considered the bells. She turned, peered through the ranks of warriors, and caught her sister's gaze. Teela flicked an eye toward the top of the tower and gave a sudden, beautiful smile.

"Did you ever play the chasing game when you were small, G'kaa?"

"Games?" The warlord whirled to stare at the sisters, suspicion and disgust brimming in his eyes. "I have never wasted my time on games."

"A shame." Oosha raised a hand to sign to Teela, and the two sisters bowed their heads and closed their eyes. "Here it comes, G'kaa. . . . Ready or not, here it comes. . . "

Chapter 12

Choking the dunes with vast masses of warriors, the Itheem army suddenly were on the move. One instant, they had been nothing but a dark shadow that lapped at the metal towers. The next, they had crossed three hundred spans of ground. They moved like lightning.

Dog soldiers, tired after a long night's march, began to rise. Officers stared for a moment, and then shouted in panic to their men. "*Stand to! Stand to. Here they come!*"

An instant later, the entire world went mad. Rats attacked in an arrow storm, launching themselves like missiles to smash into the canine lines. Rats sprang high into the air, clawing in a frenzy at helmets and heads. Others cannoned straight into the waists of the canine ranks, dodging and parrying spears. The air filled with the carnivorous screams of countless Itheem, and the night instantly dissolved into a red blood storm of hate.

There was no battle – no maneuver. The Itheem were a raw wave of anger, pure life energy blasting its foes. The Uruth in their deep spear phalanxes took the shock of impact, and then found themselves locked in one vast wall of flesh and steel that reeled and shuddered under waves of attack. Reserves charged in to bolster the Uruth battle line, and the ranks held firm. Packed shoulder to shoulder and thrusting with their spears, the dogs held the Itheem hordes at bay. The rats frenziedly tried to fight past the spear points, leaping high onto their enemies. Dogs fought furiously for their lives. The push did not falter; more rats climbed over the bodies of stalled comrades, rodents rolling over one another like sea foam. Dead rats piled high atop fallen dogs, and still Itheem battle waves came on and on. They mounded into deep, churning masses that would ebb from the fight only to gather, bunch, and rush again. The night overflowed with a deafening storm of battle cries.

Deep in a pike phalanx, Aela crouched beside the old seer and his sorcerers as they flung scraps of rat hide into a brass bowl filled with flames. The girl clamped her hands against her ears and screamed in fear.

Itheem battle rage shuddered through the skies. Locked in the front of the canine lines, Koja heard the girl's scream and roared encouragement to the soldiers all around.

He fought with sword and buckler, hacking and stabbing individual Itheem that wriggled past the forest of spear points. The young warrior ran crouching along the front line of his soldiers, hurtling himself at one gap after another – here pinning a rat that dodged beneath a pike, there chopping a creature that hung screaming on a pikeman's chest. A dense wedge of rats smashed into the lines, and Koja slipped and fell, stabbed one Itheem even as another shoved a blade through his thigh. The rats laid claws on him and dragged him out among their ranks, blades skipping from Koja's armored suit. The noble flailed helplessly, his sword too unwieldy to face Itheem blades.

A hooked pike reached from the Uruth side, jabbed through Koja's scale cuirass, and dragged him back toward the dogs. The pikeman held Koja back from the Itheem as dogs lunged forward. A raccoon armed with a shield beat the Itheem back, and soldiers snatched hold of their lord. Guarded by a dozen spears, Lord Koja was dragged back to safety, bright blood spilling from his injured thigh.

§

The battle once again stalled, the Uruth army shoving at the lethal wall of Itheem.

G'kaa the warlord merely sat upon a dune and gave a slow, bloodthirsty smile. His one eye turned toward Oosha. The seers who held Teela put a blade against the young girl's throat.

Oosha and Teela ignored it all. A slow throb of power began to ripple upward from the ground. The Itheem lines seemed to take a breath as distant thunder sent a shiver through the sands.

§

The first stab of lightning flashed so brightly that the battle froze in its tracks. The blast of sound numbed the war cries. A great blue tongue of power licked up along a soaring metal tower. For agonized seconds, the pylon wore its crown of light. The brightness suddenly vanished to leave an impenetrably dark night.

In the violent purple after-dazzle, Tupan and Surolf glimpsed the entire battle in the dunes. G'kaa and his shamans hung well away from the battle lines, isolated and alone as they forced Oosha to summon the ancient powers.

Lightning stabbed skyward a second time, blue sparks clinging like deadly silk about a metal tower.

As stark light froze the battle and the dunes, the two canines scanned the sands and cursed their dazzled eyes. "*There it is!* Over there by the fork-shaped pylon!" Surolf shook his head, trying to clear his night vision. "The Gur gate's coming!"

The gate loomed over far-distant dunes, rolling with a deceptive laziness but drawn to the lightning like a fly to carrion. A third bolt sheeted the battlefield with light, freezing it in a tableaux of slaughter.

Surolf rose from cover to kneel on the edge of the tower, judging the approach of the fast-moving Gur gate. The black sphere of the gate – a circle of annihilation two dozen spans wide – came seething through the dunes leaving a frost scarred path in its wake. "Here it comes!" The greyhound raised one hand, then chopped it down. "Blow for pathway three! Pathway three!"

Tupan drew in a vast breath of air and blew three shrieking blasts on her whistle. Far below, little nestlings erupted out of hiding in the sands, and ran past G'kaa's astonished shamans to flick wet kelp away from the bases of two towers. The nestlings worked in a flurry of feet and sticks, and then fled for cover as Tupan blew another piercing whistle blast.

G'kaa looked up at the broken pylon while behind him the captive sisters summoned another power surge. The nestlings flung themselves into cover as a lightning pulse rushed up from the ground below. Teela and Oosha hunched, eyes closed. Power leapt into the tower, struck the kelp channel, and suddenly raced off sideways beneath the sand. Steam blasted up beneath the surface, showering scraps of molten glass. A split second later, the lightning climbed a distant tower. Sparks danced and crackled about the pylon's crown.

From their lookout high above, Tupan saw the Gur gate swerve instantly aside. "*Done it!*" Surolf rose to watch the gate. "It's coming perpendicular to the battle lines! Blow for line four!"

G'kaa gave a roar of rage, saw Tupan's snout blowing a raspberry at him from above, and ordered his bodyguards to climb the broken tower. The huge rat watched Ra'hish's nestlings streaking to safety across the dunes, saw the line of blackened kelp that lay smoking on the sand, and cuffed Oosha's guards away.

"Go! They've made paths to divert the lightning! Dig up the weed! *Go! Go!*"

Freed from all but G'kaa and a single guard, the two sisters flexed their fingers in the sand. The ground rumbled as fresh lightning swelled somewhere deep below.

G'kaa whirled to see his army still locked in an even fight with their enemy. He reached out to shake Oosha wildly by the fur. "Stop! Hold the lightning!"

Oosha kept her eyes closed and gave a savage smile. "Too late, G'kaa! The game's begun!"

Between two pylons nearby, G'kaa's guards began frantically digging at the fresh-turned sand, striking kelp half a span below. The warriors snarled and began digging the seaweed from the hole. A blast of light came crashing into a tower a hundred spans away. The lightning seemed to bulge before racing through the sand, right toward them. The rat warriors flew apart, burned to scraps by the lightning as it ripped along the seaweed trail.

Snarling Itheem meanwhile climbed the broken pylon.

Peering down at them from above, Tupan gave a curse and thrashed her tail. "The lines are broken! G'kaa's rats are running back and forth over our damned kelp!"

"We can still drag the gate away!" Surolf stared down at the sand, his mind making a dozen calculations. "There are still lines running between towers six and five! We can link them to Oosha's tower by another line! Get down to the ground!"

"Wait!" The Itheem guard were clambering up the broken tower at an impressive rate. Tupan let the rats climb a deadly thirty spans above the ground, then snatched Surolf by the hand and leapt onto the slippery slope that led to the sands below. "Come on, Gray-Butt! Let's slide!"

Surolf screamed like a frightened weasel as Tupan launched him whizzing down the shiny metal slope beside the climbing path. As they whizzed past the Itheem, the rats slashed at them with their blades. One rat leaned out too far, lost its grip, and fell screaming onto the slide. As she passed, Tupan threw her bladder of fish oil at the climbing path below the remaining rats and cackled as she shot toward the ground.

"Enjoy the view, rat boys!"

The rat that had fallen now slid just below Surolf and Tupan. He thrashed and tried to hack them with his blades. Surolf battered the creature with his spear haft, fighting back and forth as they slid at breakneck speed toward the ground. Finally, Surolf managed to flick the Itheem off the polished path. The rat tumbled like a mad toy. As the slide flattened out, the rat crashed into a pile of soft sand and, in turn, became a landing pad for the canines. Tupan shook sand out of her pelt, dusted off her smoking rear, and instantly relieved the unconscious rat of his two batons.

"Quick! Gimme your spear!" Tupan planted the weapons butt down in the ground, the business ends pointing straight up the slide.

High above, the Itheem guards bickered at one another like furious squirrels trapped up a tree.

Tupan thumbed her nose at the creatures, slapped Surolf on the shoulder, and began to run across the sand. "Go repair the line you need!

I'll try to get Oosha to give you time!"

§

G'kaa's shaman held a blade to Teela's throat while the warlord clutched Oosha and screamed a frantic order at her.

A third lightning blast came. The Gur gate paused, swung slowly about, and gathered speed as it charged the Uruth battle lines.

G'kaa laughed aloud and snarled to his guard, "The gate is on course!" He flung Oosha aside. She ran into her sister and tumbled to the ground. "Kill them! Kill them both! Throw the Hastaasi's body in a fire!"

"Teela! *Run!*" Oosha sprang at Teela's guard, biting deeply into his face. Teela blinked and found herself running across the sands.

G'kaa snarled an order, and the shaman let Teela run free. "We have the Hastaasi! She's the only one we need!"

The shaman fell upon Oosha, stabbing her in a frenzy of hate. Oosha clamped her fangs all the harder, ignoring the knife that hammered into her, and ripping her claws into the shaman's flesh. In time, the shaman staggered backward, bleeding and mad with pain, and crawled away in agony across the sands.

Oosha panted, her wounds closing slowly on her sides. She laughed, the sound growing louder and madder, her mirth soaring huge and wild as she saw her sister running free across the sands. "You have lost, G'kaa!" Swollen with rage and panic, the warlord watched Teela run and felt a sudden thrill of fear. Oosha's laugh tore at him like fire. "Yes, G'kaa! I can't call lightning. I am a worthless trophy – the power was Teela's, never mine!"

From the sands nearby, something large and muscular emerged. First came one leaf-shaped ear and then another. Then arose a pony, cascading dust and weeds from his back. He lumbered after Teela and scooped her up with his neck. Clinging to his back, the rat gave a little wail of fright as the pony stretched out into a gallop and made his way toward a distant dune.

G'kaa's eyes widened in horror. He whipped about and saw Teela racing away. With his guards scattered and his shamans down, the warlord gathered his huge muscles and launched himself in a dead run after the pony. "*Witch!*"

§

On a high dune between two towers, Teela leapt from Hern's back and hurriedly conferred with Surolf. Behind them, G'kaa closed in pursuit, the gigantic rat roaring as he scented Surolf's blood.

Suddenly a chorus of shrill little battle cries erupted from the dunes. Twelve tiny nestlings burst out of the sands and drove the warlord to his knees, leaping and kicking as they fell on the vast creature with their tiny little blades. Dripping blood, G'kaa battered infants aside, sending Rika sailing far off into a dune. A whip of his weighted tail scattered the nestlings like chaff. The tiny creatures spilled madly across the sands. G'kaa found Eeka lying dazed on the dune beside him and rounded on the girl, flicking out his blades.

From behind the warlord, a hated voice hissed a low, cold challenge. "*G'kaa.*"

"Traitor!" The warlord lashed his tail and slowly turned about. "Race traitor!"

"All just words." Ra'hish stood with blades bared and wind whipping past him. "You want the Itheem to remain parasites. Oosha thinks we can become something more."

"Oosha is a freak! A giant-blighted freak!" G'kaa drew closer, foaming and shuddering with hate. "We are the Itheem – and our creed is fight or die!"

The gigantic black rat lunged with a double punch, his long blades stabbing for Ra'hish's heart. He had scarcely begun to move when Ra'hish simply faded aside. The young warrior moved with whiplike speed, twisting to spear his blades at G'kaa's extended arms. Sparks flew as G'kaa parried. He slammed his forearm straight into Ra'hish's face. The smaller rat went flying, hurtled half a dozen spans by the sheer force of the blow.

Ra'hish shook himself, wove to his feet – and leapt aside as two giant blades punched down into the space his spine had occupied a moment before. Ra'hish hit the sand, leapt again, and ripped with his blades as he streaked past G'kaa's black hide. He tore a long shallow wound across the warlord's flank.

The black rat ignored the hurt and came snarling after Ra'hish's blood. G'kaa punched left and right, making Ra'hish parry with his forearms one by one. The massive force of each blow rammed Ra'hish backward through the sands, the shock almost fracturing his arms and slowly buckling the tube-shafts of his blades. "*Teela! Whatever you have to do, make it quick!*"

The girl had run to a dune overlooking the armies and twittered in confusion, unsure what to do. Beside her, Surolf watched the armies buck and surge. He laid a hand on the girl's back and spoke quiet, calming words. Sitting cross-legged beside her in the sand, he pointed to the onrushing Gur gate and drew lines of possible pathways in the air. Teela stopped her panicked panting and listened to the dog, realization dawning in her eyes. The girl closed her eyes and hunched in a little ball, concentrating fiercely as she tried to bring the lightning to her call.

G'kaa flicked a glance at Teela, and then at the Gur gate rushing straight toward the canine battle line. Traveling along the flanks, it would carve through the rear of their formations, scattering them like ants. With a roar, the warlord fought toward Teela, but Ra'hish desperately flung himself in the way. The warrior was hurtled aside – sprang back and punched a blade hard into G'kaa's ribs. He struck again and again, in a frenzy of rage. Lightning flashed. G'kaa shrieked and whirled, smashing Ra'hish aside with a baton blow. One arm broken, the warrior wheeled through the air and crashed limply to the sand.

"*Hey – laughing boy!*" The voice sounded from just behind G'kaa.

The warlord whirled and gave a savage snarl.

Tupan – nude from the waist down – blithely threw her skirt over G'kaa's eyes. Nestlings came running from the dunes, pelting the warlord with dripping seaweed. The gigantic rat ripped the skirt in two and saw Tupan standing a few dozen spans away, smiling and waving her fingertips. The warlord lunged toward her, fangs wide in rage. His feet pelted hard on a carpet of wet seaweed blobs and sand.

Tupan changed her coy little wave to a salute of fond farewell. "Bye-bye!"

G'kaa whipped his head to stare at Teela – and suddenly lightning blasted into the nearest tower. The crackling blue light wrenched sideways and leapt and crackled along the seaweed strand, whipping straight through the kelp at G'kaa's feet. The warlord screamed and tried to jump away, but a thick snake of lightning arced up and lashed across his hide. The black rat fell, clawing, to the ground. He writhed on the seaweed as lightning blasted through him. The blue surge of power vanished. G'kaa fell in a scorched and hissing mass, his blades molten red and his lifeless claws gouging at the stars.

Taking a bow to the nestlings, Hern, and Ra'hish, Tupan shook her head in wonder. "Oooooh, sometimes I'm so good I just wish I could marry myself." The scrawny coyote gaily wagged her tail as the nestlings gathered on the sands. "Great going, kids! You're honorary coyotes from this day forth." A cold wind blew below Tupan's waist, and the girl gave a sudden frown. "Hey – any of you kids know a reliable tailor?"

The lightning blasts had zigzagged the Gur gate. It now came rolling on a mindless line right along the contact line between the two struggling armies. As the gigantic sphere approached, rat and canines, cats and raccoons, frantically retreated. Teela brought small crackles of lightning from opposing towers, carefully parting the two armies and holding the hovering sphere between the hordes of warriors.

From the dunes behind the rats, a supple figure walked quietly forth, a creature that shone ghostly white beneath the light of the moon. Oosha's hide was scored with wounds that closed to leave her utterly unmarked.

Unearthly eyes of blood pink scanned soldiers and warriors, who stared and shrank away. Unafraid, the little rat paused next to the seething, ice-cold Gur gate, looking briefly into the blasted landscape within. She perched herself on mounds of the dead and scathed the living with her eerie gaze.

"This war is over."

Seers and officers started forward, but the strange, calm creature spoke out first in the Uruth tongue, and then in Itheem, forcing the outcries instantly to stop. "We are Uruth and we are Itheem, and we say this war shall stop. If you do not stop, we shall let the Gur gate have you. You may fight each other in the land of the dead and leave our world for those who care to make it sweet."

Someone roared and threw a spear at Oosha, she winced and closed her eyes, letting the weapon cut a wound along her side. Teela gave a cry and made the Gur gate instantly start forward, but Oosha lifted a hand and stilled her sister with a single word. Her fingers dripping with her own silvery blood, Oosha walked toward the dog that had tried to strike her down.

"Pointless. Utterly pointless. You have no idea the horror that you face – the horror that is our lives. Kill an Itheem, and countless thousands take the dead one's place." The girl's wound turned silver as *something* came from her bloodstream – building, healing, replicating – knitting her whole even as she stared into the eyes of the retreating dogs. "Churning, seething – breeding like maggots in a corpse. *That* is the secret of the Itheem. And that is why I cannot allow my race to seize your world."

From the Itheem came a sudden surge, and again the Gur gate moved. The rats froze in place as Oosha turned and signaled to both sides. The thin white rat stepped down from her rostrum of the dead. "We will meet the leaders of your races in one hour's time. Until then – tend to your wounded and minister to your dead."

A spark glittered inside the Gur gate – a sense of *presence* that suddenly gave the evil sphere life. Oosha spared the gate one brief glance, and then withdrew toward the towers high above.

§

An hour later, the truce remained in effect. Injured fighters were pulled cautiously away into the rear lines, each side fearful of coming too close to the enemy.

On a sandy ridge overlooking the battlefield, Ra'hish and Hern settled on either side of Oosha, joining the thin white rat in staring at the nervous battle lines. Tupan, Surolf, and the nestlings lingered nearby, tending wounds.

Hern gave a deep, expressive snort and flicked his ears. "Will they talk?"

"They'll talk." Oosha was pale and tired, desperately glad to have Ra'hish and his friends at her side. "Let's go make sure."

Favoring his newly repaired arm, Ra'hish escorted the girl quietly downhill. Oosha walked hand in hand with her sister. Surolf followed beside Hern, who bore a rag-skirted Tupan and a set of weary nestlings. The little group made their way to the bottom of the sand hill, where canine nobles and rat matriarchs gathered nervously beside the sinister black shape of the Gur gate.

As Oosha's party approached, a haggard old figure rose from among the dogs and shook his fist at the coyote girl. "*Race traitor!*"

Tupan saw Aela supporting the old man, and instantly her face was wreathed in smiles. "Aela – and the mummy!" The coyote prodded her outstretched fingertips together in sudden glee. "The first item on the agenda is for you two to kneel and plant a kiss upon my perky – "

"*Tupan!*" Oosha snapped, more than a tad the worse for wear. "This is serious. Please be still just for a little while."

Going into a magnificent sulk, Tupan sat cross-legged on Hern's back and pretended to ignore the whole peace conference.

Oosha and her sister took their place at the council of war. "Are you ready to speak?"

From among the rats, Oosha's mother suddenly loomed; a creature grown sleek with good living and furious with the current turn of events. "You are my daughters! You will obey! Attack these canine creatures at once!"

Teela hissed and bared her fangs, and her mother shrank away. "We have had enough of matriarchs. It is the likes of you who have kept our race in hell for centuries!"

Tired and almost bored, Oosha raised her hand. "Enough. Have the Itheem and the Uruth agreed to speak?"

From among the dogs, the old seer gave a sneer. "Are you not Itheem yourself?"

Oosha merely gave a shrug, as though she did not know.

Standing with one leg bandaged and one arm held against his chest, Lord Koja of the Uruth made a weary gesture at the plain of sighing towers. "And if we refuse to come to terms with one another?"

The white rat gave a tired sigh. "Then we shall use the gate to thin your armies. You will be forced to draw apart." Oosha looked at Teela and shrugged. "We will not allow either race to destroy the other. It would interfere with our plan."

An Itheem officer shifted stance, feeling strange to be bereft of his war blades. He spoke in Itheem – translated by Eeka, who perched prettily before the Uruth nobility. "What plan? What would you have us do?"

The white rat quietly closed her eyes. "The Itheem must change. We must control our breeding and win a place as partners with the other races of the valley. I want us to have the chance to blossom. I want to give us the chance to save ourselves." The white rat looked across the assembled valley peoples with her weird pink gaze. "I want you to allow us to build a joint town on the border; a town where rats and other races may try to learn to live in peace. It will be administrated by a council made of all the intelligent races of the valley – Lammada, Taezam, Miir, Amiir, Equine – plus the Uruth and Itheem. We shall make the town together, side by side."

The old seer leaned on Aela and gave a hiss of hate. "So, you intend to force us into letting these . . . these *creatures* flood out into the valley!"

"There will be rats in the valley, Seer. But rats shall not *breed* in the valley." Oosha looked back toward the waiting masses of Itheem. "Only those rats that the committee licenses as worthy will be allowed to move out among you."

The rat desperately searched among the canines for a friendly face or an understanding eye. "The Itheem can offer you so much as friends! Will no one even try this experiment? Think of all the things we can be together if we succeed in making peace!"

Lord Koja listened. Evading the old seer's eye, he quietly settled his wounded arm. "The rats will still breed here in Acomar. How do we know the rats will not simply invade us again once our army has withdrawn?"

"If either race attacks the other's homeland, we will use the Gur gate to stop the war."

Dogs and rats all murmured, some in shock and some in hope. The old seer of the dogs grumbled violently against it. Koja looked at the Itheem and seemed to truly see them for the first time. They were on the verge of an agreement, and Oosha gave a wan, tired smile.

"*Look out!*"

Ra'hish hurtled Oosha and Teela aside. An instant later, a smoking, screaming figure crashed into their midst. G'kaa, his fur charred and red with burns, raked Ra'hish with his claws and snatched Oosha by the tail. He flung the white rat toward the Gur gate nearby. Koja somehow snatched at her in passing and batted her aside. Oosha landed on the sand beside the sizzling black sphere.

G'kaa lunged at the girl again. Weaponless, Ra'hish leapt to the attack, springing on the black rat's back to bite his spine. G'kaa bucked and leapt, flinging off his assailant. With a triumphant roar, he lunged at Oosha and reached out to snatch her up in his blackened, smoking hand.

A deep, amiable voice rumbled at the black rat from behind. "Excuse me – but now you've become annoying." Hern the pony – still bearing Tupan – pivoted and kicked once, twice.

Stunned, G'kaa staggered backward and brushed up against the crackling Gur gate.

"I think you should leave." Hern kicked a final time.

G'kaa screamed as he was hurtled into contact with the sphere. The surface instantly sucked him in, and the warlord's figure dwindled into the endless abyss.

With a sudden stab of power, the Gur gate became once again *aware*. The thing became a sphere of brooding colors that seethed and swiveled slowly, as though drinking in the sight of the armies on the dunes. The gate swiveled to face Oosha, fixing her beneath its horrible gaze, and then snapped suddenly into dead, dull blackness once again.

Thousands of faces stared in silence at the Gur gate. G'kaa was gone without a trace, and now the metal pylons began to softly moan beneath the wind.

Quite pleased with himself, Hern flicked his tail and twitched his long spotted ears. "Can we talk about making this town now? It really sounds rather interesting."

The old seer snarled, but Koja calmed him. The young soldier consulted with the valley lords, and then came quietly over toward Oosha and took her by the hand. "We shall allow your town to grow. You will have five years for it to prove itself as a place of peace."

Oosha's mother gave a scream of protest – the sound drowned out as rats and canines drew into groups to talk. Oosha made to speak again, but Ra'hish hushed her and lifted the girl onto the pony's back, and Tupan welcomed the girl on her lap. The armies reluctantly began to part, moving off into the sands.

Hern plodded his way uphill, nodding quietly with his ears. "I think we did a good thing."

"I think so, Hern." Surolf watched the rats drawing slowly back into their ruins and caves. "I think I'd rather like to make a town."

As they wandered between the wondering armies, the nestlings began dancing in the silvery light.

"Is it all right now, Auntie Tupan? Is the war all done?"

"Hey, it's all fine. I told you Tupan fixes things." The coyote helped tiny Rika clamber onto the pony's neck. "Let's go sit on the hill and sings some songs."

Warriors and soldiers watched the strange little party make its way toward the broken tower, while all around the plains, the pylons drifted an unearthly music up to greet the moon.

Epilogue

In the warm airs of spring, the Ghost Mountain hovered like a glorious white wraith high in the clear blue sky. Far below, the lowland forests soared tall and dark and green, and the grasslands were starred with little flowers. At the forest fringe, white hawthorn frothed with brilliant blooms, and lazy butterflies wig-wagged their way between the trees. Birds chirped and fat bees hummed, washing the borderlands with a timeless sense of peace.

Amid new-plowed fields, a strange ring of walls had miraculously appeared. Perfectly smooth and faced with plaster made from pounded shells, the outer battlements were bright and clean. There were no sharpened stakes or battlements, no pit traps or catapults. "Squeaktown" had made a study of preparing itself for peace.

It was a strange town – part shelter and part school; an armed camp where no weapons were allowed. The low shapes of Uruth houses made a ring about a huge new central howling mound, while between the dog huts, tunnel entrances led to warm rat burrows beneath the soil. A police force of picked canines kept order in the streets – and Oosha's peace keepers kept a quiet watch on life below. The first cautious trade fair had been announced for three months hence, and the Uruth and Itheem communities were already pondering what to offer.

Already the town was becoming the wonder of the valley. The first windmill had begun operation only days before, Surolf lounging back on a sack of ground grain to watch his handiwork. The mill also pumped water, providing Squeaktown a public bath – a place much frequented by local rats. Canines blinked in astonishment as they realized that the ancient enemy were really rather vain. Rats would sit at the baths and gossip for hours, combing whiskers as they dried their fur in blasts of air from the mill sails that whirred in brilliant splendor above.

Surolf had made many, many miracles – a sewer system to keep the streets and tunnels neat and clean, public water pipes running in from a nearby spring, and even lantern poles to illuminate the streets at night. He was an engineer in paradise – with Tupan ever present to slap him like a squealing weasel whenever his plans lost touch with reality.

Quietly strolling the well-swept streets, Oosha walked on all fours next to her beloved Teela, their tails forever entwined. Ambling along beside them in unaccustomed springtime finery, Lord Koja matched the rat's slow place and enjoyed the morning sun. Tall and handsome, the young dog stroked his tan-colored nose and sniffed at the clean scents drifting on the wind.

"I have so looked forward to the spring. . . ."

"It is beautiful here." Oosha looked around at the flower boxes planted outside every canine family's door. "The colors in the valley are almost like a dream."

"Were there no flowers, then, in Acomar?"

Teela tilted her head, watching a bumblebee as it struggled aloft with great beads of pollen clinging to its feet.

"Oh, yes. Sunflowers are there – giant things growing row by row. We plant them for the seeds. And bean flowers, and thistles, too." The girl let her gaze drift down to see a little stand of daisies shining in the sun. "But nothing like these. Nothing that was just there *because.*"

Lord Koja turned to look at the rats with his fine brown eyes. "Is it always so ugly there, then?"

"No. There is a majesty. A stark, essential majesty." Teela looked back toward her home a few hundred spans away. "The rocks shimmer in summer fog banks when the nights are dark. In the mornings, the tower song echoes out across the sands. And the night lights come out each evening to dust the soil like tiny stars."

"I should like to see it someday."

"You shall, Lord Koja. We shall show it to you ourselves."

They had reached the base of the howling mound and stood in the bright, airy central square. The surface was subtly curved to lead water down into the gutters – one day perhaps the streets might even be paved. The three creatures – white rat, gray rat, and dog – looked out across the square and tried to imagine it as a marketplace filled with travelers and life.

Koja looked at a dozen rats avidly playing fighting tops with three raccoons and a bat. As he watched the little crowd cheer on their champions, he let a wistful mood creep into his eyes. "Will the trade fair be a success? Is there anything one species has that the other possibly can need?"

Oosha shrugged. "Itheem smiths are better than yours – and our craftsmen make better gadgets." Mostly traps for killing, hidden weapons, and spring-loaded blades – but other things could be made, given time. "And everything the valley people have is new to the Itheem. There is art, pottery – all the strange things you so take for granted.

"The Itheem will want such things someday soon. If you are not constantly having to leave your hole and flee, you have a chance to make it comfortable. I foresee an endless stream of possibilities. . . ." Oosha strolled past hanging rugs that shone with all the colors of the sun, and then suddenly leapt aside as two runaway fighting tops came buzzing wildly down the streets. "I can at least think of one novelty we'll make here better than anywhere in the world!"

The Uruth section of the town was still mostly empty. Although Surolf's little civic amenities made the town an attractive potential home, few other races could bring themselves to live alongside Oosha's rats. Even so, the town had gained perhaps a hundred canine citizens, and the streets no longer seemed empty and forlorn.

Koja looked up past the square, toward the howling mound. "I heard Ra'hish's nestlings sing last night on the howling mound – a most remarkable thing." The dog scuffed his bare feet on the soil. "Is it still peaceful down below?"

"Somewhat." Oosha spent far more time in Squeaktown than her sister, who had duties in Acomar. "We talk about what to do about the others – how to save the other rats in Acomar. Somehow the fertility problem must be solved. They must simply learn not to breed so wantonly."

The dog pulled at his collar and essayed a polite little cough. "Ah – yes. . . . But you will admit that mere self-restraint offers few guarantees."

"There is another way. Something . . ." Oosha shrugged, "something that bears working on."

Biting her lip in pity, Teela looked away; Koja turned very, very still as Oosha looked at him with her strangely powerful pink eyes.

"The Giants gave me a gift, Koja. I am infected with . . ." The girl grappled with concepts, and tried lamely to explain. ". . . not a disease – but perhaps a parasite is a better term. It lives inside me, rebuilding me minute by minute, hour by hour. "It is the curse the Giants must have wished on themselves: virtual immortality. I am hard to kill, Koja – and I believe that I will not age. Not for a very long, long time."

The white rat paused, looking out over an area of blank blue sky. Koja fought an impulse to stroke the Itheem's beautiful, clean fur. "How does this help your people, Oosha?"

"I know that I am sterile. It is a side effect of the infection; it has rebuilt me from the inside." Oosha blindly reached out for Teela's hand. "Sterility and madness. Immortality comes at a heavy price." The white rat looked quietly back toward Acomar. "It might one day be possible to infect Itheem with droplets of my blood. If I am sterile, perhaps a smaller dose might . . . might make my people breed less swiftly."

Oosha walked thoughtfully down the streets, waving her naked pink tail. "Teela speaks to the old gods. If she can reach out to an oracle, perhaps it might be done." The rat looked at her own hand as though staring through the skin and down into her bones. "In time . . . in time, I might give us the key."

Koja looked from Teela to Oosha, and felt a crawling sensation beneath his skin.

"You mean . . . you would bleed yourself for them. To offer blood to the oracle to treat every single Itheem?" The dog thought of all the teeming thousands of rats in Acomar. "How long would it go on?"

"Until it is done." Oosha shook the topic away, deliberately turning her companions toward the springtime sun. "And what of you, Lord Koja. Does your new town suit you, after all the pain of the past?"

"It suits me, Lady." Koja smiled, but it did not reach his eyes. "I suits me well enough."

"But you are not happy."

"I am . . . unlucky in love." The dog gave a sorry sigh. "I believe I spent a fortune on a pearl of little price."

Teela ran little calculations through her mind and pursed her lips in thought. "Where is Aela now?"

"Somewhere." Koja gave an unhappy wave of his hands. "My grandfather the seer thinks the sun never sets on her. But I have an inkling she is a creature of small character."

"She's a scorpion crossed with a venomous snake!" Teela chuffed in distaste, unconsciously sitting up to scrub her paws across her snout. "She hasn't been seen today?"

"No – not since breakfast." Koja gave a sorry shake of his head. "The public toilets and the sewer system start up today. I had at least hoped she might attend the opening."

Oosha raised one eyebrow and turned away as Teela let her own whiskers feel the wind.

"Ah." Teela made a slow circle of her tail. "Well, who knows? Perhaps she will!"

In the skies overhead, a bright object suddenly veered above the howling mound, laughter circling in its wake. The three companions stood and stared as a gigantic kite swooped low over the town, a little figure sitting in the rigging gaily waving its tail.

Oosha stared upward in alarm. "Is that Ra'hish? He'll break his neck!"

"Oh, dear. Another novelty." Koja looked up toward the howling mound. "I wonder where it came from."

"I *wonder.*" Teela led the way to the howling mound's stairs. "Come on. This one I simply have to see!"

On the howling mound high above the roofs, where the warm spring air sparkled with drifting clouds of thistledown, a mighty project had begun. Little nestlings leapt and pulled on ropes at Surolf's command, making a huge green kite veer gracefully above the town. Sitting in a basket under the kite and joyously staring about, Ra'hish laughed with delight. He waved to Teela and Oosha far below, calling out to them with words that lost themselves in the sky. The entire population of the town came drifting out of tunnels, fields, and homes to stare up at the rat and gape in wonder.

Dressed in brand new ribbons and shiny bells, Tupan stood working away merrily behind a long line of tabletops. With her tail wagging, she hoisted a big tub of purple juice onto the bench and began mixing it happily with sugar and good wine. Sitting on the table beside her, one half-grown rat pouted and tugged pleadingly at Tupan's sleeve.

"I want to go next! Can't I have the next ride in the sky?"

"Hey – we did 'fisties' and settled it!" Tupan licked her mixing spoon and then stuck it straight back inside the juice. "It goes Eeka, Rika, Shika, Oota, Goota, Koopa, Marta, Barta, Loopi, Hoopi, Shoopi, and Jez!" The spoon jabbed the little nestling on the nose. "And you're Jez! Next time, let me show you how to cheat at 'fisties' before we start – okay?"

The little male rat kicked at the giant juice tub in a sulk. "Why am I always last?"

"Because you're the most special, so we like to spend some extra effort on you." Tupan stirred eagerly. "And if you believe that one, I've got lots of stuff you'll just love to buy! Anyway, you're not last. The last one up is Hern!"

"I'm still not going up in it, you know." Hern walked around and around in circles, treading berries in a giant tub. "I don't think ponies were ever really meant to fly."

"Aaaah – you'll love it!" Tupan waved her spoon, showering drops of purple juice on one and all. "Surolf made you a big sling and everything!"

Surolf heard his name and left the nestlings and their helpers to at last lower Ra'hish to the ground. As the pulleys whirred behind him, the greyhound scampered eagerly over to Tupan's side. He waved expressive hands toward the kite, his heart soaring. "Does it work? Did you like it?"

"It's hoopier than hoopy!" Tupan passed her friend a drink, tugging happily at his ear. "Are you pleased with it?"

"Pleased? It's wonderful!" Surolf flapped his hands like an ungainly bird, unused to such *joie de vie*. "You're going up?"

"In a bit. The ratties get first call, otherwise they'll bust like popcorn."

The kite grounded, and Ra'hish tumbled from the basket, somewhat unsteady on his feet. He wove his way toward Oosha and Teela and babbled madly to them about the ride. Oosha held him, simply loving him, and Teela watched them from the corner of her eye.

More spectators had wandered in from the workshops and fields. Her juice tubs ready at long last, Tupan ran to the edge of the mound and waved her spoon to the people staring from the streets below.

"*Come on up! Dogs and cats, mice and rats! Hey, raccoon boys – come on up and have a turn!*" The coyote made manic little running motions to coax her audience into racing up the mound. "*Food, drink, sky rides! Forget what you're up to and come and have a hoopy time!*"

Beside the kite, Ra'hish held Oosha's hand and stared at her with eyes made brilliant with joy. "I can fly!"

"So, you can!" The white rat fixed her fingers in the warm fur behind Ra'hish's tattooed ears. "Where on earth did this thing come from?"

Eeka answered before he could. "We made it for Ra'hish. He always wanted one." She was already climbing up into the basket and lashing herself to the safety lines. "Surolf helped a bit. Isn't it hoopy?"

Oosha sat and stared at the kite in puzzlement. "How can you want something you never even knew existed?"

"Ra'hish is clever! He knows about things." Eeka gave a squeal of delight as Surolf released the winches and the kite's vanes caught the springtime wind. *"So, we made him a giant thistledown . . . !"* Her voice faded as the nestling went winging into the sky.

Townsfolk began to top the mound, staring at the brilliant green contraption high above. Rats and canines mingled side by side to stare in wonder into the sky.

Eagerly ladling juice into wooden cups, Tupan thrust drinks into every passing hand.

"Free beer! Berry juice! Lemon juice, and sparkling tea! Just the thing for a ratty thirst! Just the stuff to dampen your raccoon!" Tupan threw herself into her domestic task with a strange, ferocious energy. "Don't pee in the bushes, folks! Save it all for the grand opening of Chelth Valley's first-ever public facilities in ten minutes time. Yes, sir, contribute to the tide of history!"

The first hundred drinks were served in a rush; with unaccustomed domestic efficiency, Tupan put on an apron, washed dirty cups, and made sure the entire town was served a second round. Finally breathing an exhausted sigh, the coyote rested on her latest tub of berry juice and patted Hern's flanks as he trudged by.

Oosha and Teela came over to the juice stand and held up little cups for a taste of berry wine. "Tupan, have you seen that girl, Aela – the one Surolf won't speak to any more?"

"No, why?" Tupan topped glasses all around, the very heart and soul of innocence. "Why ask me?"

Teela gave a long slow coil of her tail. "It's just that the steering vane of your kite is the same colored cloth as her good silk dress."

"Aaaah, that stuff's lying around everywhere right now! We'll bring you guys more when we get back from the wilds." Tupan gave herself an extra large glass of foaming berry juice and drank it in a great rush of energy. She wiped her mouth with the back of her hand and gave a satisfied sigh.

Her ears rising, Teela stared at the coyote girl. "Where are you going?"

"Like I said – the wilds! Over the mountains, or maybe we'll find a way to cross the sea!" The coyote smacked her empty cup down on the tabletop. "So, how does your population control thing work? Bleed Oosha into a cup and plunk it down in front of a holy hill of dirt? Sounds a little shaky to me." Tupan gave an airy wave of her hand. "There's got to be another way. Maybe another bunch of rats solved the problem somewhere – maybe there's a gadget or a medicine or a spell written on a pillar a hundred spans high! So, I thought we'd go look for it for you – Surolf, the ratties, and me!"

"And me." Hern stood in four tubs of water, washing off his hooves.

"I thought of the idea."

"Yeah, he thought of the idea – so I started asking around. We'll find something hoopy and solve the problem. You'll see!"

"Really?"

"Really!" Tupan served Hern a brimming bowl of sugared juice. "Hey – Surolf and I fix things. It's what we do!"

With kite rides happily taking place and drinks being had all around, Tupan laid a hand across Hern's neck and walked him down the steps toward the little town. Nestlings leapt and cheered as their turns on the kite came, and the air was filled with drifting fluff from dandelions. Walking past the brand new buildings, Tupan turned her snout into the breeze, felt the sun on her fur, and joyously closed her eyes.

"Aaah – a new invention, a decent lunch, and a day of utter fun." The girl's bells jingled as she strode along the warm dirt of the road. "Still, this Aela thing; is a little guilt becoming?"

"She *did* try to have you killed." Hern gave an expressive swish of his long tail. "I rather like her where she is."

"True, true." Tupan made a turn through the town gates and walked beside the pony out onto a hill of brilliant green grass. "You tie pretty good knots for someone who only has hooves."

"It's a talent." Hern settled himself beside a particularly juicy patch of wheat. "Do you think it will take her long to get untied?"

"Hoo hoo! Just long enough!" Tupan sat so that she could see the exit pipe for the newly opened sewers, waiting for the first trickle of water to go off on its merry way. "I think I hear her now."

Bladders swelled with berry juice, the public trotted one by one into Surolf's latest building. The doors were opened, and water was diverted off into the sewers. A distant female scream echoed out from the sewers, and Tupan lay back in the sun, wriggling her toes with glee.

"I'm not normally a vindictive creature – but like I say, every now and then the universe wants you to help bring the balance back the way it should be."

"It's a talent." Hern chomped on green wheat stalks and idly watched a passing butterfly. "We should go fix some more things later in the afternoon."

"Maybe." Tupan made herself a bed inside the weeds and gaped clean white fangs in an enormous yawn. "For now, old horse, I think everyone has a perfect schedule for the day."

Over the town, the kite swayed like a magical green cloud. In the field, all seemed quiet save the sound of nestlings' laughter in the breeze. The sun shone through drifting streams of thistledown, and at last all was right with Tupan's world.

Printed in the United States
1295400005B/40-45